Rush OH!

Shirley Barrett

virago

VIRAGO

First published in Australia in 2015 by Pan Macmillan Australia Pty Ltd
First published in Great Britain in 2016 by Virago Press

1 3 4 5 7 9 10 8 6 4 2

Illustrations (except for those on pages vii and ix) by
Matt Canning / The Illustration Room

Hardback ISBN 978-0-349-00662-8
C Format ISBN 978-0-349-00663-5

Printed and bound in Great Britain by
Clays Ltd, St Ives plc

Papers used by Virago are from well-managed forests
and other responsible sources.

MIX
Paper from
responsible sources
FSC
www.fsc.org FSC® C104740

Virago Press
An imprint of
Little, Brown Book Group
Carmelite House
50 Victoria Embankment
London EC4Y 0DZ

An Hachette UK Company
www.hachette.co.uk

www.virago.co.uk

For

Sabrina and Emmeline

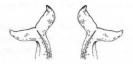

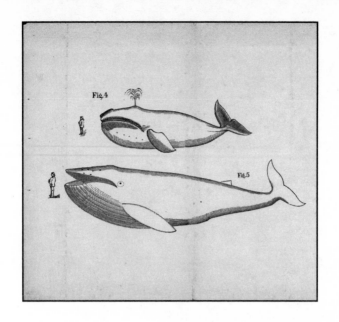

If you ever ever ever ever ever
If you ever ever ever see a whale
You must never never never never never
You must never never never touch its tail
For if you ever ever ever ever ever
If you ever ever ever touch its tail
You will never never never never never
You will never never see another whale.

ANON.

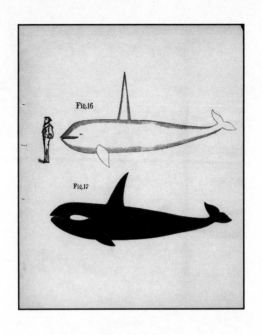

Fig.16

Fig.17

There are few people, if any, who have not
heard of the Killer Whales of Twofold Bay –
of the great help they render to the whaling
crews at Eden and the names they bear, such
as Tom, Hooky, Humpy and Cooper …
And yet those who have known these strange
creatures for a lifetime look upon them as
friends; yes, just as much friends to the
whaling crews as the cattle dog to the drover;
just about as much, if not a little more so.

EDEN OBSERVER AND SOUTH COAST ADVOCATE
27 NOVEMBER 1903

A Visitor

OUR HOUSE WAS SITUATED UP THE HILL FROM THE TRY-WORKS, which meant not only were we enveloped in the stench of boiling blubber for five months of the year, but also that our garden must needs incorporate various vestiges of dead marine life. The jaws of a large white pointer shark, in which the children liked to pretend they were being eaten, formed an ornamental feature near the front gate, while the path leading up to the house was laid with the pulverised remains of whale vertebrae, creating an effect not unlike pebbles, although considerably sharper underfoot. The towering rib cage of a ninety-foot blue whale sat amidst a winter display of jonquils; my father had had the men haul it closer to the house that he might contemplate its grandeur while enjoying his evening pipe. In a bid to soften its stark appearance (and incidentally create a kind of pergola), I had attempted to train a wisteria over it; however the wisteria had never taken to the task and its gnarled tendrils did nothing to dispel, in fact seemed generally to enhance, the somewhat gloomy aspect of the mammal's parched remains. Certainly they cast an impression upon the visitor now standing before them, for he issued a low whistling sound through his teeth and shook his head slowly.

Before proceeding further, I should pause to mention that at the time my sisters and I were slave to a great many 'kitchen superstitions', some of which we had learned from others, and many of which we had simply invented ourselves. For example, if when washing dishes a cup or a plate is overlooked, then that is a sign that you will soon hear tidings of a wedding. This particular superstition had failed us many times, but was later to come true in circumstances so close to home that we have persisted in believing in it, even in spite of the frequency with which we forget to wash things and the relative infrequency of hearing about weddings. Perhaps owing to our distance from the township of Eden, we had developed a whole series of superstitions regarding the impending arrival of visitors. If the kettle was accidentally placed on the fire with the spout facing backwards, then a stranger was coming to see us. If, after sweeping a room, the broom was left in a corner, then the sweeper would shortly meet her true love. Of course, as can be imagined, this led to a greater interest in sweeping and a good deal of leaving brooms about in corners, until we decided that the leaving of brooms had to be accidental or the effect was otherwise null and void. I convey this information simply for the purpose of setting the scene, for late that particular afternoon in June 1908, I had almost finished sweeping out the bedrooms when I glimpsed from the window the visitor gazing solemnly at the rib bones as I have just described. Throwing off my apron, I hurried out to the verandah, and in doing so, *I left the broom in the corner of that bedroom.*

'Good afternoon,' the visitor called out to me. 'I'm looking for George Davidson.'

'He's in town,' I responded. 'He should be back before sundown.'

'I hear he's putting together crews for his whaleboats,' said the stranger, stooping to pluck a jonquil, which he proceeded to place in his buttonhole. (The jonquil display had been another of my attempts at 'softening' the rib cage, yet in truth the effect was not entirely harmonious.) 'Does he need another, do you know?'

'He does,' responded my younger brother Dan, who had joined me on the verandah. 'Tell me, can you row hard?'

'I can.'

'Have you chased a whale before?'

'I've not,' confessed the stranger, strolling up the path towards us, whale bones crunching underfoot. 'But I can fish.'

'They're bigger than fish.'

'Much bigger?'

'Oh yes, quite considerably. Have you never seen a whale up close before?'

'I've not.'

'Well then, you're in for quite a surprise.' Dan took an old clay pipe from his pocket now, and tapped at it thoughtfully. 'Mary, perhaps if you showed our visitor your artwork, it might convey more clearly some sense of their dimensions?'

At this, the stranger turned to me, and his face broke into a broad grin. I'm not sure what prompted this; perhaps Dan's lofty manner amused him (Dan was a small boy and looked younger than his twelve years).

'You sketch?' enquired the stranger.

'Yes, somewhat; mainly whaling scenes,' I replied. My cheeks reddened. How dreary and bluestocking it seemed suddenly, to enjoy such a pastime. Nor was this impression helped by the fact that I was indeed wearing my blue stockings.

'One of Mary's depictions received a Highly Commended at the Eden Show just past,' said Dan stoutly. 'Go and fetch it, Mary,' he encouraged, giving me a shove.

Although I am not usually one to put myself forward, I did as I was bid, for I felt an urge to cast an interesting impression of myself upon this gentleman. When I returned, I saw that Dan had perhaps been affected by a similar impulse, for he was now engaged in the act of demonstrating to the stranger the action of my father's whale gun. Dan had been expressly forbidden to so much as touch the whale gun since he and one of the Aboriginal children had used it for shooting minnows in the creek and only with the greatest good fortune avoided blowing away their own legs. Calmly I wrenched it from his grasp and placed it aside.

'My father rarely uses it,' I explained to the stranger. 'It scares the Killers away. Besides, it has a powerful kick that can knock you clear out of the boat and into the water. Dan here tried it once and had a bruise the size of a dinner plate on his chest.'

'Show him your picture for God's sake, Mary,' muttered Dan, having no wish for me to go into further details on the subject.

'Very well,' I replied.

Stern All, Boys! (which, as formerly mentioned, had received a Highly Commended in the Eden Show just past) depicts the moment when the whale receives the fatal lance and lashes the water in its death flurry. My father, the headsman, is standing at the bow of the boat applying the lance, and it is he who is calling out for the men to row hard astern in a bid to escape the fury of the tormented monster. You can see from the position of the whale's enormous flukes that its tail will crash down upon the boat at any moment. It is spouting blood; also, there is a fountain of blood issuing from the point where the lance enters the whale's vitals, spraying over the men and giving them a most ghoulish appearance. One of the striking features of the painting is the look of abject terror on the faces of the crew, with the exception of my father, who is known locally by the sobriquet of 'Fearless'. My brother Harry is the most terrified of them all. He is gazing up beseechingly at the giant flukes and wringing his hands like a girl (in fact, he was quite annoyed with me about this representation, and the subject was to remain a sore point between us). Amidst the commotion, one of the men has fallen into the sea and is in the throes of drowning, while another is depicted struggling valiantly for life in the grip of the whale's mighty jaws. Meanwhile, in the water circling the thrashing leviathan, are the Killer whales Tom, Hooky, Humpy, Typee, Jackson, Charlie Adgery and Kinscher – each of them identifiable by the distinguishing characteristics of their dorsal fins. Hooky is pushing at the whale from below to ensure it does not sound. Tom is jumping across the creature's blowhole. Jackson is endeavouring to force open the jaws of the whale in a bid to tear out a portion of its tongue, while Humpy looks on approvingly.

All in all, it is quite a dramatic representation, and a great favourite with the children. Some considered it ought to have been awarded first prize; however, for reasons of their own which remain mysterious, the judges deemed otherwise. Admittedly, there were some small inaccuracies (the whale I have depicted started off as a humpback but, after some difficulty rendering the head, it ended up as a sperm whale; truth be told, however, sperm whales have never been sighted in Twofold Bay). It was rumoured that the judges may have found the painting too gruesome – if this was the case, then I consider it curious, as I know that one of these judges was to be seen on the cliff tops cheering heartily whenever such a scene unfolded in real life. In truth, I suspect that the real reason *Stern All, Boys!* was deemed unworthy of a prize is that the subject matter was considered unsuitable for a young lady. Far better that I had employed my talents depicting three cows in a paddock at sunset, as did Miss Eunice Martin of Towamba, for which effort she received the coveted blue ribbon.

'Whales eat folk?' asked the stranger finally. He had been gazing steadily at the painting for some moments.

'Not commonly,' I replied. 'I have embellished a few small details.'

'There's nothing to say a sperm whale wouldn't eat a man,' said Dan. 'Didn't Moby Dick eat Ahab?'

'I don't know. I can't remember,' I said. 'He may have done.'

'Well, in any case, there's nothing to stop a fellow from falling into a whale's mouth,' said Dan. 'The whale may be just about to spit him out as so much gristle.'

The stranger continued to study the painting in silence. I could see his brows knit and the muscles of his jaw tighten, and for a long time he gazed at it and said nothing. Evidently it was the first time he had seen whaling depicted in detail, and given that he had just volunteered for the job, perhaps he was experiencing misgivings.

'There's a lot of blood,' he said finally. 'Perhaps you could have shown less of it.'

Stern All, Boys!

I stiffened. A surge of indignation rose up within me.

'Forgive me, but I felt it my responsibility to deliver an accurate pictorial representation. There *is* a lot of blood. Isn't there, Dan?'

'Oh yes,' agreed Dan. 'Whaling's not for the queasy.'

'I never said I was queasy,' said the visitor, seemingly slightly annoyed at the implication. 'I just said how there's a deal of blood.'

'Then perhaps you would prefer I confine my pictorial efforts to pastoral settings,' I responded. 'A cow or two in a paddock – would that be a more suitable subject for a young lady?'

'Leave it, Mary,' said Dan.

'Never mind that one of Miss Martin's cows seemed for all the world to have five legs! I've never heard of a five-legged cow, have you?'

'There was a calf born in Bega with five legs,' said Dan.

'That story was completely *apocryphal*!'

Just at that moment, our youngest sisters Annie and Violet cried out from the bottom of the garden – my father's motor launch, *Excelsior*, had rounded the headland and could be seen approaching. They galloped down to the jetty to meet him, followed by our dogs hot on their heels, anxious to convey the impression that they had remained vigilant and not spent the entire afternoon dozing in the sun. Forgetting his worldly manner, Dan stashed his pipe in his pocket and took off down to the jetty also. My father had been into Eden to pick up stores, and there was always the chance that he had thought to include some small confectionery or trifle.

'Well, sir,' I ventured at last, turning to the stranger. 'Are you still up for adventure, or has my painting put you off?'

'No,' he said. 'I mean, yes. In truth, it has scared the bejesus out of me.'

A wave of alarm overtook me. I may not have yet mentioned that our visitor was remarkably handsome, and whalers as a rule were not celebrated for their good looks.

'Oh no, you mustn't let my picture deter you,' I entreated. 'Whaling is generally considered no more dangerous than fishing, albeit whales are larger than fish.'

'Yes,' he replied. 'I think I am clear on that point now.'

'Also, to be perfectly honest, we don't catch that many whales,' I continued. 'Oh, enough to get by certainly, and make a decent – well, a living of sorts, but . . .' Here I trailed off, for he glanced at me curiously. 'The truth is, sir, my father could certainly use an extra hand at the oars.'

I gazed at him imploringly and hoped that my spectacles were sitting straight. So often they sat askew, which gave me the appearance of a character in a musical comedy.

'This comment I made regarding the amount of blood,' he said. 'That was unwarranted. Forgive me.'

'There's no need,' I replied, surprised and, in truth, greatly pleased. 'Your comment was perfectly understandable. However, I think you'll soon find that there *is* a lot of blood, perhaps more than one would reasonably expect.'

'Yes,' murmured the stranger, gazing off. 'That is so often the case.'

He fell silent now, apparently absorbed in his own thoughts. I strained to think of some additional remark that would assist my cause but could think of nothing, so instead stood sucking my lower lip between my teeth, a habit of mine when nervous. The dogs were barking furiously as my father manoeuvred the *Excelsior* alongside the jetty; my brother Harry, at the bow of the vessel, tossed the rope to Dan, who jumped at it eagerly and missed. It ended up in the water. Harry pulled it out again, cursing Dan freely.

'Well, then,' said the stranger at last. 'Here goes for a cool, collected dive at death and destruction, and the devil fetch the hindmost.'

And with that, he smiled at me, tipped his cap and strolled off down the hill to meet my father.

I stood for a moment and watched him go, then turned and hurried back inside. An odd feeling of distraction overcame me: I proceeded to sweep again with great thoroughness several rooms I had previously swept.

A Minister of the Methodist Church

GIVEN THE SHORTAGE OF WHALE MEN AFTER THE MISFORtunes of last season, my father was pleased to make the acquaintance of John Beck (for that was the name of our visitor).

'And what kind of experience have you had?' he asked, after the initial introductions.

'Well, sir, up until recent times I was a minister of the Methodist church,' John Beck replied. At this, the children stared and Harry embarked upon a series of snorting sounds (my brother had a problem with his adenoids). My father silenced him at once with a look.

'That is well and good,' said my father, turning back to John Beck. 'But what kind of experience as regards whaling?'

'Ah,' said John Beck. 'None, to be exact.'

At this, both men gazed down sadly at the wooden boards of our jetty.

'It's a bad thing we lost Burrows,' said Uncle Aleck that evening, as we sat around the kitchen table. 'He was a good man when sober, and a fine oarsman. What makes you think this clergyman can row?'

'If he can't, then he'll learn soon enough,' said my father.

'Perhaps he will row for Jesus,' offered Dan, who was at the time a Junior Soldier with the Salvation Army. They would sometimes visit in a bid to minister to our Aboriginal whale men, but had so far only succeeded in recruiting Dan to their ranks. The Aborigines enjoyed the hymn singing, but that was about it.

'Also, Dad,' said Harry, 'I bumped into Robert Heffernan in town today and he mentioned to me that he would be very keen for you to consider him, if you are still short of oarsmen.'

At this, my father turned and gazed suspiciously at my sister Louisa, but she continued to eat, paying no attention to the conversation around her. (I have not mentioned Louisa in detail yet, but I will get to her soon enough.)

'Well,' he said. 'I may have to at that, if we're to run two boats.'

'God help us, George, two new chums and one an ex-clergyman!' cried Uncle Aleck. 'You'll sink like a stone out there.'

Voices Whisper

That the usual preparations for whaling in Eden will be ready by the 15th.

That the Killers, true to their custom, are about; and whales may be expected soon to show – or cry 'hello,' and bellow.

That Hopkins, our local butcher, who will never be beat in the dispensing of meat, in charge of bullocks whose fat would fill full street.

That our Eden horse, since last referred to, has masticated a fishing net and pair of boots.

That if he is not watched he will swallow a whale after the Killers are done with it.

EDEN OBSERVER AND SOUTH COAST ADVOCATE

A Good Fish is Tom

WHILST IN TOWN, MY FATHER TOLD US, HE HAD HAD occasion to stop in at the Great Southern Hotel, where a gentleman recounted to him an amusing incident. It seems that very morning the gentleman had been fishing for schnapper in the bay when all of a sudden he experienced a different 'bite' to that which he had been anticipating. A group of Killer whales had materialised alongside his dinghy and, amidst the general spouting and breaching, one of their number had grasped the boat's kellick between his teeth and proceeded to tow the vessel at speed in the direction of the open sea. The man clung to the gunwales and began to weep, for he feared he might never again see his loved ones; yet just as they passed South Head, the kellick was dropped as summarily as it was taken and the Killer and his entourage departed. Finding himself thus abandoned, the unhappy fellow was then forced to row a distance of some several miles back to his starting point.

'Whereupon I discovered that the schnapper had long ago dispersed,' he concluded, amidst general laughter in the front bar of the Great Southern.

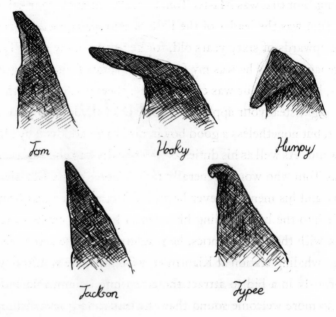

Tom   Hooky   Humpy

Jackson   Typee

When the good-natured joshing had subsided, my father asked the gentleman if he could describe to him the appearance of the particular Killer whale who had taken the kellick.

'Why yes,' the fisherman responded. 'He was of about twenty-five feet in length, in rude good health, shiny black in colour with gleaming white marks around his middle.'

My father nodded thoughtfully. 'And tell me, did you observe any peculiarity of the dorsal fin?'

'Well, sir, it was probably six feet in height and boasted a small knob or protuberance about midway up its trailing edge,' replied the fisherman.

At this, many of the surrounding drinkers at once erupted into knowing chuckles.

'Then you should count yourself privileged,' my father said, smiling. 'For that was Master Tom himself who took your kellick.'

Tom was the leader of the Killers, and his age was calculated to be upwards of sixty years old, for he had been my grandfather's lieutenant, just as he was my father's. In spite of his distinguished years, his demeanour was ever that of a cheeky schoolboy, the sort that might steal your apples or throw rocks at you from across the street, but nonetheless a good boy in his heart and loved by all who knew him. As well as his duties as Chief Scallywag and Rouseabout, it was Tom who would generally take it upon himself to alert my father and his men whenever he and his companions had herded a whale into the bay. Leaving his team to keep the hapless beast in check with their usual antics, he would make haste across the bay to our whaling station at Kiah Inlet, whereupon he would flop-tail vigorously in a bid to attract the attention of the whalers. There was no more welcome sound than the resounding *smack!* as Tom's mighty tail crashed down upon the water. The men would cry, 'Rush oh!' and run to the whaleboats. Once the boats were put out, Tom (an impatient fish by nature) would lead them directly to the spot where his chums had corralled the whale. Occasionally, if engaged in a particularly exciting scrap that demanded his full attention, Tom would send an offsider to rouse us, but mostly he preferred to take this task upon himself. Rather like my father in this way, Tom was the sort of fish who liked to see a job done properly, even if it meant doing it himself.

Any account of Tom and the wonderful assistance he and his team provided our whalers, however, should not exclude the fact that this mischievous Killer whale could at times be as much hindrance as help. Several times over the years, we had experienced a number of incidents involving Tom and the whale line, resulting in the loss or near-loss of the whale. I shall endeavour to explain.

When stuck with a harpoon, a whale's natural response is to set off at great speed in a bid to escape the sting of the iron. The men chock their oars and are thus towed along behind it, great walls of water rising up on either side of their boat. Much skill is required to ensure that the whale has rope enough to run (and thus exhaust itself) without pulling the whale line out of the boat entirely. There is no more disheartening sight to a whale man than that of a whale swimming out of the heads with an iron in its side and fifty fathoms of rope trailing after it.

In all the danger and uproar of this hair-raising 'sleigh ride', the last thing that is needed is for a Killer whale to suddenly attach himself to the whale line and hang on for grim life, and yet this is exactly what had occurred on several occasions. As if losing his head in the excitement, Tom would throw himself upon the taut rope and hang there by his teeth, thus causing himself to be towed rapidly through the water along with the whaleboat. (I have never had the good fortune to witness this, but have had it described to me in detail; I had even attempted to re-create the scene in oils for the Eden Show the year previous, once again with little success.) Why Tom engaged in this behaviour, no one could say; whether it was a bid to slow the whale's progress by adding his own body weight; or simply for the enjoyable sensation of being pulled forcibly through the water. Whatever the reason, his antics were not well appreciated by the whale crew, as the sudden application of his weight could result in the line being pulled entirely from the boat and the whale subsequently lost. On several occasions, a stoush ensued between whale man and Killer whale; once a boathook was brought into play in a bid to dislodge the errant cetacean, but this annoyed Tom considerably and he hung on all the more tenaciously.

Another story involving Tom, and somewhat of an infamous one, concerns the time the Hon. Mr Austin Chapman (the federal member for the region at the time) was hosting a pleasure cruise on the bay. Various visiting parliamentarians were on board, including the Hon. Mr G.H. Reid and the Hon. Mr Joseph Carruthers, the purpose of the excursion being to persuade the assembled dignitaries that, with its beautiful bay and natural harbour, the township of Eden was the obvious location in which to establish the national capital. With good fortune, they had chanced to witness the closing moments of a particularly exciting whale chase. Now that my father and his men were securing the carcass, Mr Chapman took the opportunity to bring the pleasure craft over so that his guests might inspect the dead whale more closely. The visitors had a great many questions to ask of my father, and my father, a shy man but anxious to promote the attractions of Eden, responded to the very best of his ability. Yet all the while he was aware of the Killer whales' increasing agitation, and the growing urgency of securing the whale with anchors and marker buoys before they dragged the carcass to the depths below. As it was, they were already circling impatiently and tugging at its side fins.

'You certainly put on a fine show for us,' said Mr Chapman, after the initial introductions were made across the vast expanse of whale flesh.

'Yes, she led us on a bit of a dance, the old girl,' said my father, with characteristic understatement. The chase had in fact been a desperate one and taken almost five hours, the men rowing from South Head to North Head and back again, with multiple diversions along the way.

'They call Mr Davidson "Fearless" in these parts, and I think you can now see why,' Mr Chapman remarked to his party. 'I hope he won't mind me telling you that he has a wrought-iron constitution and a heart like a blacksmith's anvil!'

My father was always embarrassed by this sort of talk, but his men raised a hearty 'Hear, hear!'

'Tell me, Mr Davidson, what kind of whale is this?' asked the Hon. Mr Reid, later to become the Prime Minister of Australia, if only for a period of eleven months.

'This is a southern right whale, sir, the most valuable of all on account of the whalebone.'

'Is that so? And what would you estimate to be its worth?'

'Well, sir, the whale oil on a whale this size would be in the order of two hundred pounds, and the whalebone itself – well, we're talking in the league of a thousand pounds, sir.'

The whalers raised an even louder cheer at this news, but my father could tell by the threshing of the water that the Killers were none too happy about the hold-up in proceedings.

'And tell me, Mr Davidson – may I call you Fearless? – tell me, Fearless, what are you up to here with the anchors and buoys and suchlike?' enquired the Hon. Mr Carruthers.

'Well, sir, we let the Killers here have first dibs at the whale.'

'It truly is quite remarkable,' explained Mr Chapman, eagerly. 'The Killer whales will now take the carcass underwater and feast upon its tongue and lips – am I right, Mr Davidson?'

'That's right, sir.'

'How extraordinary,' exclaimed Mrs Reid. 'I was not aware that whales had lips.'

'Oh yes, ma'am,' said my father. 'A whale has lips all right.'

'Then, some twenty-four hours later,' continued Mr Chapman, 'after the Killers have enjoyed their repast, the remains of the carcass will fill with gas and rise to the surface, whereupon our stout-hearted friends here will tow the brute home and begin the process of rendering its blubber into whale oil.'

'So you share the bounty, as it were,' said Mr Reid.

'That's right, sir. Well, the Killers help us catch the whales, and have done for sixty years. Also, to be honest, sir, I doubt we could get the whale off them now if we wanted to.'

And just at that moment, as if to demonstrate this last point, Tom surged up out of the water and grabbed hold of the rope my father had in his hands, hanging on to it with his teeth for twenty seconds or thereabouts and crushing several of my father's fingers in the process. The assembled dignitaries cried out in horror; the whalers – terrified that the Killer would pull my father into the water – threatened Tom with whatever implements they had at hand until finally he relinquished his grasp and slid silently back into the water. Throughout the ordeal, my father's expression remained impassive, nor did he utter a sound; a slight wincing as he tucked his mutilated hand out of sight was the only hint of any discomfort he was experiencing.

'That's Tom,' he said by way of explanation to the visitors, who were staring at him aghast. 'He wants us to hurry up, by the looks of things. I daresay we'd best get back to work, if you'll excuse us.'

'Yes, for heaven's sake, don't let us keep you,' cried Mr Reid, who was still recovering from the shock of this sudden attack. (Mrs Reid had to sit down with her head between her knees.)

'Before we take our leave, one final question concerning Tom,' said Mr Chapman, anxious that the exchange end on a more cheerful note. 'Would you agree with me in saying that there would not be a more loved and revered cetacean alive in the world today?'

My father paused to consider this. (It was always his custom to weigh matters carefully before giving an opinion.)

'He's a good fish is Tom,' he said at last. 'Though he has his funny ways.'

Seeing that Mr Chapman was smiling at him encouragingly and feeling that somehow something more was expected of him, especially in light of the incident they had just witnessed, he added: 'He would be a tremendous asset to the nation's capital.'

'Hear, hear!' cried the whalers.

Whenever I think of this story, I can almost see my father standing there atop the dead whale, a lean and wiry figure, yet somehow heroic with his bloody hand and his marker buoys and boathook, the sun setting behind him and the Killer whales circling and calling to one another with their high-pitched twittering calls. And even in spite of a subsequent infection and the amputation of the top two-thirds of his index finger, my father never went along with the thinking, popular amongst some in the township, that this particular episode contributed in no small way to the fact that Canberra was ultimately selected as the site of the nation's capital, and that therefore the blame could be sheeted home to Tom.

Non-Appearance of Whales

THE SIGHTING OF TOM AND THE KILLER WHALES IN TWOFOLD Bay (punctual as ever, for it was the first week of June) signified that the humpbacks and the right whales would soon be making their way up the coast. Whaling season was about to begin.

'He sounds to be in fine trim and looking for action!' chuckled Uncle Aleck, when he learned of Tom's escapade with the fisherman. 'It's a good sign; it's a very good sign!'

The truth is, we had lately been feeling, in a more marked fashion than usual, an increasing anxiety as the season approached us. I experienced it as a gnawing sensation in the pit of my belly; in my brother Harry, it was evidenced by an outbreak of scaly eczema on his elbows. With my father, the anxiety manifested itself in his restless agitation, his endless inventory of ropes, lances and harpoons; also, unusually for him, in a shortness of temper. The fact of the matter was that the previous season had been the worst on record in sixty years of whaling at Twofold Bay. Not a single whale had been captured, and for this, I regret to say, the Killers had to bear some responsibility.

For reasons best known to themselves, the whales had elected to keep well clear of the coast that year, and from July through to October, barely a whale had ventured close enough to warrant the putting out of boats. Every morning at dawn my father and his crew would row over to South Head to keep lookout from the vantage point of Boyd Tower; every day their long vigils passed unrewarded. Week after week the *Eden Observer and South Coast Advocate* ran the same small item under *'Voices Whisper'*: *'That the whalers are wailing on account of the non-appearance of whales.'* This did nothing to improve the morale of our whale crews. The men were grumbling and fighting amongst themselves; one of our best men absconded and it was all my father could do to keep the rest of them from following suit. The Killers, too, seemed restless and dissatisfied. Tired of toying with seals and grampus for their amusement, they took to cruising long distances out to sea, often staying away for days at a time. This was most unlike the Killers; their customary practice was to keep vigilant sentry at the heads, ready to escort the first unsuspecting whale into the welcoming waters of Twofold Bay. Even if a whale chanced to enter the bay without their initial encouragement, they could always be relied upon to join in the chase once they saw our whaleboats in the water. For the Killers to be absent without leave in the height of the whaling season was a most unusual occurrence.

Very late in the season, almost at the end of October, two very large black whales unexpectedly hove to in the bay. My father and his crew put out at once and rowed hard in pursuit, expecting that at any moment the Killers would enter into the chase. The Killers, however, failed to present themselves. The crews toiled ceaselessly all day, rowing back and forth across the bay in futile pursuit, but were unable at any stage to gain sufficient proximity to engage the harpoon. Many times in their desperation my father and his men employed their usual means of summoning their assistants, by bringing the flat side of their oars down hard upon the water in unison. The Killers did not respond. Finally, as darkness descended, the whales escaped out to sea and the exhausted men made their way home. We later learned from the lighthouse keepers that the Killers had spent the day off Green Cape, idly tormenting seals for their amusement.

Rarely have I seen my father so despondent as when he returned that night. He sat at the kitchen table with his head in his hands and would take no supper. By all accounts, these two whales had been the largest seen in this vicinity for many years. Furthermore, they were right whales, the most greatly sought after owing to the immensity and value of their whalebone. These two whales, for their whalebone alone, were together worth possibly as much as three thousand pounds. This is without even taking into consideration the quantity of oil, which could be reasonably estimated at about sixteen tonnes. Hence it is not difficult to appreciate my father's disappointment.

The next day, the Killers were back, having a grand old time chasing a couple of worthless finbacks, right under the noses of the men on lookout, who cursed them bitterly. Shortly thereafter, my father was forced to disperse his disgruntled crews. He and Harry kept lookout a while longer; however no more whales of any commercial value were sighted, and the fruitless season was closed by the middle of November.

Fastidious Diet of Whale Men

MY OWN FEELING OF ANXIETY REGARDING THE ONSET OF whaling season was exacerbated by the fact that it seemed I was expected to be Cook again. It is true, my mother had cooked for the whalers along with all her other duties, but as I was only thirteen when she died, my father had gone on to employ a series of cooks. None of them lasted long at the post; it seemed they were either addicted to drink or inclined to run off with the first person who glanced at them sideways (usually one of the whalers). Three seasons ago, our cook (a bad-tempered redhead by the name of Ginnie) complained of tiny insects burrowing out of her skin and promptly took herself into town on a drinking spree with the money my father had given her to buy provisions. After two days she fell down dead in the back room of the Great Southern – a fitting end. However, I had little cause to celebrate, as I was thrown in at once to replace her.

I have read that cooking for shearers is a thankless job, yet I would volunteer for it happily if offered a choice between that and cooking for whalers. Naturally, whalers are ill-mannered as a rule and boast enormous appetites – that is to be expected. What is less to be expected, however, is their extreme finickiness as regarding their 'slops'. It seemed that each one of them suffered from some manner of digestive imbalance which required the most fastidious tending. Bastable could not tolerate any form of marsupial, so kangaroo and wallaby were out of the question. Albert Thomas Junior complained that oysters gave him a terrific bellyache, which was unfortunate because oysters were abundant, and useful for stretching out many of their stews. Although rabbit was reasonably plentiful and cost nothing, the whalers became disgruntled when I served it too frequently; canned rabbit was out of the question. Mutton was tolerated if roasted in goose fat or fashioned into rissoles with finely chopped bacon and parsley. Stewed ibis, attempted once, was deemed unpalatable. Further, the whale men were extremely particular about seasoning and would pull me up sharply if they considered a dish under-salted. All meals were doused in vast quantities of Worcestershire sauce or golden syrup, with little thought as to the expense of such condiments.

Although I had no wish to add to his worries, I gathered my courage and asked my father if he would not hire a cook this season.

'They are too much trouble,' he responded. 'Besides, you are old enough now to take on the responsibility, and Louisa will help you.'

'Louisa!' I scoffed. 'She will be a lot of help, I must say. You might as well ask the cat.'

'Then get the younger ones to help you.'

'But they are completely useless!'

It was generally considered at the time amongst the immediate family that Annie and Violet, our youngest two, were not quite right in the head. For many years now, they had communicated mostly through a language they called 'Whinny', which consisted of grunting and snickering and pawing the ground. This had been mildly amusing when they were small children, but now that they were nine and ten years of age it had frankly become rather tiresome. Oddly, they had little interest in our actual horse, Two Socks, but then he was always a very difficult horse to get along with.

'Well, Mary, it is up to you,' said my father, rising to his feet. 'You are the little mother of the household now. You will have to organise the younger ones accordingly. I have enough to deal with regarding the whales.'

What a burden it is to be the firstborn daughter when your mother has died! It was not as if I was unused to work – I did almost all the cooking and all the washing (with some assistance from Louisa, admittedly) and cleaned the house and darned their clothes; I even taught the little ones their lessons as best I could. But to cook for the whalers seemed to push me to the very limit of my forbearance. As I say, it was not even the fact of the extra mouths to feed – it was the lack of appreciation for my efforts. Not enough salt? Then here, sir – have the entire container, upended over your fat head.

Another difficulty we faced in feeding the whalers was that in order to carry down their slops from the kitchen each evening, we were required to 'run the gauntlet' of a pair of masked plovers known to us as Mr and Mrs Maudry. These plovers had for some years staked their claim to our front garden and, by unhappy coincidence, timed the great drama of their annual nesting with our whaling season. I cannot say for sure why we came to know them by these names, or even if it was the same Mr and Mrs Maudry who year after year tormented us; it is entirely possible, since they are indistinguishable from each other, that succeeding generations took over the roles. Suffice to say, these ill-tempered birds provided a wholly unwelcome element of annoyance to the short but dreary journey down to the sleeping huts each evening – and back.

For that part of the year when they were not preoccupied with matters nesting, Mr and Mrs Maudry contented themselves with stalking broodingly about the garden and glowering at us. Mr Maudry in particular possessed a malevolent air similar to that of a Land and Tax officer or Customs agent, an effect enhanced by the plovers' plumage, in which nature appeared to be imitating the

black-collared suit coats of the kind favoured by my late paternal grandfather. By all accounts entirely capable of flight, the Maudrys for the most part elected not to, preferring to spend their days instead lurking ominously amongst the jonquils. Occasionally they might materialise suddenly out of 'thin air' where previously they were not, prompting the thought that wings may have been utilised in some fashion in order for them to do so. For reasons of their own, however, Mr and Mrs Maudry felt it necessary to maintain the illusion that they were solely ground dwellers.

Soon after whaling season commenced each year, Mrs Maudry would get broody, and from that moment on, any inter-loper (by which I mean any person who ventured foot in the front garden) was set upon at once by Mr Maudry and summarily issued with his marching orders. First he would charge towards the hapless wanderer, emitting a series of short staccato cries (I mean Mr Maudry would emit the cries, not the wanderer); all the while, Mrs Maudry urging him on shrilly from the sidelines. Should the unhappy party not immediately desist from his or her intended journey, then Mr Maudry would launch at them with his wings extended, revealing a fearsome kind of spur he had hitherto concealed in his plumage and which he wielded wildly, all the time with a look in his eye that meant to say he would have no compunction in using it if pressed. No amount of stick-waving or shouting at Mr Maudry would discourage him, and this is what we faced every evening in carrying down the pots to the ungrateful whalers. If one of us was assigned the task of distracting Mr Maudry whilst the other scurried past, then Mrs Maudry would willingly abandon her nest to tackle the other party, proving herself every bit as spirited as her husband. Nor were the dogs of any assistance to us: alas, cruel experience had taught them well, and in the height of nesting season they simply refused to accompany us at all.

Eventually the Maudrys stepped up their campaign to the point where we had no choice but to take an alternative route around the back of the house and through the blackberry bushes, the last section of which journey required sliding perilously down a steep set of rocks onto the beach. Thus we arrived scratched, bruised and pulling off leeches; scant wonder the whalers received short shrift if they complained that their slops had gone cold.

Commencement of
Whaling Season, 1908

I HAD RISEN EARLY TO MAKE THE DAMPER, AND NOW I HURRIED down the hill to the boat ramp with tuckerbags for the whale men. They stood about beside the boats, flapping their arms in a bid to warm themselves and grumbling as usual about their conditions. Our Aboriginal crew members had recently returned, as they did annually, from Wallaga Lake: Arthur Ashby, my father's long-standing harpooner; Albert Thomas Senior and Albert Thomas Junior; and Percy Madigan and his son, Darcy. We were always relieved to see them, for without them my father would have struggled to continue. They were stronger oarsmen overall; Darcy especially had extraordinary eyesight, and their nerve was better in a pinch. Consequently, my father preferred to use them on the Number One boat, which saw most of the action. As well, electing to return finally after protracted consideration was Salty Mead, one of my father's longest serving whale men (in fact, he had served as an oarsman for my father's father), and Walter Bastable, a veteran of the Great Shearers' Strike of 1891, who now considered himself the 'whale man's shop steward'. I spotted John Beck almost immediately; he was standing to the side with two other new chums.

'And what brings you here to try your hand at whaling?' asked my father of one of these newcomers, a tall, stooped man with a drooping moustache.

'Well, sir, not a soul on this earth cares whether I live or die, so I suppose I have naught to lose,' responded the man in a thick Scottish brogue.

'We haven't lost a man in thirty years, Mr Shankly,' said my father, glancing up from his ledger book. 'So I'd be pleased if you'd adopt a more optimistic outlook. Can you row hard?'

'I can,' said Mr Shankly.

'All right then, I'll try you out as oarsman in the pick-up boat. You'll get a seventieth lay, less board and slops, take it or leave it as you please.'

'I'll take it, sir, thank you kindly.'

'And you?' said my father, turning to a callow, pimpled youth of seventeen.

'Yes, sir, Mr Davidson, my name is Robert Heffernan, I'm a mate of Harry's.'

'I know who you are,' said my father. 'Why are you so keen to go whaling all of a sudden?'

'Well, sir, I thought as a way of meeting girls.'

Harry gave Robert a shove in the ribs, but it was too late. The whale men stared at him; Bastable, removing the pipe from his mouth, surveyed the young man balefully.

'There are no girls whaling, lad,' he said. 'I believe you've been a labouring under a terrible misapprehension.'

'I've worked on whaleboats forty years and never met a girl yet!' cried Salty, and judging from their responses, it would seem that this had been the experience of most of the whale men.

'No, you want to be trying the Presbyterian Sunday school picnics,' offered Uncle Aleck. 'Now there's a way to meet ladies of all shapes and sizes.'

'That's right,' concurred Salty. 'Or the Plain and Fancy Dress Balls up at the School of Arts, though it will cost you five shillings to get in.'

'I haven't got five shillings,' said Robert.

'Ah well then, I see your point. You might as well try the whaling.'

My father held up his hand to indicate that that was enough on the subject.

'Listen to me, young man,' he said. 'If you've volunteered for whaling in the hope of getting yourself better acquainted with Louisa, then I had better put you out of your misery. She won't be courting till she's eighteen years of age.'

'Yes, sir,' said young Robert, his cheeks aflame.

'So, in light of that information, are you still keen?'

'Yes, sir. I'm still keen, sir,' he replied.

My father nodded, and signed him on. The young man did not look very keen. I imagine the prospect of having to go out in all weather and row back and forth across the bay in endless pursuit of enraged leviathans must have seemed exceedingly grim, especially now any chance of courting Louisa on the side had been discounted. He threw a dirty look at Harry; it seemed this might have been all his idea.

I have the ledger book in front of me now, and in my father's handwriting is the following, inscribed on that blustery morning:

Boat Number One	*Boat Number Two*
Headsman: Geo. Davidson	*Headsman: Harry Davidson*
Harpooner: Arthur Ashby	*Harpooner: Salty Mead*
Oarsmen: Walter Bastable	*Oarsmen: John Beck (Rev.)*
Albert Thomas Senior	*A. Shankly*
Albert Thomas Junior	*Robert Heffernan*
Percy Madigan	
Darcy Madigan	

'Right, men,' cried my father, handing the ledger to Uncle Aleck. 'Let's get the boats in the water. We're off to the Lookout!'

'And here's to a prosperous season, this nineteen hundred and eight!' cried Salty.

There were general grunts of 'Hear, hear!' as the men dragged the boats into the water.

'And let's hope it's a damned sight better than last year,' I heard someone mutter.

Urged on by my father now, the men bent to the oars and the two dark-green whaleboats pushed past the first line of breakers. My father stood at the stern of the first boat, wielding the mighty steer oar with expert authority; he was much practised at negotiating the moods of the bar, and his crew had a better time of it than those in the second boat. On the jetty, Violet and Annie jumped up and down, shouting goodbyes and whinnying. Our two dogs, Patch and Bonnie, raced up and down the beach, barking in excitement.

Bonnie even had the notion of swimming after the boats in a show of enthusiasm, and leapt into the shallows determined to do so; once testing the temperature of the water, however, she thought better of the idea and clambered out again, shaking herself miserably at my feet.

'Louisa!' cried Salty. 'How old are you now?'

'Sixteen!' she called back. 'Why?'

'No reason! None at all!' Over the water, we could hear him chortling. 'Two years of whaling, you poor hapless b-----d!'

Once the boats had rounded the Point, we headed back to the house. Glancing back, I saw that Uncle Aleck was standing in the shallows, clutching the ledger, unaware that water was now washing around his knees. I called out to him, and as he turned and came towards me, I saw that tears were streaming down his cheeks. This was not unusual; he had only stopped whaling a few years ago, and it was on occasions such as this that he seemed to miss it most keenly. Knowing better than to offer any soothing words, I put my arm through his and together we made our way back up to the house, the children galloping on ahead, all mad with the cold and excitement.

Once inside and warmed by the fire, Uncle Aleck soon recovered himself and was within half an hour berating me over the consistency of the oatmeal. In fact, he only ate a few spoonfuls before pushing it away and stomping off down to the try-works to see that things were in order for the men's return. The oatmeal was not wasted, however; Louisa applied the rest of it to her face and throat as she had read in the newspaper of its improving effects upon the complexion.

A Most Prepossessing Young Lady

I SHALL NOW PAUSE A MOMENT AND DESCRIBE MY SISTER Louisa, as I notice she is creeping into my story and perhaps warrants an explanation. At that time (I have decided to confine my literary endeavours to an account of the whaling season of 1908), Louisa was sixteen years of age and widely admired for her appearance. Her hair was a pale straw yellow in colour, her features dainty and her figure slender, with an overall effect which many found pleasing. (I myself value qualities such as kindness and consideration for others above mere symmetry of form; however, it seems I am out of step with public taste in this regard.) That same year, I had painted Louisa's likeness in a bid to try my luck in the Portraiture section of the Eden Show. While it too failed to secure a ribbon, the portrait nonetheless attracted a great deal of interest. Certainly, I had captured a reasonable facsimile of her appearance, even in spite of the fact that, at Louisa's insistence, I had elongated her neck untruthfully and painted out a small blemish on her chin. But beyond the relative accuracy of its physical representation, I felt that the portrait also indicated something of her character; a glassy vacancy about the eyes, perhaps, and a sullen insolence in the pouting of her lips. For whatever reason, whether in admiration of Louisa's pleasing physiognomy or the skill that I had demonstrated with my brush, there seemed always to be a small assembly of men gathered about this portrait as it hung in the Exhibits Pavilion. After several offers were made to me, I finally agreed to sell the painting for the sum of ten shillings to Mr Caleb Cook, a sheep farmer from Burragate. Mr Cook then went on to award Louisa the prize of Best-dressed and Most Prepossessing Young Lady, a sum of one pound in the form of a gold sovereign which he himself had personally donated.

Louisa

It is true that, even at this young age, Louisa seemed to exert a mysterious power over the opposite sex. If I was down at the try-works, for example, perhaps bringing the men their evening slops, the whalers might manage to restrain themselves for fully five minutes before they reverted to blasphemy and expectorating. My father was often forced to rebuke them on this matter, with little lasting effect. And yet if I succeeded in having Louisa accompany me, they would come over all quiet and queer and generally conduct themselves with far greater decorum. It seemed they were mesmerised by the afore-mentioned dainty features and the will-o'-the-wisp way she floated about, avoiding anything that might look like work. The various flaws of her character seemed to pass undetected by these fellows.

I will say in Louisa's defence, however, that in one area she did contribute to the household, and that was in the matter of dressmaking. After the particularly prosperous whaling season of 1899, in which twelve whales had been captured (five of them right whales), my father had purchased as a gift for my mother a Singer sewing machine from Mr Crowther, the travelling agent. I recall clearly the great day of its arrival on the back of Mr Crowther's sulky, for it was the first time we realised how much afternoon tea Mr Crowther was capable of ingesting, and in fact he went on to stay for dinner and a hearty breakfast the following morning. Still, if the larder was depleted, it was worth it, for never had we seen anything so beautiful as the machine he unveiled to us in the front room.

It was an especially fine example of the Singer, with a handsome timber cabinet and an ornately detailed Egyptian Sphinx emblazoned in gold upon the black lacquer of its chassis. I can remember feeling even then, at the age of ten, a sense of shame, as its startling glamour seemed only to throw into stark relief the shabbiness of our dwelling and furniture. The haughty demeanour of the golden Sphinx did nothing to ameliorate this feeling.

In between slices of Madeira cake and long anecdotes about unpleasant cows he had had run-ins with in his travels, Mr Crowther took some trouble to demonstrate to my mother the various features of this wonderful machine. By the time he had departed the next day (with corned beef and mustard pickle sandwiches to be going on with), my mother had sewn all by herself a flannelette chemise and an apron made from a fifty-pound calico flour bag. Her next task was to sew together hessian wheat bags, which she then painted with calcimine to form dividing partitions between rooms. She sewed singlets and underpants, petticoats and bloomers; shirts and trousers for the boys and pinafores for the girls. Her work was plain and straightforward; she rarely bothered with anything so fanciful as lace trimmings or ruffled hems; there were no crocheted necklines or blue embroidered forget-me-nots about our collars. I suppose this was the Presbyterian in her nature, or perhaps she just simply could not be bothered. It was not like there wasn't already enough to do about the place.

Much of my memory of my mother, I realise, is of her leaning over her Singer in the evening, murmuring quietly to herself as she strained to thread the needle, and the gentle comforting whirr of her treadling as we drifted off to sleep. Although she attempted to teach me how to sew on it, she did not meet with much success. A dull child, I was always slow to acquire any new skills, and the footwork involved in controlling the machine was beyond me. Further, the hand wheel seemed to wish to deliberately defy me, revolving in the opposite direction to that which it was bid, thereby causing the thread to snap. Even when I finally got it going, the furious action of the plunging needle frightened me, causing me to leap back and the needle to veer wildly from its path. For these crimes, the Sphinx regarded me scornfully.

Louisa was always too flighty a child to be bothered with such a tedious task as sewing; on the one occasion in which my mother coerced her into sewing a pillow case, she registered her protest by sewing the wispy curls at the end of her own plait to the linen. The half an hour spent unpicking the stitches in order to release the furious child was enough to discourage my mother from further attempts in this direction.

Thus, when my mother died, the sewing machine sat silent and still, the Sphinx glowering at us accusingly from across the room. My father must have been very sorry about this, not only for the memory it held of my mother, but also because he was still paying it off on Mr Crowther's hire-purchase plan (he would continue to do so till November 1912). I attempted a few simple garments for the little ones, but the Singer did not choose to cooperate with me; its bobbin jammed and its stitches looped and finally I gave up in frustration. I put the cover over it, ostensibly to keep the dust off, but truthfully to stop the Sphinx from judging me. And then one day, around her thirteenth birthday, Louisa removed the cover and began to sew.

A Cinderella ball was approaching. Admiring an illustration of a pretty girl on a biscuit tin, Louisa decided she would attempt to copy the girl's dress for the occasion. Right from the beginning, she demonstrated an uncanny ability. Pulling apart a blue percale skirt of my mother's, she fashioned for herself a very reasonable approximation of the biscuit-tin dress, though deeming it too plain ('too Presbyterian' were her actual words), she embellished it with a ruffled hemline, and made the sailor collar and sleeve cuffs of a contrasting white cotton, trimmed with a fine pink ribbon she had had my father purchase in Eden.

I would like to report that she sat quietly at the Singer, constructing her garment with a minimum of fuss. This was not the case. She spent most of the week in a vile temper, snapping at anyone who dared approach her, and hurling at the Singer all manner of briny epithets she had picked up from the whalers. By the end of the week, however, she had gained the upper hand; the Singer had cowered into submission. The contest had been hard fought, with casualties on both sides, but now the Sphinx seemed to have lost some of his hauteur. The dress turned out very nicely, and Louisa was singled out in the *Eden Observer and South Coast Advocate* as a '*budding beauty in cornflower blue*'.

I would also like to report that from that point on, she took upon her slender shoulders the entire burden of clothing her family, but in this regard Louisa again thwarted hope. She would not condescend to sew such workaday items as shirts and trousers and under-garments – these items my father was forced to purchase at Howard the Price-Cutter. However, if a ball or a concert or the Presbyterian picnic was approaching, and my father could spare the money, she and I would hasten into Eden and choose ourselves a floral cretonne of some description (there were prettier fabrics, but they were too expensive), and Louisa would apply herself to the task of making our dresses. As long as I made no suggestions as to what I would prefer by way of trimmings or style, they always turned out very well indeed. She would study the pictures in catalogues and newspapers, and without aid of any pattern, produce something very similar; I say 'similar' because invariably Louisa improved upon the original. She had mastered the Singer's many fancy feet, and she pintucked and ruffled, smocked and shirred and puffed. And although squalls of foul temper continued to pass through the front room whenever a dress was in progress, for the most part the activity greatly improved her moods and certainly improved our wardrobes. She had bent the Singer to her will; but then Louisa's will was always formidable.

The Bandages

WHEN MY FATHER AND HIS MEN RETURNED FROM South Head after their first day of lookout, I had boiled a flap of mutton for their dinner, and served it with white sauce, cabbage, carrots and potatoes. We had a reasonable supply of stores since my father's trip into Eden, so I also fixed a tapioca pudding with marmalade sauce. The men were pleased to have meat and pudding, and spoke in a complimentary way of my cooking.

'You keep this up, we'll have to change our name for you,' said Salty.

'Oh, and what is your name for me?' I enquired.

Here, the men grew fidgety and feigned great interest in whatever small activity they were engaged in at the time.

'That's all right, I have names for you also,' I said, and they took this in good part, chuckling humorously. The truth is, I was pleased that the men had enjoyed their meal, for I was keen to make a good impression on John Beck.

I had espied him when Dan and I carried down the food; he was sitting on a log outside the sleeping hut, ruefully examining the palms of his hands. Like any new chum, he had incurred blisters from rowing. Further, he sported a fresh bruise upon his chin, for at one point the oar had apparently slipped from his grasp and smacked him soundly in the jaw. It seemed he was somewhat less experienced at rowing than he had claimed to be.

'You'll want to bandage those blisters,' offered Dan. 'Mary has some rags up at the house if need be.'

'No,' said John Beck. 'I don't need bandages.'

'They'll be a damned sight worse after tomorrow,' said Dan, who often lapsed into language around the whale men. 'And what if a whale hoves to? You can't chase a whale with girl's hands.'

John Beck's face darkened, and he stood abruptly and walked away. He did not return, so I left his portion in a tin dish and covered it with a saucepan lid.

Later that night, as Louisa and I washed the dishes, I came across this same dish scraped clean, and took it as a sign that my culinary efforts had met with his approval. I immediately set about planning what meal I might prepare for the following evening. It would have to involve mutton, but perhaps there was some new way I might enliven it. As I was reflecting on the limited possibilities available to me, I heard the shrill cries of Mr Maudry in full attack: several moments later, a small knock sounded on the kitchen door. There outside in the darkness stood John Beck, looking somewhat harassed.

'I have just been set upon by an unpleasant bird,' he said, as if to account for the state in which he presented.

'Yes,' I said simply. 'That is Mr Maudry.'

'I see,' said John Beck, regarding me strangely. 'Well.' He paused for a moment. 'I was wondering if you might have some rags to spare.'

'Yes, of course,' I replied. 'Is it for your blisters?'

'Yes,' he said.

'May I see?' I asked.

He gave me his hands, palms facing upwards, and I took them by the wrists and examined them closely. (I had to examine them closely, as for some reason I was not wearing my spectacles.) They were good hands, well-shaped and strong – perhaps stronger than one would reasonably expect of a Methodist minister – the pads of each palm sporting a set of fresh blisters.

'You should wash them in salt water,' I instructed.

'I did, in the sea,' he replied.

'And rub in some sand.'

'You mean rub sand into the actual blisters?' asked John Beck.

'Yes, several times daily.'

'Did you just make that up?'

'Yes. I mean, no. No, it's actual advice that I have read somewhere. In a medical text of some kind. I believe the coarse granules, ah, slough away the damaged skin.'

'Won't that hurt?' he asked.

'It may.'

'Can you recommend something less painful?'

I glanced up at him; he was smiling at me.

Many times in the ensuing years, I have run this moment through again in my mind; taken it out of my small box of precious things and turned it over, examining its every facet minutely.

There was something about his smile that was unlike that of any minister, Methodist or otherwise, that I had ever encountered. It was a gentle smile, amused but not mocking, the subtle, curving movement dispersing small creases around his eyes and mouth; even the purple bruise upon his jaw did not detract from the effect. How fortunate had been his congregation, I marvelled, to have had that kind, handsome face beam down upon them from the pulpit, intoning a psalm perhaps or leading them in a Wesleyan hymn.

A small movement of his hands alerted me to the realisation that I had been holding on to them for a longer period of time than was appropriate; I dropped them at once.

'Well, of course, you could simply bandage them,' I said. 'Let me fetch some rags at once.'

I hurried back inside and rummaged about, and in fact it was several minutes before I was able to put my hands on anything suitable. Upon returning to find him waiting patiently, I held them out to him. He hesitated.

'I don't suppose ... would you?' he asked. 'It's just that it's awkward to do it oneself.'

'Yes, of course. I would be happy to,' I responded, and set about bandaging his hands in as businesslike a fashion as I could muster, given my own hands seemed to be trembling violently.

'Do all the whalers get such pretty bandages?' he asked softly. (I had torn a strip of broderie anglaise from the bottom of my clean petticoat, as there were no other suitable rags available.)

'Not all of them,' I responded, not daring to look up at him.

'May I ask, is it from a petticoat?'

'Possibly.'

'Then when I am chasing whales tomorrow I shall think of that poor petticoat's sacrifice, and it shall spur me onwards.'

So overcome was I at the unexpected turn that the conversation had taken (albeit somewhat at odds with my image of him leading the congregation in a Wesleyan hymn), I was unable to think of any response, and simply tied the bandages as securely as I could. When I had done so, he thanked me and moved off into the darkness; several moments later the piercing shrieks of Mr Maudry resounded through the night.

I stepped back inside the kitchen and closed the door. I would have valued a moment of quiet to reflect upon this exchange; however, Louisa was keen to pass judgement on our newcomer. Initially, she expressed surprise that he had incurred blisters from simply rowing the short distance to South Head and back. When I reminded her that new chums often suffered blisters, she responded that this might well be the case if they had rowed eight or nine times across the bay in pursuit of a whale. I was then compelled to remind her that since John Beck was formerly a Methodist minister, it was small wonder his hands were more delicate than those of our regular whale men. Louisa twisted her mouth into a scornful expression, and said nothing; I then informed her that this was most unbecoming and made her look like she had recently ingested something disagreeable, to which she responded, 'Yes, dinner.'

'What kind of bandages do you call them?' asked Salty the following morning, as they pushed the boats into the water.

'Why, I'm not sure,' said John Beck. 'I think it's broderie anglaise.'

'Looks like a lady's undergarment is what it looks like!' cried Salty. 'Oi!' he called out to the occupants of the other boat. 'You should see the Reverend's bandages!'

'What's that?' called Arthur Ashby, unable to hear him properly across the water.

'Reverend's got some girl's bloomers as bandages! Show them, Father!' Here, he raised one of John Beck's hands so they could see it more clearly. 'All frilly and lacy! Some lady's pantaloons, I'll wager!'

John Beck pulled his hand away in annoyance, and bent to the oars. He did not look to be enjoying Salty's ribaldry. Nor did it appear from his expression that my father much liked the sound of what he heard. It was fortunate that he was preoccupied in guiding his boat across the bar, otherwise John Beck would have felt the full force of Fearless Davidson's whale-killing gaze.

The Old Grey Kangaroo

THE OLDEST CHILDREN – THAT IS, HARRY AND LOUISA AND I – had been taught to read and write by our mother, who had herself been a governess before she met our father. She had come out from England at the age of twenty-five on a loan from the Female Middle-Class Emigration Society (I know this because they continued to write for many years after her death, demanding that the loan be repaid). There was no one to meet her when she arrived, and she was forced to impose on the goodwill of strangers; not wishing to be a burden, she proceeded to endure a series of situations, each worse than the last, until finally she arrived at the Walcotts' near Pambula. Soon after her arrival, she took ill with the measles and very nearly died; in a bid to reduce her fever, they cut off all her hair. Considering her too sickly to work, the Walcotts subsequently discharged her. As luck would have it, my father was called upon to convey her back to Eden (he had been cutting railway sleepers in the area at the time, a job he often took out of whaling season). He did not think much of her immediately, as she was thin and pasty and her hair was cut short like a boy; also, any attempts at conversation were thwarted by her continual crying and blowing her nose. However, my father, always a kindly man, felt sorry for her and he took her back to stay at his mother's house (this house in which we still live) as she had no place else to go, and barely a shilling in her pocket. Over ensuing weeks, they developed sufficient feeling for each other that they became engaged. He was thirty years of age at the time and she was twenty-nine; each of them had given up hope of ever marrying, and yet they shared thirteen happy years together and produced six children. I was the firstborn and named Mary, after my late maternal grandmother.

It was January when they met and March when they married, and although my mother knew my father was a whaler, she little realised what that meant until the first whale of the season was captured and tried out in July. My mother suffered frequently from sick head-aches, and the stench and the blood and the ramps awash with whale oil greatly exacerbated her condition; however, she did her best to keep the extent of her suffering from my father. I well remember the sight of her returning from the try-works after delivering the men their meal; scrambling up the hill with her hand clasped tightly over her mouth, veering suddenly into the shrubs to retch violently. Once inside, she would bid me squeeze a lemon and add a teaspoon of baking soda, and this she would force herself to drink down to quell her biliousness. I don't think that she was ever a woman of strong constitution. Even on her good days, I can only recall her eating small portions of dry toast, dipped in a little Worcestershire sauce. 'It's my nerves,' she would tell me. 'They get raggedy sometimes.'

We have a photograph of her which I sometimes find myself studying. She had broad cheekbones and prominent teeth; people say I take after her, although I cannot see it myself. She has baby Dan on her lap and I stand very close beside her, as if attempting to hide behind her skirts. She is smiling (in fact, she is the only one who smiles, as the rest of us children are either glowering or grimacing), but there is a look about her, almost in the slope of her shoulders, that indicates a person who struggles with her health. Nonetheless, her expression is one of gentle kindness, and that is how I remember her. The *Eden Observer and South Coast Advocate*, in noting her passing, commented: '*She was highly esteemed by all who knew her.*' This was true; I could only add that small children and animals esteemed her most of all.

One of my strongest memories of my mother is the way she used to talk to an old grey kangaroo that would come and graze about the house in the dawn and the early evening. My mother liked this kangaroo, and whenever she saw him, she would go out and talk to him in a kindly fashion. 'Watch him, Mary,' she would say. 'Watch him go all sleepy when I talk to him.' She would then proceed to tell him how handsome he was, what a fine kangaroo, how nicely his fur gleamed in the sunshine. On and on she would murmur these compliments; after a little while, the old kangaroo would start to close his eyes as if falling asleep. His battered old head would start to sink. Occasionally he might open his eyes and gaze at her dreamily, then close them again as if in a trance. He seemed to like to listen to the sound of her voice. I liked to listen to her, too. I would sit very quietly on the back step and watch. When it was time to resume her chores, she would bid the old buck goodbye; he would rouse himself softly, as if from a reverie, and hop slowly away.

The morning after she died, I was standing in the kitchen, feeling rather sad and lonely for our mother, when I looked out the door and saw the old grey kangaroo. He was standing beneath the jacaranda tree, and he seemed to be gazing at me in a very deliberate way. A sudden feeling of hope lifted me; I felt at once compelled to go outside and talk to him, just as my mother had so often done. Approaching him carefully, I began by assuring him that he was indeed a fine old kangaroo. I told him that our mother was dead, but that his handsomeness was beyond question. I remarked on his fine posture and how magnificently his fur gleamed in the morning sunshine (in truth, he was rather battle-scarred and moth-eaten in appearance). All the while, the old kangaroo eyed me steadily. As I continued, I noticed that his expression seemed to be growing increasingly indignant. Every now and then, he would swing his head around sharply, as if in scornful disbelief. Then, after several minutes and with an air of the greatest disdain, he turned his back upon me and hopped away. I have never forgotten it. A feeling of the utmost despair came upon me. I was thirteen years old and motherless; I wanted only that he stand there and listen to me. The old grey kangaroo could not have chosen to hurt me in a more deliberate fashion.

On subsequent occasions, whenever I saw him about the place, I would greet him curtly and continue on with my chores. After a while, he stopped visiting at all. I assumed he was dead, and felt glad about it. However, some months later, while taking baby Violet for a walk in the bush up behind the house, I suddenly came upon him. He had been basking in a patch of sunlight, nearly asleep; I had caught him by surprise. He lurched to his feet in a most ungraceful manner, and hopped away into the scrub. This unexpected sighting infuriated me. The fact that he was still alive but chose no longer to visit us seemed to be his final insult; I felt that he could scarcely have been more pointed in indicating what a poor substitute for my mother he thought me to be. Overcome with anger, I flung at his retreating form all the various anathemas I could think of; startled awake by my shrill cries, Violet commenced howling afresh. She was teething and unhappy, I had taken her for a walk in a bid to settle her. This was the last occasion on which I saw him. Over the ensuing years, we have had many wallabies come to eat the new grass around the house. I much prefer their company; they are timid and deferential by nature.

But I see I have gone on at length about my mother, and in fact I only mentioned her by way of explaining that she had taught us older children to read and write. After her death, our father employed a governess briefly, a Miss Gurney; however, she did not stay with us for long. I do not remember much about her except that she was very tall, and took the largest size in boots and gloves; also, we were a little afraid of her as she seemed very harsh and once referred to my brother Harry as a 'bl---y b-----d'. On one occasion, she asked my father if she might accompany them on a whale chase; of course he was horrified and would not hear of it. He did consent to let her take the rheumatism cure for her lumbago, and she was subsequently submerged up to her head in the carcass of a dead whale. (This treatment was quite a popular sideline for my father at the time; the combination of the natural benefits of whale oil and the heat generated from the fermentation process was known to have a curative effect.) I remember her staggering up the hill afterwards, looking as if she might faint; shortly after this she departed abruptly without giving notice, a paltry thanks for my father's kindness.

Preoccupied as he was with his own concerns, it seemed not to occur to him to employ another governess, and we were left to our own devices. Years passed and the little ones grew out of babyhood. One day I realised that Dan, almost nine years of age at the time, did not know so much as his ABC. I immediately took it upon myself to educate the younger ones, and from that day on devoted an hour or so daily to their schooling, sometimes including the Aboriginal children in my 'classroom' – that is, the children of our Aboriginal whalers, if it was whaling season and they were willing to be confined indoors.

They were good little children on the whole, and eager to learn, with the possible exception of Darcy, whose natural high spirits seemed to incite mischief in others, especially Louisa. I remember the pair of them once encouraged the younger children to eat tree sap wrapped in tinfoil, claiming it was caramel toffee. My classroom rapidly became the sick room; I spent the afternoon administering salt water and ground mustard as a purgative. On another occasion,

I found Darcy terrifying the younger children with an account of a bunyip he claimed to have witnessed emerging from our creek.

'The water was bubbling and the ground started shaking, and there he was, with a huge white head like a bull, and terrible rolling eyes...' And here Darcy rolled his eyes alarmingly while the little ones clutched at each other and whimpered. 'They say if you done something wrong, he'll come looking for you. You'll hear him panting like this' – and here Darcy began to pant stertorously – 'and then he'll start to roar, and you better watch out, because if he bites you, you die.' At which point, the little ones erupted into shrill screams, and I was forced to intervene. Fortunately for me, Darcy commenced whaling at thirteen. As fond as I was of the boy, I was glad to banish further talk of the bunyip from the classroom, for reasons of my own which I will now describe.

As a very young child, perhaps two years of age, I had once wandered away from the house as far as the creek that runs along the back of our property – that same creek where Darcy claimed to have seen the bunyip. It was most unlike my mother to let me roam so far; her anxiety of losing us was such that she used to tie a small bell around each of us so she knew at all times where we were. It occurs to me now that on this occasion she may have been indisposed with another of her sick headaches; perhaps she had been lying down in a darkened room. For whatever reason, I nonetheless disappeared for several hours, and it was only as darkness approached that my mother found me, playing happily with a pile of stones I had collected by the side of the creek. My little bell had apparently been caught on a branch and broken free, and I was soaking wet from head to toe, as if I had fallen in; however, the creek runs deep at the point at which I was discovered, so if that had been the case I would surely have drowned. I certainly have no memory of having fallen in, or indeed of anything prior to my mother's discovery of me, but that I recall very vividly; in fact, it is my earliest memory. Her face was very red and her features contorted with fear as she gathered me up and clutched me tightly. Suddenly, almost as if we were being chased (although I don't believe there was any pursuer), she began to tear wildly through the undergrowth so that it ripped her skirt and scratched our arms and faces.

Even now, I can make no sense of this memory when I think of it. Why did she take off like this? Why did she not simply return the way she had come, where she would have emerged very quickly from the scrub and returned safely to our house? If there was no one pursuing us, why did she run? Of course, the only explanation for this was my mother's terror of the bunyip, for she had heard the blackfellows talk of it.

As the creek was our primary source of fresh water, my mother was required to venture there several times a day. She claimed that on one occasion she had seen the bunyip scampering through the trees; also, that she heard it crying out at night and, on several occasions, had even come upon the ragged bones of the creatures it devoured. She was convinced it was the bunyip that had lured me up to the creek, torn my bell from my clothing and thrown me into the water; she feared it would very likely have eaten me had she not stumbled across the scene in time. When we asked her what the bunyip looked like, she would clamp her lips tightly shut and shake her head, as if its appearance was too monstrous to describe. At night, sitting by the fire, especially if my father was out chasing whales, she would suddenly stop what she was doing and motion for us to be quiet. In silence, we would listen. Mostly, we heard nothing but the sound of our own panicked breathing; sometimes the crack of a branch outside. '*Bunyip*,' she would whisper to us triumphantly. 'Prowling about.'

Of all of her children, I became the most frightened. Having been lured away by the bunyip once, I became fearful of venturing far from the house lest he entice me again. My fear of the bunyip was such that I felt a great need to stay close to my mother at all times, and became very agitated when separated from her. When my mother died, my fear of the bunyip only escalated. I now refused to go to the creek at all, even in broad daylight. This was a great nuisance to my father, as he had enough work to do without having to fetch water for our domestic needs.

'Don't be foolish, Mary!' he said to me one day, in exasperation. 'There's no such thing as bunyips. Don't you realise your mother only told you that to keep the little ones away from the creek?'

At first, I was deeply shocked by this, for if it was true, then she had lied to us, and my memory of my mother was sacred to me. But after a great deal of thought on the subject, I concluded that my father had only told me this in a bid to dispel my fears. Of course my mother had feared the bunyip; I remember vividly her great panic on the occasion on which she rescued me. This was something I had witnessed which my father had not: her terrified whimpering, her wild blundering through the undergrowth. Naturally, she would have tried to keep her fears from him, not wishing to concern him with her private anxieties when he had already so much to worry about. Also, and this was something I could not emulate, my mother was, in spite of her terror, somehow still able to visit the creek to fetch water every day. Given this, it is perhaps little wonder that my father concluded that her fears were not genuine.

The situation was only alleviated by the arrival of a book entitled *Mr Bunyip*, charitably bestowed upon us by Mrs Pike of the Great Southern Hotel, along with several other books her own children had outgrown. I opened it with some trepidation; however, once I commenced reading I could not stop until I had finished it (admittedly it is a slim volume of twenty-four pages). By the time I put it down, I felt altogether differently about bunyips, and my one regret was that my mother had not had an opportunity to read it also.

The story concerns a little girl named Mary (coincidentally the same name as my own) who is sitting by the river one day when a huge monster (the bunyip) rises out of the water and approaches her. Paralysed with fear, she is surprised when the creature addresses her not with a fearsome roar, as Darcy had described, but with a mild, gentle voice:

> '"*Don't be in the least alarmed, my little dear," says the Bunyip. "I know who you are. You are Mary Somerville, the best-conducted girl in your class. I wouldn't hurt a hair of your head for all the gold in Ballarat."*'

He then describes to her something of his life (he is one hundred and eighty years old), and talks of how important it is for boys and girls to apply themselves to their schoolwork. He advises all children to put money away for the orphanages in Melbourne, to listen to old people and not be too trusting of strangers. He talks of how he dealt with a cruel white settler, Peter Hardheart, who used to shoot down the Aborigines as if they were wild beasts.

> *'I kept my eye on him till one day I saw him chasing some of the poor*
> *fellows along the bank here, and I was out of the water and had him in*
> *a moment.'*

He dealt similarly with Tommy Turbulent, a small boy who used to steal other boys' marbles and play truant.

> *'When you see Susan Slattern, tell her I have my eye upon her, too. I*
> *know all about her capsizing the perambulator and throwing her baby*
> *out in the thistles.'*

Although I knew it was only a story, it nonetheless made a great impression on me, for this was an altogether different bunyip to the one of my terrified imaginings. This bunyip seemed a gentle fellow. He acted harshly only when appropriate, and his words were remarkably instructive and of value to all. But the greatest revelation for me was the way in which the bunyip's physical appearance was described:

> *'He had fins at his sides, which gave him the appearance of a whale,*
> *and as he had a difficulty in moving along the ground, and seemed much*
> *more at home in the water, she came to the conclusion at last that he must*
> *belong to the whale species.'*

I found this remarkable, given that we are a family of whalers and surrounded by whales, mostly dead, and from that point on, my fear of the bunyip diminished. What did I have to fear? My father was a whale-killer. Even a bad bunyip (presumably there were bad bunyips as well as decent bunyips) would be no match for his lance.

I myself had stood upon the bloated underbelly of the ninety-foot blue whale whose ribs now form our pergola, as it lay belly-up in the shallows (this was for Mr Wellings, our town photographer, in order to best demonstrate the whale's vast dimensions); how could a bunyip be more fearsome than that? I read the description aloud to my father, who raised his eyebrows thoughtfully and considered it a moment.

'Next time you go up the creek, take the whale gun with you,' he said at last. 'If there's no whales, we'll try bunyips.'

And, in fact, I did take the whale gun with me up to the creek the next few times in the hope of contributing to our family's fortunes; however, I soon desisted as it was a cumbersome great thing and the water was enough to carry. Suffice it to say, the terrible fear I had suffered was now gone – I could go to the creek alone. For this reason, *Mr Bunyip* remained a book close to my heart, and I endeavoured to use it as a means of instructing the youngest two in particular. They had much they could learn from a little girl like Mary Somerville, '*who seemed to carry sunshine with her wherever she went, and was a universal favourite*'. Annie and Violet did not think much of the book however, except to cackle in the most uproarious fashion at Susan Slattern throwing the baby out of the perambulator into the thistles.

An Unhappy Experience

THREE WEEKS INTO THE SEASON, AND NOT A WHALE WAS sighted. Please God, we prayed, not another season like the last. Every night my father would return from another fruitless day of keeping lookout at Boyd Tower; every night he would seek something different to blame. It was a parasite, a worm of some kind burrowing into the whales' brains and thus diminishing the population. It was the Norwegians with their factory steamers and their explosive harpoons. The whales had changed their breeding grounds. The water was too warm, or possibly too cold. After his dinner, he would sit by the fire and forbid us from speaking, lest he miss the call of a wandering humpback. Please God, we prayed, bring our father a whale. Make it a big one, with plenty of whalebone. Let him pay off all his debts, and stop from worrying.

To add to my discomfort, I was becoming increasingly pre-occupied with my feelings for John Beck. Since our exchange over the bandages at the kitchen door, I had seen him only briefly when I served the whale men their slops; thus I found myself looking forward to this time of day with a mixture of eagerness and nervous dread. Unlike some of the other whalers, John Beck was invariably pleasant towards me; sometimes he even joked with me a little or teased me in a friendly way. Although I tried to respond in kind, I found I was often at a loss to know how best to reply to his remarks. Having lost my mother at an early age, I had no feminine example in matters concerning intercourse between the sexes. (I do not wish to give the impression that I am forever moaning about the loss of my mother. Most of the time, I do not think about it.) Being somewhat earnest by nature, I greatly feared I would make a dull companion; consequently, I had looked to romance novels for direction in these matters (the School of Arts had a small collection available for loan, although the waiting list was long). In so doing, I had often noticed a certain archness deployed by the heroines when addressing members of the opposite sex and I strived to emulate this tone whenever the opportunity arose, which was infrequently. I had been forced to practise on my brother Harry, or my father; however, I did not meet with much success, as my playful tones seemed only to irritate the former and bewilder the latter. In desperation, I had even attempted to engage my Uncle Aleck in repartee, but it was difficult to sparkle when constantly having to repeat things in a louder voice.

I now attempted to adopt this lightness of manner when speaking with John Beck, to the extent that I became quite nervous and excitable in his company and had even been cultivating what I had hoped to be a gay and tinkling laugh. However, my brother Harry took me aside one evening and said to me, in his surly fashion: 'Stop with this dreadful false merriment you've been assuming of late.

You're greatly embarrassing me.' Admittedly, as my brother and closest sibling, Harry was the least forgiving of my foibles; be that as it may, I was nonetheless aghast that I had perhaps been creating an unfortunate impression of myself. I now seemed to lose what little self-confidence I possessed; I began to find it difficult to simply look at John Beck in a casual, nonchalant fashion, or even to meet his gaze when he spoke to me. The responses I gave to his queries seemed to suffer, at best, from a stilted quality. In trying not to be falsely gay my conversation became overly self-conscious and strained. It soon reached the stage (over a period of two to three weeks) where, in my anxiety not to offend, I seemed to be losing the capacity for speech altogether. And what was the reason for all this agony? Because I had bandaged John Beck's hands and he had smiled at me.

I had suffered a similar experience before, in fact during the previous season, with a man called Charley Burrows. He had been one of my father's best oarsmen; in fact, my father thought so well of him that he had elevated him to the position of headsman of the second whaleboat. Burrows was a ruddy-faced young man, well-liked by all for his readiness with a joke or a quip. He was at first very amiable towards me; we had a little joke together where he would call me 'Curly' or 'Curly-Top' (owing to my hair) and I would call him 'Ginger' or 'Gingernut' (owing to his hair). He would often volunteer to carry the pots and dishes up to the house for me after dinnertime, and it was always 'Curly, let me get the door' and 'Curly, have we got any jam for our bread and butter?' and 'Curly-Top, tell us what's new in the newspaper'.

Flattered by his attentions, I found myself rapidly developing feelings towards him. As with John Beck, these feelings manifested themselves in my becoming rather nervous in his company, and unable to converse with him any longer in a relaxed fashion. The other whalers noticed this and began to tease me, making a great joke of my blushing and so forth. Hoping that Burrows would speak up for me, I found that his manner seemed instead to become increasingly cool towards me. He no longer called me Curly, nor would he volunteer to carry the pots and pans for me. When I attempted to engage him in conversation (and I was careful to keep my subjects general, some topical issue in the newspaper perhaps), he would respond in a surly fashion if he responded at all. One night, as I passed him his meal, I said to him, 'Here you are then, Gingernut,' and he scowled at me and told me not to call him that. Needless to say, I was exceedingly hurt and bewildered by this apparent change of heart: after all, he had been very civil towards me at first. However, I was soon to discover the true reason behind it all.

It transpired, in fact, that Burrows was a drinker. One evening, on bringing down their meal, I found that several of the men had procured a quantity of rum. Burrows in particular was intoxicated and reeling about the sleeping huts, singing a song about a jolly tinker which contained several lewd verses. He followed me up to the house on the pretence of helping me with the pots; instead he lunged at me and attempted to kiss me. I broke free and scrambled away, whereupon he hurled insults at me and accused me of having encouraged him and led him on unfairly. Horrified, I returned to the house, saying nothing of this at all to my father.

Instead, I took myself off to my bed, and lay there wide awake, going over and over in my mind this dreadful development. Although I had many times tried to imagine myself being kissed, even somewhat roughly, by Burrows, the reality had in fact been most unpleasant and rather upsetting. His breath had smelled of liquor and his beard had scratched my face; also his tongue had become involved, which I had not expected and found alarming, as if a sea slug was flailing about in my mouth. Perhaps I should not have been surprised by his behaviour; whalers were inclined to imbibe heavily, especially if they had recently captured a whale (which had not been the case in this instance). Well aware of their propensity towards ribaldry when inebriated, my father usually ensured that we kept well away from them if there was any sign of them carousing in the sleeping huts. However, on this occasion, my father had been preoccupied with his own concerns (brooding on the absence of whales and so forth), and had thus unwittingly allowed me to venture down to the sleeping huts alone.

However, even more upsetting to me than his intoxication was the fact that Burrows had so rudely attempted to make love to me after lately treating me with such coldness. If he liked me well enough to want to kiss me, why had he been treating me with such indifference? Could it be that he drank more than I realised, and the drink was causing him to behave in such a way? I sat down and wrote Burrows a long letter, in which I discussed my bewilderment at his conduct towards me. I suggested as delicately as I could that this might be a consequence of his dipsomania and that, if he could adopt a more abstemious way of life, then indeed there might be a chance of our friendship developing into something deeper. I indicated that if he was prepared to embrace a life of abstinence, then I was certainly prepared to overlook the unfortunate incident of the previous night and start afresh.

The next day, the crews were away early as usual to spend the day on lookout at South Head. Realising I would not have an opportunity to see Burrows until evening, I worked all day on polishing and refining my letter. I crossed out entire paragraphs and reinstated them; I fretted over misspellings and attempted as far as possible to improve my childish, back-sloping handwriting. By evening, I had completely rewritten the entire five pages several times over.

That night, the crews returned later than usual; in fact, Dan and I had been waiting for them at the jetty for some time. We had hoped that their late return might be a consequence of them capturing a whale; however we soon learned that this was not the case. It seems they had rowed over to Eden for the purposes of letting Burrows off; he had 'had a gutful' of whaling (according to Harry) and was not coming back. Whether he had indeed given up in disgust at the shortage of whales or had been released from his duties by my father, I was never able to discover. I had certainly said nothing of the incident the previous evening to anybody, and yet my father instructed my brothers to accompany me to the sleeping huts that night and from thenceforth. The men were exceedingly subdued that evening; I felt a tension in the atmosphere that I could only surmise contained a degree of resentment towards me. As I say, Burrows had been well-liked by the men; I imagine they were sorry he had gone. But I was also sorry, and I kept my letter in the hope that he might return.

The reason I go on at such length about this unpleasantness is in part because Harry himself had introduced the subject of Burrows on the occasion that he had taken me aside to berate me for my false merriment and for being an embarrassment to him. 'Don't be doing to the Reverend what you did to Burrows,' he had cautioned me. When I asked him to explain more fully what he meant, he indicated that I knew very well what he meant, and on that note ended our conversation. I can only conclude by this that my personal feelings for Burrows had been so plainly evident that they were somehow construed as granting him permission to make improper advances to me.

'Why don't you talk to me anymore?' asked John Beck one night, as I gathered up the dirty dishes outside the sleeping huts. 'Have I offended you in some way?'

'No,' I stammered. 'You have not offended me.'

'Because you used to like to talk to me, and now you don't.'

'That's because I am busy with my chores,' I said.

'Did you not want to see how my blisters have healed?' he asked, with a smile coming over his face again.

'No, I don't,' I replied quickly, and scurried away just as fast as I could.

Tom Raises the Alarm

I AWOKE SUDDENLY TO HEAR A DISTANT BUT DETERMINED *SMACK!* It was a Killer whale flop-tailing, surely? *Smack!* There it was again, and no doubt about it this time. I jumped out of bed and hurried out to the verandah – my father was running stiff-legged down to the sleeping huts, shouting, *'Rush oh! Get up, boys! Rush oh!'*

Hurrying around the side of the house, I climbed up the ladder to where the boys slept inside the roof. Both Harry and Dan were sound asleep – what heavy sleepers boys were as a rule! I sometimes thought it might be necessary to detonate the whale gun in order to rouse them. 'Harry, get up, there's a whale!' I cried, shaking him vigorously. He opened his bleary eyes, and lay there inert for a moment; however, upon poking him sharply and reiterating my point, he finally seemed to rouse fully and started groping for his trousers.

I clambered down the ladder and rushed to the kitchen now to hastily fill two waterproof canvas bags with yesterday's damper and some salted beef. I thrust these at Harry as he scrambled down the ladder. 'Don't forget the kegs!' I cried, and he scooped up a keg of water with his free arm. 'Dan, take the other!' I instructed, as Dan jumped down off the last few rungs. He picked up the second keg and set off down the hill at a gallop, although with some difficulty as the keg was heavy for a small boy.

Back on the verandah, I could see the men now rushing for the whaleboats. There was John Beck, scrambling to jump in. Annie and Violet were awake now, and at my side. 'Come on, girls, let's see them off,' I cried. We ran for our coats, which we pulled on over our night-gowns, and we raced up the hill to where we could gain a reasonable vantage point of the bay.

'It's Tom!' cried Annie, and there he was, our famous Killer whale, leaping out of the water and crashing down his tail, impatient for the whalers to join him. As ever, I felt something of a shock when I saw him. He was so crisply illustrated, as it were; his black head so shiny and his white patches so luminous that he struck me as absurdly cheerful in his appearance as a carousel horse at a fairground. He had none of the dismal, barnacled grey of the humpback: no, he was a portly and dapper fish in white tie and dinner jacket. How homely and dull humpbacks seemed in comparison, I thought to myself. (Or at least they certainly seemed so as the men at the capstan prepared to haul off their blubber, which is when I had had most occasion to observe them.) Sometimes, at night, when we heard the anguished cow-like moan of the humpback, my sister Louisa would say: 'Listen! A humpback has just seen its own reflection,' which set the younger ones to giggling. My father told us that on several occasions he had witnessed younger humpbacks bedecked in seaweed, as if in a bid to improve their appearance.

The girls occupied themselves by calling out excitedly to Tom, in the hope that he might somehow acknowledge them. He paid us no direct attention, except to perform more spectacular breaches; perhaps he was showing off for our benefit. Meanwhile, I scoured the bay in the hope that I could spot the whale, and thus assist my father. Was that a plume of smoke rising up near

Tom

Snug Cove? My eyesight was not reliable at a distance, but yes, I felt certain that that was smoke. Somebody had obviously sighted the whale, perhaps a fisherman at Eden wharf, and had lit a fire in order to alert my father as to its whereabouts. Now my father's boat appeared below, his men pulling hard at the oars. *'Smoke!'* I cried out. My father, at the steer oar, looked up at me; I pointed towards Snug Cove and cried out, 'Smoke at Snug Cove!' I could see him squinting in that direction. He called out to me, 'Where?'

'Snug Cove!' I cried again. Was there smoke at Snug Cove? I wondered suddenly. It was certainly quite difficult to see at the moment, given the heaviness of the clouds.

'I don't see any smoke,' said Annie, standing beside me.

'Smoke at Snug Cove!' my father was now calling to Harry. Harry was headsman of the second boat, which was coming up quickly behind my father's boat. I could see every head turn in the direction of Snug Cove, straining to see. Where had it gone, that plume of smoke? Perhaps the fire had been accidentally extinguished?

'Where did you say?' cried Harry.

'Snug Cove!'

'I don't see any smoke at Snug Cove!'

'Nor me!' This from Darcy, who had the best eyes of all.

'Mary thought she saw smoke!'

'Mary?' riposted Harry. 'She's blind as a bat, for Christ's sake!'

I could see John Beck look up towards me now and felt suddenly mortified. I had leapt out of bed in such excitement that I had not considered my appearance and my hair was now blowing about wildly in the stiff breeze. Just then, providing a welcome distraction, Tom rushed up suddenly out of the water and flop-tailed directly between the two boats, thoroughly drenching the occupants. The men cursed the Killer whale vehemently.

'Stop your complaining!' I heard my father cry. 'At least now you might wake up a bit! Come on, put your backs into it!'

The men leaned into their oars and took off in pursuit of Tom, all talk of smoke now forgotten. I felt a rush of excitement as I watched the two dark-green boats fighting their way through the breakers. A hard north-easterly wind ripped across the bay; it was not at all a good day for small boats such as these, and now as I gazed upon the churning sea I wondered that they were going out in it at all.

'Good luck!' I cried to my father, and also to John Beck, although they were well past the breakers now and could not hear me. The girls jumped about in excitement; also in a bid to keep themselves warm. Uncle Aleck staggered up the hill to join us; Dan bounded up as well, anxious to see them off. Together, our little group watched until

Killer whale and whaleboats had rounded the point and disappeared from view.

'Godspeed,' said Uncle Aleck. 'Bring us back a humper, Georgie boy.'

We spent the rest of the day trying to occupy ourselves with the usual mundane chores; however, I doubt that many minutes passed between one or other of us scampering up the hill in the vain hope of witnessing our warriors engaged in battle. I should add that Tom had led them off towards Honeysuckle Point, which is in the opposite direction to Snug Cove, so perhaps I had been wrong about the smoke.

Canst Thou Draw Out
Leviathan with a Fish Hook?

MY FATHER AND HIS CREW RETURNED AT ABOUT FOUR IN THE afternoon, covered in whale blood, weary but triumphant. The second boat returned some forty minutes later with Harry in a foul temper and his crew looking exceedingly shame-faced. A humpback had been captured; however, another had somehow managed to escape. The crew of the second boat had been found sadly wanting.

In short, from what I could glean, the chase and ensuing capture had gone as follows: Tom had led the men to where the Killers were engaged in harassing two whales; they succeeded in separating the whales just as the boats arrived and the Killers subsequently applied their attentions to the smaller of the beasts. My father and his men immediately set off in pursuit of the larger whale. It zigzagged desperately in a bid to shake them off, and considerable time elapsed before my father was sufficiently close for his harpooner to throw his iron. My father always used Arthur Ashby in this capacity; he was one of our longstanding Aboriginal whalers, and tremendously accurate with his aim. From this point, I will quote from the *Eden Observer and South Coast Advocate*, in which an account of the chase appeared several days later:

> *'The Killers had been engaged with the smaller whale, but no sooner had the larger animal been harpooned than they were present, attacking it with desperate energy; and its loud and continuous bellowing told clearly the deadly battle that was being waged beneath the troubled waters of the bay. The spray flew continuously over the frail craft, in quantities sufficient to dampen the ardour of any but George Davidson and his plucky men, who don't seem to understand the meaning of the word danger or have a total disregard for it.'*

We were fortunate to have such a fine writer as Mr Phillips, the editor of the *Eden Observer and South Coast Advocate* at the time. Although the men would often mutter that he'd got some small detail wrong here or there, his accounts nonetheless offer a tremendous record of my father's work. We made sure to cut out every article and preserve them in a scrapbook, sometimes making small annotations in ink on the side. Uncle Aleck would often have me read aloud his favourites by the fireside of an evening, and although my father acted like he didn't much care, you could tell he was listening intently.

> *'Crowds of people occupied the different headlands, and, notwithstanding the bitterly cold wind which was blowing, watched the chase with keen interest. From the heights of Cattle Bay could be seen almost every movement of the whale as it tore onwards from Quarantine Bay,*

from time to time rising above the surface of the water and throwing great bodies of foam in all directions, as attack after attack was made upon it by the Killers, whose persistent onslaughts were witnessed with great wonder by visitors. While a number of Killers always remained close by the head of the whale, tearing at its jaws and impeding its progress by many methods, others were acting as sentinels well ahead and in its wake, and as they rose to the surface, spouting up the water, exhibiting their bodies and long black fins, they presented a sight never to be forgotten.

The roughness of the water prevented a free use of the lance for some time, and then one of the Killers, being in a frolicsome rather than a business mood, caught the whale line in its mouth and hung on to it for considerable time . . .'

Although Mr Phillips has refrained from naming the guilty party, clearly this was Tom up to his usual tricks.

'. . . and as the whale turned in the middle of the bay and steered a course for the open sea, it was feared the crew might suffer a loss; but nearing the lookout, George Davidson, standing in the bow of the boat, was seen to be using the lance with great effect. Just here the whale made a quick turn and for a minute or so whale, Killers and boats seemed to be an inextricable mass, and the crowds of people on shore looked on with feverish excitement lest an accident should happen. It is such a position as this that coolness, seamanship, and complete knowledge of the tactics of the whale show out to great advantage, and all these qualifications are possessed by George Davidson. Another turning movement and the whale was bound seawards again; but his life was a short one for, as it rose to the surface, upwards went a volume of blood, and the whole surface of the

> *water was seen to be dyed with the crimson fluid. Onwards, however,*
> *the whale went until off Lookout Point, when suddenly it collapsed,*
> *and a few final thrusts of the lance and the first whale of the season was*
> *killed.'*

The second boat, led by my brother Harry, meanwhile made several attempts to fasten to the smaller whale, but, as reported in the same account:

> *'his somewhat amateurish crew were either unable or unwilling to get*
> *within the required distance to throw the harpoon with any chance of*
> *success and consequently he had to be content with following the "fast"*
> *boat to render aid in the event of an accident taking place.'*

Here I see that I have underlined the words *unable or unwilling* and inscribed a tiny question mark in the margin.

I should explain that the second boat is often relegated to the role of 'pick-up boat'; that is, if the whale line, tearing out of the boat, flicks a man into the water, then the second boat picks him up. Similarly, if the whale stoves in a portion of the boat (this happened rarely, again mainly due to the aforementioned qualities of my father). Sometimes, if a whale was particularly large or possessed of unnatural vitality, or if the first boat's harpoon had not gained a secure purchase within the whale's flesh, then the second boat would also make fast to this same whale; however, this was dangerous in practice as the two lines could become crossed in the ensuing chase, and the two boats end up ploughing into one another at high speed. If the Killers had apprehended more than one whale, then the duty of the second boat was to harpoon and capture the second whale or, at the very least, to remain fast to the whale until such time as the first boat could render assistance. In this instance, it seems that the crew of the second boat was deemed *'unable or unwilling'*. Certainly the crew included three new chums (John Beck amongst them), but I wonder if the blame could not be at least in part attributed to my brother's inexperience in the role of headsman.

I should perhaps pause here to outline in more detail the duties of the headsman. He is sometimes described as the chief officer of the boat; he steers the boat from the stern with the long sweep or steer oar, until the boat has gained sufficient proximity for the harpooner to employ his tool. It is a highly skilled position and calls for a man with experience; when a whale has sounded, it falls upon the headsman to predict where it might resurface and set his course accordingly. Here it must be said (and perhaps Mr Phillips of the *Observer* was alluding to this when he referred to my father's *'complete knowledge of the tactics of the whale'*) that my father had an uncanny instinct for the underwater manoeuvrings a whale might attempt. Frequently was a whale surprised by the cold steel of a harpoon when it at last came up for air.

At this point, once the boat is attached to the whale by means of the harpoon, the headsman then changes position with the harpooner in order to lance the whale from the bow of the boat. This 'changing of the guard' between the headsman and harpooner is a time-honoured practice, but puzzling to the uninitiated. Here is the whale stung by the harpoon and desperately trying to outrun its tormentors, yet just at this critical and dangerous moment, the headsman and the harpooner must each scramble to opposite ends of a thirty-foot boat, doing their utmost not to become entangled in the whale line which is whipping out of the boat at such speed that the friction as it pulls around the loggerhead will sometimes cause it to ignite.

'But why does the headsman not simply harpoon the whale himself?' I once asked my father.

'Because that is the job of the harpooner,' he replied in a kindly fashion, as if to a halfwit.

'Then could not the harpooner just stay at the bow and lance the whale?' I asked, feeling as if I may have unwittingly stumbled across a simple solution to a vexing problem.

'Oh no. No. No chance of that.'

'Why not?' I persisted.

'Because that is the job of the headsman.'

I could tell by the tone of his voice that he did not wish to continue this line of conversation, so I desisted. However, I do not pretend to know better than my father; there is much about whaling that my father chose not to explain to me, although I took an avid interest; indeed, there is much about whaling that he tried to spare me. The truth is that throwing the harpoon and wielding the lance are two quite distinct disciplines. Certainly, great skill was required of the headsman to hasten the whale's demise; a mortally wounded whale in its 'death flurry' is extremely dangerous. The headsman would take aim at the whale's vulnerable spot, about three feet back from its side fin; sometimes, a single thrust of the lance, a mighty shudder and it would all be over. At other times, however, many more thrusts of the lance were required; occasionally, the vitality of the whale was such that it simply would not die. On one moonless night in 1905, a large humpback set such a determined course out to sea after having been repeatedly lanced and even fired upon by the whale gun, that my father was forced to cut it loose, deeming the operation too perilous to continue. They had chased this whale for six hours and over many miles; in spite of its injuries, it showed no sign of weakening, and yet my father considered it could not possibly live. In cutting adrift, my father lost a harpoon and eight fathoms of line.

I go into detail here about the role of the headsman because I feel it is important to understand that it is a demanding and difficult position, the headsman's skill in both steering and lancing being crucial to the outcome. Harry at that time was only eighteen years of age, and had been promoted to the position of headsman of the second boat only owing to my father's extreme difficulty in finding crew members. Harry maintained, in this instance, that his crew had not rowed hard enough, that they seemed leery of getting too close to the whale, but I wonder, was that really the cause? Surely it is up to the headsman to steer the course whereby they are best positioned to encounter the whale when it next resurfaces? Surely it is up to the headsman to encourage and inspire his men with his own steady nerve? These are questions that I felt needed to be asked of Harry; however, given his foul temper that evening, I thought better of doing so.

At mealtime that night, the crew of the second boat was given a pretty thorough bucketing by the others. When Dan and I brought down the evening meal, John Beck seemed not his normal self, but rather pale and shaken; he took his plate from me without a word and moved off to sit alone, some distance from the others. This concerned me; it was not unheard of for new chums to 'do a runner' after their first taste of whaling, and my father could ill-afford to lose an oarsman.

I brooded over this as I washed the dishes, and as soon as I was free of my duties, I sought him out with the idea of offering him some words of encouragement. Night had fallen and, apart from a slush lamp flickering within a sleeping hut, all was in darkness. It seemed that the whale men, worn out by their exertions, had taken themselves off to bed. With some difficulty, I negotiated the path down to the try-works and stood for a moment on the slipway, holding up my lantern in a bid to peer further into the darkness.

'Well, you were right, Mary,' said a voice behind me.

I turned quickly and saw that John Beck was leaning up against the capstan behind me.

'What about?' I responded.

'There's a great deal of blood in these whales.'

'Ah,' I said. 'Yes.'

Although pleased to be vindicated, I had no wish to gloat at this moment, so I said nothing further. Moreover, I felt suddenly uncertain as to what I might say that would best offer comfort or encouragement at this time. John Beck also remained silent, seeming greatly preoccupied, although owing to the darkness it was difficult to be sure. Several moments passed; it was John Beck himself who finally spoke.

'*Canst thou draw out Leviathan with a fish hook?*' he asked.

'I beg your pardon?' I said. In truth, his comment startled me.

'*Or press down his tongue with a cord? Canst thou put a rope through his nose, or pierce his jaw through with a hook?*' he intoned.

I was now genuinely at a loss; unfamiliar as I was with much of the Bible, I was uncertain whether a response of some kind was expected of me.

'*Wilt thou play with him as with a bird?* No, that's not right . . . How does it go again, I wonder? Do you know the passage I mean, Mary? I find I cannot quite remember it, and yet it now seems so important that I do.'

As I feared, he certainly did sound discouraged.

'I gather you found your first encounter with a whale to be startling,' I said, summoning all my nerve to speak directly. 'It put you in mind of something biblical.'

'Yes,' he said. 'Yes, it did. Oh, Mary, such a sight to behold.'

'I have never seen one actually alive,' I confessed. 'A spout in the distance, perhaps. Mind you, I've seen plenty of them dead, of course, belly-up here on the slipway.'

'Ah yes,' said John Beck. 'That's a pity. For it's a sight to surely fill one with awe.'

'I gather that you were perhaps too filled with awe to bring yourself to row close enough to the drat thing?'

There was silence in the darkness.

'Who told you that?'

'That is just the general impression I have formed.'

'Has there been a complaint?'

'No. Not really. Look, it's common for new chums to be scared –'

'I wasn't scared.'

'Filled with awe then – whatever you wish to call it. Frankly, I mostly blame Harry. He doesn't have the experience to be headsman yet. I don't know what Dad was thinking. Anyway, first whale of the season! Plenty of time to get your nerve up! I'm sure on the next occasion you won't be letting one get away.'

I gave a light laugh. I had meant this speech to instil in him a sense of optimism and verve, but even as the words spilled out, I began to doubt their efficacy. For although I could see him only dimly by my lantern light, I could sense in him a mounting irritation. There was silence; then a short sigh, as if of exasperation.

'Well, Mary, I will try not to let you down again,' he said. 'Goodnight.'

And with that, he wandered off towards the sleeping hut.

The Trying-Out

H ERE I WILL ATTEMPT TO DOCUMENT THE INTERESTING process of 'trying-out'; that is, rendering the blubber into whale oil. Although the smells were abhorrent and the spectacle gory, I often tried to find time to study at least part of the trying-out process, and sometimes brought with me my sketch-book. Looking at these sketches now, I see that I had a great deal of difficulty with the subject; in fact, the longer I stare at them, the less I am able to make sense of what these earnest scratchings are supposed to represent. For if a whale is difficult to draw when alive and kitted out in all its blubber, it is nigh on impossible when just a mountain of indeterminate, unwholesome flesh, denuded of blubber, fins and features, and left abandoned in the shallows. I would sometimes catch our house cat Philly sitting on the slipway staring at these remains – as keen as she was on fish scraps, the very sight of these seemed somehow to defeat her.

The humpback recently captured had 'gassed up' within a day or so and risen to the surface; the Killers had taken their portion, and now the whalers towed it back to the try-works and immediately set to the task at hand. It was not a job they greatly relished, yet they applied themselves to it in a determined fashion, the new chums learning from the old. First, armed with the blubber spade, my father clambered to the top of the carcass and, making an incision near the tail end, cut a piece along the length of the whale about twenty feet long and six feet wide. A rope was then attached to one end of this piece and fastened to the capstan. Seven or eight of the men (including John Beck on this occasion) then put their weight to turning the capstan, thus slowly prising the 'blanket' away – for it did not come easily – my father hacking at it with his blubber spade whenever it should stick. In this laborious fashion, the belly side of the whale was flensed of its blubber, and with aid of heavy tackling and much heaving and grunting on the part of the whale men, the whale was then turned over for the same process to be repeated on the other side. This particular humpback was not an especially large one, yet the process still took a great many hours.

Those men not engaged in flensing would commence cutting the 'blankets' into 'junks', which were then sliced into smaller pieces, called 'horses', and tossed in a vat to render into whale oil. After a period of time, these pieces were pulled out again and placed on the mincing horse to be sliced into thin leaves, and thence into the try pot itself, where they would liquefy into valuable whale oil. The oil would then flow automatically into a series of coolers, and from there be ladled into large iron tanks, and then into casks for storage.

Uncle Aleck himself took the task of supervising the try pots, standing by with his skimmer and every so often pulling out a piece of crispy blubber and examining it closely. Only when he was satisfied that every last ounce of oil had been extracted would he toss it aside. It could then be used to fuel the fire, although the smell was not pleasant.

'I have a question for you, Father,' said Uncle Aleck. Glistening with blood and oil, he looked like a creature from the bowels of hell as he stirred the foul contents of his cauldron.

'Oh yes?' said John Beck. He also glistened with blood and oil, yet somehow the effect on him was more pleasing.

'It's a theological question of sorts.'

'By all means. Ask away.'

'I believe you were a minister of the Methodist church?'

'That's right, for a time.'

'In your frank opinion then, Father,' said Uncle Aleck, 'how do you find the Methodist ladies compare with Presbyterian girls? I'm speaking purely of appearance – never mind personality for the moment.'

Uncle Aleck had never married, and his thoughts often lingered upon such topics.

'Well, I couldn't rightly say,' said John Beck, and at this point he glanced over to where I sat sketching, some small distance away. 'I've not had a lot to do with Presbyterian girls.'

'More's the pity! Presbyterian girls are the prettiest by a country mile!' volunteered young Robert. Some of the whale men then proceeded to offer their own opinions on the subject; Bastable took the case for the Anglican lasses while Salty admired the good women of the Salvation Army. The conversation was just turning to the Little Sisters of the Sacred Heart when my father instructed me to get back up to the house.

'But why? I've nothing to do up there.'

'This is no place for you, that's why.'

Annoyed with him, I gathered my drawing implements and headed off up to the house; the whole area was awash with blood and whale oil, but thankfully I did not slip.

Excursion to Boyd Tower

S ITUATED ON THE CLIFF TOP AT SOUTH HEAD, BOYD TOWER was built by Benjamin Boyd, one of the founding fathers of the Eden district. He was a pastoralist, banker, adventurer and whale man who later went broke and took off in his schooner, only to be killed and eaten by natives somewhere in the Pacific. Such is life. The structure is some sixty feet high, and constructed of sandstone: across the four stones at the very top of the monument is carved the word BOYD. Inside, a series of perilous ladders lead to the top, and if one is game to climb them, tremendous views of the ocean may be enjoyed. It was from this uppermost vantage point that our whale men took turns in keeping lookout each day from dawn to dusk.

It was now seven weeks into whaling season, and we had captured only the one moderately sized humpback. Since then, any whales that passed by on their journey north must have veered so wide of the coast that they eluded even our vigilant Killers. Could

Boyd Tower

it be that the whales were growing more cunning? Strange to think that after almost a century of whaling in Twofold Bay, the whales might finally be concluding that it was better to avoid the place.

'You've never engaged in this line of work before then, Father?' asked Salty. They were leaning against the base of Boyd Tower, idly surveying the horizon. Other whale men were playing cards or draughts, or fishing off the rocks below.

'No,' said John Beck. 'This is my first time whaling.'

'Well, then. That's grand. Good luck to you,' said Salty, sucking at his pipe. 'Can you bear a word of advice from an old hand?'

'I'd be glad of any advice you could offer me.'

'I've been doing this for thirty years now, and I've encountered a few whales in my time. I think I might know what I'm talking about.'

'I would not doubt that,' said John Beck.

'Nevertheless, you may dismiss it as the rantings of an old fellow, if you so choose. It is entirely up to you.'

'Anything you have to tell me would be of great interest to me.'

'I was not fortunate enough to get much in the way of schooling as a youngster; however, there is one area in which I am learned, and that is the subject of whales. In fact, some folk call me the Professor of Whales.'

'I have no doubt that you are a great authority on the subject,' said John Beck. He was beginning to think that Salty was something of a blowhard, and might never get to his point.

'An authority? Some may consider me so. The truth is, I would estimate that I've harpooned over two hundred whales in my time.'

'Over two hundred whales in his imagination,' said Darcy, rather cheekily. But Salty did not appear to hear him.

'And that is why I say to you, Father, do not fear the humpback. Nor fear the black whale, the blue whale or the white whale.'

'All right,' said John Beck. 'Thank you. I will bear that in mind.'

'No,' said Salty, for he had not finished, 'it is the spotted whale you must fear.'

Darcy coughed quietly to himself.

'Spotted?' said John Beck.

'Aye. That's what I said. Spotted.' At this point, Salty paused to stoke his pipe.

John Beck began to wonder if Salty was having some kind of joke at his expense, although he could not be entirely sure. He looked to Darcy, but Darcy was now bent over his work. He was carving a serpent out of a piece of driftwood.

'Do you know why it is you must be fearful of the whale who has spots, Father?' resumed Salty, having satisfactorily tended to his pipe.

'No, I do not.'

'Those spots are old harpoon scars.'

'I see.'

'What I am telling you is this: *the whale has been harpooned before.*'

'I understand.'

'Three things you must bear in mind now. First up, she'll be a boat-breaker, for likely that is how she got away. And if a whale has broken a boat once, she likes to do it again; oh yes, she enjoys it, as a child enjoys jumping on a sandcastle. Secondly, the whale knows all our tricks; oh yes, she has our measure. We can no longer surprise or outsmart her. Thirdly, and this is the worst of it . . .'

'Yes?' said John Beck.

'She is consumed with thoughts of vengeance.'

Here he puffed away on his pipe to such a degree that his face became momentarily enshrouded in smoke. Again, John Beck looked to Darcy, but Darcy was now bent so intently over his work that his face was entirely hidden from view.

That day, I had decided to take the children on a picnic to Boyd Tower; they had been fighting amongst themselves and we had all been feeling cooped up. The fact was that we lived a long way from anywhere, and had not much in the way of transportation. Three or four seasons ago, we had had three good horses, ten head of cattle and several sheep, but the varying fortunes of whaling were such that we were now reduced to Two Socks, a good pulling horse although moody in temperament, and Betty, our milking cow. Betty was by no means an especially prepossessing cow, and yet she comported herself with an air of great self-satisfaction which oft times reminded me of my own sister Louisa. Certainly what bovine charms Betty possessed worked their spell upon Two Socks, for over the years he became inordinately attached to her and demonstrated the strength of his feelings by protesting strenuously if any attempts were ever made to separate them. Never a cooperative horse even before this infatuation, he could now only be persuaded to venture from the back paddock if Betty felt inclined to accompany him. This was not such a problem if we proposed a short journey, such as this one to Boyd Tower, which Betty could manage comfortably. However, it was a different thing altogether to have Betty accompany us all the way into Eden. Not only did the journey take three times as long, for Betty was a terrific dawdler and must sample the foliage, but also the exercise exhausted her and was bad for her milk. Suffice to say, there were times when, owing to a shortage of provisions, we had no choice but to go through this ordeal with cow in tow, but wherever possible, we waited till our father was going into town by means of his motor launch *Excelsior*. Of course, at the moment he was always on lookout, so this was not a possibility. Thus, the long months of whaling season loomed before us, stranded at Kiah, with slim possibility of outings.

Two Socks & Betty

Our three remaining chickens had managed between them to lay two eggs. In a rush of excitement I attempted the Economical Madeira cake from my mother's Presbyterian Women's Missionary Union cookbook. It turned out presentably enough and, while it was still warm, I wrapped it in a tea towel and we set off. Louisa and Uncle Aleck decided at the last minute that perhaps they would come after all, then the dogs took exception to being left at home, so all in all, we made quite a procession. The six of us would not fit in the buggy, so had to be taking turns walking, except Uncle Aleck, who was suffering with his lumbago. A lengthy and heated discussion ensued. Finally, it was resolved that there would be a changeover every two hundred paces; however Violet, the youngest, considered that somehow she should be exempt from this ruling and registered her protest by taking tiny, tiny steps and Annie, in her customary fashion pretending to be a horse, insisted on being a very nervous horse that shied at the slightest leaf rustle and finally baulked altogether. At this point, our real horse, Two Socks, decided that he would only continue if Betty walked alongside him (up until then, Betty had been tied to the rear of the buggy), but Betty did not care to walk ahead because she did not like Patch, and Patch always had to take the lead in any expedition as he imagined himself to be our advance guard. So that meant we had to make Patch ride in the buggy, sitting across our laps, but he struggled so much that finally I walked just ahead of Betty and Two Socks, carrying Patch in my arms so he wouldn't annoy Betty. This worked well enough until a magpie got it into her head that we were after her babies so she began to swoop us; this frightened Betty and she baulked, whereupon Two Socks baulked, so now Dan had to get out of the buggy in order to hold Louisa's parasol above Betty's head so she could not see the magpie. But then Bonnie (who had been the least trouble of anyone) got a prickle in her paw, and made such a performance of bravely limping onwards that it was agreed she should ride in the buggy, at which point Patch decided, somewhat contrarily, that if Bonnie got to ride in the buggy, then so should he. I was glad of this, because Patch had been getting very heavy, but once in the buggy he became excited and commenced jumping about from one side of the buggy to the other until everybody screamed at him to 'Sit!', whereupon he sat himself down on my Madeira cake.

'Stop yelling at Patch, Mary!' implored Annie.

My nerves were frayed and I had lost my temper; it was the way Patch was grinning at me whilst wagging his tail stump about in my Madeira cake.

'He's just a dog!' cried Violet, hugging him violently. 'He can't help it!'

At which point, Patch noticed he was sitting in the Madeira cake and so commenced to eat it.

Soon after, we arrived at Boyd Tower, where the whale men stared at us perplexed.

'Why is the boy holding an umbrella over the cow?' asked Albert Thomas Senior, to which there was no sensible answer. The magpie had stopped swooping some distance back, but Betty seemed to enjoy the shade that the parasol provided her.

One of the pleasures of visiting Boyd Tower was that it afforded, on occasion, an excellent vantage point from which to observe the marvellous work of the *Orca Gladiator*. The steep cliffs overlook Leatherjacket Bay, the preferred headquarters of the Killer whales when residing in Twofold Bay, and often they would pass the time between the real action of chasing whales by teaching the younger Killers the complex tactics and manoeuvres involved in such a sport. Sure enough, much to the children's great excitement, a game of 'Chase the Finback' was underway. An unfortunate finback had been enticed into the bay, and now found himself being herded back and forth and roundabout by several squads of Killer whales.

Each squad, consisting of seven or so Killers, seemed to have its own responsibilities. The first squad was involved in the direct chasing and harassment of the finback; the second concerned itself with heading off the creature from its desired course while the third squad formed a sentry line across the bay to contain any attempts at escape. The entire business was conducted at tremendous speed, and on several occasions the finback (who we estimated to be thirty feet in length) leapt entirely out of the water in his desperation to escape his tormentors. At one point, he charged towards the shallows as if to beach himself, but Hooky and Charlie Adgery would have none of that; they darted ahead and turned him round again, as if to say, 'Oh no you don't, sir, we're not finished with you yet!'

As the finback grew more exhausted and began to slow down, he was dealt a sharp nip to the tail by Tom and instructed to get a move on. Up and down and roundabout and do-si-do your partner; in this fashion, the game continued for most of the morning. Finally, they tired of it and got down to the real business. There was a great threshing and foaming of the water, and the finback disappeared from view.

My father watched their antics with amusement; however,

I imagine he wished that the Killers were expending their efforts on chasing a real whale. Occasionally, if the Killers had driven a finback onto the beach, the men might tow the carcass home and go through the rigmarole of trying-out, but as there wasn't much blubber on them, it was hardly worth the effort. As for myself, I had found the Killers' play discomforting. Although the other spectators laughed and cheered as each bid to escape was thwarted, it struck me that the Killer whales were nothing more than a pack of schoolyard bullies. Their behaviour demonstrated that they had not once ounce of compassion between them. I found myself overcome with sorrow for the hapless finback, to be hounded to death in such a fashion.

John Beck was on lookout in the tower for much of this time, and then he came down and said hello, to which I responded, 'Hello.'

We stood side by side in complete silence watching the blood and the oil spread across the water, and then he turned to me and said: 'I would not much like to be a grampus, would you?'

'A grampus? Why do you say that?' I said sharply. I was sensitive on the subject as Harry used to tease me and say that I reminded him of a grampus he had seen washed up on a beach, and that it was lucky that the grampus had not been wearing spectacles, otherwise we would have been virtually indistinguishable from one another, and everybody would say, 'Oh look, there's poor Mary Davidson washed up on a beach and covered in kelp.' This never failed to upset me, and finally my father had ordered him to desist.

'Well,' said John Beck, 'because it has just been torn apart by the Killer whales.'

'That was not a grampus; that was a finback. They are completely different.'

'Really? Are you sure? Because Salty told me it was a grampus.'

'Oh, Salty calls everything a grampus,' I said dismissively. 'What would he know?'

For some reason, I was sounding very bad-tempered, although I did not mean to. It was probably because I was hungry and had not thought to bring any food besides the Madeira cake which Patch had sat in. Yet even as I spoke, I recalled an article that I had cut out from the newspaper, entitled '*How a Woman Becomes Popular*', from which I quote below:

> '*She was not a pretty woman, rather plain than stylish, but of a cheerful temper. When asked to give a reason for her popularity, she answered: "A man is a sensitive creature, and in dealing with him, I bear that in mind. He does not like to be reminded of his shortcomings, nor does he care to hear another man praised for the attributes he lacks. He dislikes to be interrupted when telling a story, or set right over unimportant matters. I always try to talk to every man as he talks to me, and treat young men as if they were old and old men as if they were young. I can think of no other reason for my popularity."*'

The homely woman had made it her practice never to remind men of their shortcomings or set them right on unimportant matters, and here I was this very minute setting John Beck right on the subject of the grampus.

'Well,' said John Beck, 'I might take myself for a walk along the rocks then.'

'Yes, all right then, why don't you,' I said. I could certainly not be described as being '*of a cheerful temper*'.

If he was going for a walk along the rocks, then I would

take myself for a walk in the opposite direction – along the cliffs, perhaps, where I might spot a whale and be the heroine of the day. I was just setting off when I saw ahead of me Louisa sitting on a rock, with her young admirer Robert Heffernan in doting attendance. She made no attempt at concealing her boredom, and when she saw me jumped up eagerly and called out: 'Can we go soon?'

'For goodness' sake, we have only just got here!' This was not true; we had been there for almost two hours. But for some reason, I was feeling oddly contrary. Louisa was forever setting men right or reminding them of their shortcomings, or in this case openly yawning out of boredom, and yet men admired her all the more for it! It was simply not fair. The homely woman did not know what she was talking about.

As I walked, my thoughts returned to the Killer whales, and their conduct regarding the finback. I realised that my discomfort in watching the harassment may well have stemmed from my own experiences at the hands of one Eunice Martin and her friends at Sunday school. (Incidentally, this was the same Eunice Martin who had gone on to receive the blue ribbon at the Eden Show for *Towamba Eventide*, the depiction in watercolours of a five-legged cow at sunset.) She and her friends had poked fun at me because of my spectacles and said that I smelled like a dead whale. Also they had once shoved me into the sand at the Sunday school picnic. This sort of behaviour went on for some time; however, when my mother died, my father lost all interest in attending church and so my torment finally ended. But it seemed to me that day, as I pondered what I'd seen, that the Killer whales were the Eunice Martins of the marine world.

And yet, had I known at the time what was to become of

Eunice Martin, perhaps I would have judged her less harshly. For only several years hence, she was found in Towamba cemetery after attempting to poison herself. She had left several letters indicating where she might be found, placing the blame squarely on Constable Weston, who it seems may have molested her in some fashion. My sister Annie took a dim view of this, and said, 'How difficult is it to poison yourself? And how convenient that she left so many letters indicating where she might be found so that she may be revived before it was too late.' Certainly she recovered fairly promptly, but the family was obliged to leave the region shortly thereafter. In the meantime, Constable Weston had been hastily moved on to Barmedman, where it was expected that he might engage in further unwholesome activities involving young ladies of hitherto spotless reputations; there was a brief furore about it in the newspaper.

I had been charging along through the low shrub, not looking up but just stomping angrily head down and thinking about Eunice Martin, when suddenly I heard a cry: *'Rush oh! Rush oh!'* The lookout had spotted a whale! Where? I thought, furious at myself for not having spotted it first. I looked out to sea. At first I saw nothing, and then at once I saw it – a V-shaped spout of mist and the sense of an immense dark bulk beneath the water. I stood without breathing for a moment, not daring to believe it. Then a vast set of gnarled black flukes rose up out of the water and hung there, as if suspended.

The First Black Whale of the Season

THE WIND WAS WORKING UP TO A GALE AND THE WORK WAS heavy in pulling across the water. The whale had last been seen off Jews Head but, as the boats approached, had sounded. A considerable interval had passed and it had not yet reappeared. At different vantage points along the cliff tops, groups of onlookers were gathering and their cries could be heard across the water, urging the whalers on.

'It is all very well to shout at us,' muttered Harry. 'Kindly tell us where the whale went, if you wish to be useful.'

He was out of sorts as he had been demoted from the position of headsman and was now taking the secondary role of harpooner. This meant more rowing, which was unfortunate, as whichever way they turned the wind was against them. They had already rowed many miles with only occasional distant glimpses of their elusive quarry.

'Are we just to row round and round in the hopes it will come up beneath us?' he asked, with a note of petulance.

'These whales can certainly hold their breath for a long time,' remarked Robert Heffernan.

Salty, who had taken the role of headsman, urged them to shut up. The crowd on the headland had broken into screams and shouts, and were waving their hats and handkerchiefs in the direction of Cattle Bay. There it was, spouting idly, basking in the winter sunlight. It was the length of a steamer, and even from this distance, you could see that its head was a mass of unsightly callouses.

'Black whale all right,' said my father, turning the boat towards Cattle Bay. A cheer went up amongst his boatmen. A black whale (or a 'right' whale as they are also known, because they are the 'right' whale to catch) is the most valuable of all the whales, especially a big one like this one. Its whalebone would be long; its blubber thick.

My father's boat led the way, moving quietly so as not to startle the leviathan. Arthur Ashby rose to his feet and braced his thigh in the cleat, his harpoon poised. The whale wallowed contentedly in the water, quite unconcerned, almost as if it hadn't seen them. The boat crept up to within four or five boat-lengths away. But just as Arthur pulled his arm back to launch his iron, the whale curved its broad back and slid under the water, flicking its flukes idly. The crowd let out a cry of disappointment. Arthur Ashby lowered his harpoon.

'Where was she off to then, George?' cried Salty, across the water.

My father shook his head. He gazed intently at the circle of smooth water the whale had left behind, trying to read in its shape some idea of the whale's intentions. Up above, an albatross hovered – the men looked up at it hopefully. Seabirds often provided clues as to a whale's whereabouts; they were both, after all, interested in the same food. Sometimes, if a whale was lunging through a patch of krill with its mouth open, the cheekier birds liked to swoop in and pick off any morsels of marine life stuck in the whalebone. The albatross, however, veered off on the wind.

'Where are the Killers?' asked Bastable, disgruntled. 'Have they not noticed there's a whale in the bay?'

'Too full of ruddy finback,' muttered someone.

'We try calling them, boss?' asked Albert Thomas Junior.

My father leaned on his steer oar, peering intently at the water. Finally he nodded. The men raised their oars high and, at a given signal, brought the blades down hard upon the water in a single resounding *smack!*

Up on the headlands, the crowd fell quiet; all studying the water, all eager to be first to raise up the cry. A bank of clouds passed in front of the sun. There was an eerie atmosphere suddenly, and a feeling of heaviness in the air. Gently, the boats rose and fell, the water slapping at the sides. A short distance away, a cloud of mutton-birds materialised as if from nowhere and wheeled in wild formation just above the surface of the water. The men watched in silence as the birds banked sharply to one side and skimmed low across the surface, seeming to dip their very wingtips in the water.

'Mutton-birds,' said the newcomer Shankly, darkly. 'They are not a tasty bird, by any means.'

The others looked at him in surprise. Shankly rarely spoke, and when he did say something, it generally had a portentous quality about it.

'Well, that depends!' responded Salty. 'It depends on how long you boil them.'

'I believe they are very good if stewed at length in port wine,' offered John Beck, but Shankly just shook his head grimly. It appeared he had a set against the mutton-bird.

'Salty!' called my father, whose mind was still on matters whaling. 'Head over towards Quarantine Bay. We'll go towards Snug Cove.'

'Right you are!'

The two boats separated and began moving off in opposite directions. They had not travelled far when, from the cliff tops, the piercing cry of a small boy rent the air.

'*Whale! Whale! Whale!*'

Where? wondered the whale men, turning to look up at him, and just now, with a loud spout from its blowhole, the black whale rose up directly alongside the Number Two boat. The inexperienced oarsmen reared back; their instinct was to flee, but unable to flee, they froze and stared at the sight before them. It was difficult to make sense of what they were seeing. It was huge, unmistakably, though most of its mass was concealed underwater; grey-black in colour with a flat broad back. Its ugly, misshapen head had the tumorous quality of an ancient anthill, or a tree stricken with abscesses. These tumours, one of which sat comically atop its head like a bonnet, were whitish in colour with a quality similar to lichen, and within this lichen, odd dark stalagmites sprouted from which rivulets of water streamed. Its vast coal-scuttle mouth curved downwards, and at one end of this a tiny eye, rheumy like an old man's, gazed up at them. It was grotesque and prehistoric in appearance, yet not unfriendly.

'It's big, isn't it?' said Robert in a hoarse whisper, and I suppose that is what they were all thinking.

'For God's sake, get your iron up, Harry!' hissed Salty.

Harry rose to his feet and scrabbled for his harpoon. With a sigh, the whale began to move away. The oarsmen remained stunned, their oars in mid-air.

'Row!' cried Salty, and his voice seemed to have risen an octave. 'Don't let it get away, you useless b-----ds!'

This epithet seemed to rouse the men from their reverie. They seized their oars and began to pull, all out of time with one another, their blades colliding.

'Take her, Harry!' cried my father, whose boat was beginning to catch up. 'Don't wait for us!' My brother raised his harpoon with trembling hands. The notion of plunging such an implement into this mountain of whale seemed suddenly ludicrous, like sticking a hatpin into an elephant.

'You have her in sights?' asked Salty.

'I have her,' said Harry, and he braced his thigh against the cleat in readiness. But just at that moment, the leviathan spouted a percussive *Bosh!*, and the fetid spray blew over him, stinging his cheeks. His iron was poised above his head, but for some reason he did not throw it.

'Dart, dart, you imbecile!' cried Salty. 'Into the old girl's gizzards!'

'Use your iron, son!' cried my father.

'Harpoon her!' cried the people on the cliff tops.

These exhortations were not helpful to Harry. He tossed his harpoon, but in his panicked state, it fell short and landed in the water with a dispiriting slap.

The whale dived, smacking the water with its flukes and thereby drenching the boat's occupants. The crowds howled their dismay, as did the whalers.

'God Almighty!' cried Salty, his face bright red, his grey hair dripping.

'My hand slipped!'

'He throws like a girl!'

'This is where nepotism gets you,' cried Bastable. 'The boy has been promoted regardless of merit.'

'Shut up, the lot of you, for Christ's sake!' said my father.

Chastened like children, the men fell silent. Even the crowds on the headlands desisted from hurling their derisive comments.

My father stood gripping his steer oar, his face a study of grim concentration. Minutes passed; nobody spoke. Hearts thudded in chests.

Some distance away, a Killer whale leapt out of the water, and slammed the full weight of its body upon the surface – the sound ricocheted across the water like the crack of a whip. The crowd on the cliff top let up a cry: '*Tom! It's Tom!*' The men in the boats grabbed hold of their oars and tried to steel themselves; now the chase would be on in earnest. A strange sound rose up out of the water, hard to identify at first: a piteous kind of bellowing, like a bull set upon by dogs.

I realise that I do not paint my brother Harry in a very favourable light, first of all in his failure as a headsman and now with his harpooning. Certainly, I was very hard on him at the time, and yet even as I write this account, it occurs to me that perhaps Harry was not scared at all, but simply had no wish to kill the whale. It is entirely possible, as he was a kind-hearted boy in many ways; if not with his sisters, it was certainly evidenced in his treatment of 'all creatures great and small'. As a small child, he would climb to the top of the run-off tank and endeavour to rescue any small insects that had apparently drowned. Gathering them gently in his palm, he would blow softly upon their lifeless forms till they revived. Then he would sit there quietly nursing them till such time as their wings had dried and they were able to fly away.

Nor can I believe that he would be put off by such an oft-seen sight as a whale spout, even a large one. My brother had the idea that when a whale spouted, it was actually saying, '*Bosh!*'; that is, vehemently pooh-poohing something, as would a curmudgeonly old man (in fact, it was a common retort of Uncle Aleck). As a young oarsman in the whaleboat, this notion tickled Harry to such an extent that he would endeavour to have a conversation with a whale if it was spouting nearby.

'Excuse me, Mr Whale, are you aware that the dolphin is said to be the smartest of all God's creatures?'

'*Bosh!*'

'I believe Towamba is a dead cert to defeat Eden in the upcoming semi-final.'

'*Bosh!*'

And so on and so forth, until he would set to giggling. It was all very distracting when someone was meanwhile trying to harpoon the whale. I know my father frowned upon it, and perhaps that is why he was so anxious to tax Harry with the more serious tasks of headsman or harpooner. As I say, I cannot know for sure why Harry failed with the harpoon on this occasion, and it has only just occurred to me that the reason may have been something other than fear.

A Celebration

THANKFULLY, OUR RETURN JOURNEY FROM BOYD TOWER WAS much faster than the one we had endured on the way out there. Once Two Socks was pointed in the direction of home, he invariably put a sprint on, and Betty was simply expected to keep up. We were glad about this, as we wanted to be sure we were ready for our whale men's return. As they had run for the whale-boats, several of them had thrust their freshly caught fish upon me, with instructions as to how best I should prepare them. Darcy had pulled some molluscs and mutton-fish off the rocks below, and these were also added to the bounty. Thus I had several whiting and three schnapper, and one fish the likes of which I had never seen before, plus five mutton-fish, a dozen or so oysters and a handful of other unidentified bivalves. As the boats pulled away from the cliffs, Salty was still calling out his recipe for fish stew; much of it was lost on the wind, but it seemed to involve plentiful amounts of milk and cream.

'A liberal dash of Worcestershire will improve the flavour,' was the last that I heard.

Thus when we arrived home, we set about preparing it. Such was the excitement over the long-awaited appearance of a whale that the whole family pitched in to help. Dan cut open the first oyster, but injured his thumb so badly in the process that Louisa took over (she could at times prove herself very capable), while Uncle Aleck cleaned the fish; Annie coaxed some milk from Betty, and Dan and Violet went to find parsley and chives in the garden. Meanwhile I browned some onions in a little butter, and made a gelatinous broth from the fish heads which formed the base of the stew. With a portion of Betty's cream, some boiled potatoes, salt and pepper, a pinch of cayenne powder, and of course the obligatory Worcestershire sauce, the fish morsels and molluscs cooked up very nicely indeed. It was a hearty meal for the whale men, and one they were sorely in need of when finally they returned home that evening.

'Here they come!' cried Dan. He had been keeping lookout up on the hill, and en masse we ran down to greet them. They appeared to be rowing in the most haphazard fashion; also, across the water we could hear strains of robust argument and song.

'Oh, she was wily!' cried my father, as he came lurching up the jetty. 'She was a wily wily old wily old whale.'

I looked at him in astonishment: he appeared to be intoxicated. In fact, it soon became apparent that they were all in this condition, to varying degrees. Darcy and Robert Heffernan were no sooner out of the boats than they began to punch one another, and had to be separated, while Percy Madigan had to be stopped from veering off the jetty altogether and into the water. It seems that so satisfied were the whalers with their efforts in capturing such a fine whale, they had promptly adjourned to the Great Southern Hotel before finally rowing back with a quantity of rum. It was most unlike my father to drink to the point of intoxication; however, it gives some indication of the intense relief he must have been experiencing in catching such a valuable whale.

'We must feed them immediately,' I instructed Louisa, and while the men washed themselves, we hurried up to the house to bring down the big pot of fish stew and some freshly baked damper with which to mop up the juices. They devoured it in the most ravenous fashion, and declared it a culinary triumph. We each felt a degree of pride as we had all taken some part in its creation, and for once we stayed with the men to enjoy the celebration rather than retiring to the house as we would normally do; my father was too inebriated to care. I should hasten to add that the meal had had the desired effect of sobering the men to some extent, otherwise I should never have permitted the younger ones to remain in their company.

It was a bitterly cold night but several large campfires were lit on the beach, which we gathered around, sitting on kegs and blankets and whatever we had at hand. Our Aboriginal whalers, Albert Thomas Senior and Albert Thomas Junior and Percy and Darcy Madigan, provided the music by means of blowing upon gum leaves as you would blow upon a harmonica. To this, the little girls danced a jig while we all clapped along our encouragement. Our very own Dark Town Leaf Band demonstrated complete mastery of their unusual 'instruments', and their repertoire was wide-ranging, from reels and jigs to sentimental ballads, even several hymns that they had been taught by the missionaries of the Salvation Army. We sang along as best we could whenever we could remember the words; however, it was only 'Onward Christian Soldiers' to which

Bonnie felt compelled to add her voice, with an outburst of the most heartfelt baying and howling, inducing much laughter and merriment amongst us all.

Bonnie

At one point, I looked across and saw my father gazing into the flames, wearing an expression of great weariness but also something akin to contentment. I felt a tug at my heart, for I realised I had not often seen this expression since my mother died. I went across and sat at his knee, and although we did not speak, he smiled at me and patted my hair.

As I sat there, listening to the conversations around me, I began to piece together the story of the chase and capture of the black whale. After the Killers had arrived upon the scene and set about corralling the whale, it was short work for the first boat to make fast to it. However, once stung by the harpoon, the whale – who had seemed a placid creature up to this point – put up a ferocious battle for its survival. At once, it executed a series of short, sharp turns, as if attempting to dislodge the boat now suddenly attached to it; then, when this tactic did not achieve the desired result, the creature stopped suddenly and elevated its great tail flukes to a height of some twenty feet above the water, before sweeping them most deliberately across the length of the boat. Fortunately, my father, who was of course standing at the bow, and Arthur Ashby (at the steer oar) had had the wherewithal to hastily duck down, thereby avoiding what could undoubtedly have been serious injuries. (By all accounts, the whale's tail span was twelve feet across, and of exceptional thickness.) The whale then made a spirited dash for North Head, causing the Killer whales to exert their most concentrated efforts in attempting to prevent its escape. It succeeded in rounding North Head, and was speeding in the direction of Leonards Island, still dragging my father's whaleboat after it, before the Killers managed to rein it in and turn it back into Twofold Bay.

Becoming increasingly desperate now, the whale sped towards the entrance of Lake Curalo, then thought better of the idea and skirted along Haslems Beach before proceeding to Lookout Point where, as if for the benefit of the onlookers assembled there, the Killers commenced a series of furious onslaughts. Humpy threw himself across the creature's blowhole; Tom engaged in his favourite game of pushing at the whale repeatedly from underneath, while Hooky and company endeavoured to tear open the creature's mouth. They only desisted long enough to allow my father clear access to deal the fatal lance, and with each thrust of the steel, the crowds on Lookout Point let out cheer upon cheer. Soon the spouting and bellowing and the crimson-foaming of the water ceased; the whale was *hors de combat*. The entire business, from making fast to the whale to its ultimate demise, took only an hour and a half.

Remarkably, the whale was of such vast dimensions that the Killers had difficulty in pulling the carcass below. 'We'll have our work cut out for us towing it over the bar,' said my father, and there was talk of the possible necessity of excavating a channel in order to tow the carcass close enough to the try-works. My father estimated that, given its size, it could yield up to ten tonnes of whale oil. Further, its whalebone was of tremendous length and quality. All in all, it had been a most satisfactory afternoon's work.

As the exertions of the day began to catch up with everybody, and the merriment and music died down, a stiff breeze rose up suddenly, causing the flames of the campfires to gutter. My father lifted his head, almost like a dog sensing something on the wind. He looked out towards the blackness of the water; then, without saying a word, rose to his feet and made his way down towards the jetty. I watched him for a moment, then got up to follow. As I passed, a shadowy figure, seated some small distance away from the campfire, reached out and took hold of my arm. It was John Beck.

'Mary, Mary, sit with me a while,' he said.

I hesitated. He had obviously partaken of the liquor, for his eyes were shiny, but had not taken so much as to be unpleasant, nor were its fumes redolent on his breath. He gave a small tug at my arm by way of encouragement, and so I sat myself down beside him.

'I have something for you,' he said.

He pulled from his pocket the broderie anglaise bandages, now somewhat grimy from use, and for one moment I thought that he was simply about to return them to me. But instead, he carefully unwrapped them to reveal a shell, which he held up to show me in the flickering light.

'I've been making a collection of seashells,' he said. 'But this one is by far the prettiest.'

'Oh yes,' I responded. 'It is very pretty.'

In fact, it was a common spindle shell; undoubtedly attractive, with its brown and white markings and spindle shape, but perhaps I had seen too many of them to be greatly excited by it. John Beck, however, seemed quite delighted with it. He turned it over several times to admire its delicate contours, then pressed it into my hand.

'It's for you,' he said.

'For me?'

'Yes. Do you know why?'

I shook my head.

'Because you made my blisters better.'

'Are they better?'

'Oh yes. Look,' he said, and he held up the palms of his hands. 'I don't think your little brother would be laughing at my ladies' hands now. Do you see how they've toughened up?'

He then took my hand so I could feel the new callouses where the blisters had once been.

'Yes, they have toughened up considerably,' I said. How earnest and dreary I sounded, I thought to myself. *Yes, they have toughened up considerably.* No wonder I had never been popular. Perhaps it was time to put into practice the advice of the homely woman: '*Treat young men as if they are old and old men as if they are young.*'

'You should see my arms, Mary,' John Beck was meanwhile saying. 'See how strong my arms have got from the rowing?'

Here he rolled up a sleeve to reveal his upper arm. 'Feel it,' he offered encouragingly. Twisting his fist this way and that, he made several flexing motions with his arm, causing the upper muscle to bulge most satisfactorily. Scarcely aware of what I was doing, I found myself reaching out and feeling it with my fingertips.

'Like a rock, eh?' whispered John Beck. 'Not many Methodist ministers have muscles like these, I can tell you. I'm very proud of them, as you can see.'

'They're very nice,' I replied, and instead of removing my hand at this point, I allowed it to slide down to his forearm, which was also of pleasing firmness and strength.

'I've been wanting you to admire them all night,' he continued softly. 'It's been rather chilly in my shirtsleeves too.'

He was smiling at me and his eyes were shining in the darkness, and at that point, I'm afraid that something within me seemed to seize up in a kind of panic. Any girlish gaiety that I had been blessed with at birth had stiffened and stuck from lack of use, and although I was only nineteen years of age, I felt unable to rise to the obvious demands of the occasion.

'I'm sorry. I'm no good at this. I can't do it,' I said, lurching abruptly to my feet.

Swiftly he reached up and pulled me back down again.

'Do what?'

'This light-hearted banter between the sexes that you are obviously hoping for.'

'Of course you can do it! You've been doing it extremely well up to this moment.'

'That is kind of you to say, but I am only too aware of my shortcomings. And although I've been trying to picture you in my mind as Uncle Aleck –'

'What?' he said. 'Please don't do that. Please don't picture me in your mind as Uncle Aleck. Why in God's name have you been doing that?'

'Because that way I might perhaps be less stilted in my conversation.'

'No, no. I must insist that you stop it at once. It is undoing all of my good work with my muscles.'

'But you see . . .' I hesitated for a moment, but then all of a sudden it came tumbling out. 'My fear is that you view me as some earnest, bespectacled *whale painter* – a bluestocking – which of course is not helped by the fact that I was wearing my blue stockings when we first met, but only because I had not been expecting company, let alone a Methodist minister –'

'*Former* Methodist minister.'

'– otherwise, of course, I would have been wearing my black silks –'

'Yes, but putting aside the Methodist minister bit for the moment,' said John Beck, 'and even the much more interesting question of your black silks – do you think your father would mind terribly if I kissed you?'

'*Oh!*' I exclaimed. 'Yes, possibly he would mind terribly.'

'What do you think he would do? Would he harpoon me?'

'Oh, I doubt he would waste a harpoon on you.'

'Ah! You bantered!'

'No, no. That wasn't banter. That was the truth. He is very careful in his use of harpoons.'

'I see. Is he looking?'

'Looking?'

'At us.'

'No.'

'Then dare we have just one little kiss?'

Rendered unable to speak, I simply nodded; he leaned forward and kissed me tenderly on the lips. And because I did not resist, he kissed me again, longer and more tenderly this time. Until finally I opened my eyes and found him gazing at me.

'Please don't tell me you were imagining Uncle Aleck,' he whispered.

'Oh no!' I replied. 'No, I wasn't at all –'

And at this moment, a fierce gust of wind whipped around us, pulling a sheet of tin from the roof of the try-works. It crashed down upon some empty barrels, causing them to thunder down the slipway and setting the dogs at once to barking.

'Get the boats – we're going out!' my father shouted from the end of the jetty.

The whale men cried out in disbelief; various epithets were tossed about in bitter disappointment; and yet they clambered to their feet and moved towards the boats. Such was the loyalty my father inspired.

'Wait!' I cried. 'I'll get some food for you! Dan, fill the water bags!'

'What's happening? Why are we going out?' asked John Beck.

'Because the wind has come up!'

'But what does that mean, that the wind has come up?'

'We'll lose the whale! It'll blow out to sea – oh, shut up, you stupid dogs, from barking!'

In all that commotion, I must have dropped the shell that he gave to me. The next morning, upon realising my carelessness, I went down to the beach and spent several hours combing the area thoroughly. I found a multitude of spindle shells in the vicinity, and because I could not be entirely sure which was the one he had given me, I have kept four of which seemed to most closely resemble my memory of it.

Although, as I say, I cannot be entirely sure, I feel that A may be the shell that he gave to me, as it could be argued that A is slightly prettier and more delicate in its ridges than the other three. Then

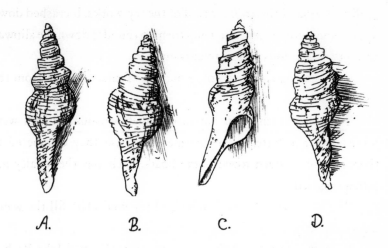

A.   B.   C.   D.

again, C has a more elegant fold to its opening, and is very softly coloured in this area. D is not really a contender as it is somewhat battered, and I cannot believe that he would have pressed that upon me so ardently; however, as it is a spindle shell and was found closest to the log on which we were sitting, I feel I must include it. All in all, it is a great pity that I did not take the trouble to examine the shell more carefully when he gave it to me.

(Of course, the thought occurs to me now that he may have simply picked up the nearest shell and pretended that he had been saving it up to give to me. Perhaps he had hastily wrapped it up in the bandages as he saw me approach. But no, I cannot really believe this of him, for he seemed so genuine in his appreciation of its prettiness, and so ardent in the manner in which he pressed it upon me. I do not understand this impulse I have developed in later life whereupon some small part of me seems to want to find fault in my memories of him, to 'burst the bubble', as it were.)

Sitting Tight

A S A RULE, A DEAD WHALE TAKES TWENTY-FOUR HOURS TO BLOAT with gas and rise to the surface; in fact, sometimes, for unknown reasons, it takes longer than this. So the reader may wonder why my father insisted they go out when the black whale had been dead for only a matter of hours. The only answer I can proffer is that his fear of losing the whale was so great that he felt it necessary to take every precaution possible. Thus, in the bitter cold and darkness, the weary men rowed back across the bay and, with some difficulty, finally located the marker buoys bobbing upon the surface. The Killers had long since finished their feast and departed. The carcass of the whale lurked deep down below. Arthur Ashby held up his lantern. He tugged at the marker buoys, and peered into the black water.

'Looks like the anchors are holding all right,' he announced. Not wishing to look as if he did not wish to be there, he perhaps made his voice sound a little overly cheerful. The men looked hopefully at my father. Perhaps they could now row back home again?

'We'll sit tight,' said my father.

A low murmur of frustration went round the whalers. They did not fancy the thought of keeping watch over the sunken remains of a dead whale. They would rather have been asleep in their bunks, especially since the rum was wearing off.

'Excuse me for saying so, boss,' said Arthur Ashby. Being my father's harpooner and right-hand man, Arthur was the only one who would dare to say what he was about to: 'The old girl's not going to gas up till tomorrow at the earliest. We might as well –'

'We'll sit tight,' repeated my father, with such a firmness of manner that Arthur deemed it better not to press the point.

And so the long wait commenced.

The great gust of wind that had knocked the sheet of tin off the roof of the try-works had been the harbinger of a biting north-westerly gale, bringing with it squalls of icy sleet. The whale men hunched over and huddled together; they pulled up their collars, pulled their hats down low over their ears and buried their hands deep within their pockets. Any part of their anatomy exposed to the elements began to turn blue and stiffen with the cold.

'We shall have frostbite of the nose,' said Salty grimly. 'And it shall not be pretty.'

This prompted Bastable to recount the story of the Parisian streetwalker he had once met. It had been a cold night and, moved by her plight, he had taken her to a small cafe that she might warm her innards with a bowl of pea soup. For in spite of her occupation, maintained Bastable, she was the most elegant and gracious lady you could ever hope to meet. In the course of their conversation, she assured him that although her work exposed her to many dubious characters, she was never afraid, for she knew how to protect herself. If any man tried to force himself upon her, she would simply bite his nose off. Then she would spit it at him.

'Spit what at him?' asked someone who had not been following the story closely.

'His nose.'

'But the nose is all gristle!' argued Albert Thomas Senior. 'It would be next to impossible to bite it off!'

'I am only repeating what she told me,' said Bastable. 'She herself had a good set of teeth.'

Generally speaking, the whale men were not so fortunate in the way of teeth, and so they refrained from commenting on this.

'Furthermore,' continued Bastable, 'after having his nose bitten off, the offender would now find himself stigmatised by his crime. If he attempted to stroll through the boulevards of Paris *sans* nose, then all would recognise at once the foul nature of his deed.'

'Why are you telling us this story?' demanded Salty. 'Are you saying that everyone in Eden will assume we have had our way with your Parisian prostitute, simply because we have had the misfortune of losing our noses to frostbite?'

Some of the men considered it unlikely that Bastable had ever spoken to a Parisian prostitute in the first place, and thus there was probably little to worry about. Nonetheless it was decided that a notice could be placed in the *Eden Observer and South Coast Advocate* to clarify the issue, if indeed it became necessary. My father, who had not entered the discussion up to this point, spoke up to say that, for

God's sake, no one was going to lose their nose to frostbite, for to do so they would have to be a lot colder.

'I assure you,' said Bastable, 'the only occasion on which you will find me colder will be at my funeral.'

'Hear, hear!' the men grumbled.

'In which case, you need not worry about the frostbite,' said my father.

The men slumped into silence. Another squall arrived, the sleet as piercing as if each icy drop had been sharpened on a whetstone. The men hunkered down into their sodden clothing, their misery complete. When the squall had passed, Salty shifted in his seat and shook the water out of the brim of his hat. To John Beck's surprise, he began to sing:

'Shallow Brown, you're going to leave me.'

It was slow and solemn, like a dirge. His rich baritone voice seemed to cut through the howl of the wind. The older whale men responded with a mournful refrain:

'Shallow, Shallow Brown,' they intoned.

'Shallow Brown,' sang Salty, *'don't ne'er deceive me.'*

'Shallow, Shallow Brown,' averred the men.

'Ye're going away across the o-ocean.'

'Shallow, Shallow Brown.'

'You'll ever be my heart's devotion.'

'Shallow, Shallow Brown.'

And then the song was over. The men had sung it without comment, and indeed without looking at each other. If anything, their gaze seemed fixed upon the water, as if it was the carcass deep below who might deceive them, who might go away across the ocean.

'All right,' said my father. 'We'll go ashore and light a fire.'

They rowed ashore to a rocky and inhospitable beach, where after the most treacherous landing, in which their boats very nearly capsized in the breakers, they staggered ashore and found a patch of sand protected by a rocky overhang. Here they succeeded in lighting a small fire with what little bit of dampish driftwood they could scratch up in the darkness. Around these thin flames they huddled. They ate some salted beef from their tucker-bags and then almost immediately fell asleep, curled up tightly together on the wet sand. Only John Beck and Salty remained awake, and they sat silently staring into the flames, occasionally rearranging the burning embers in a bid to improve the fire's heat. After a while, Salty produced a small flask of rum, which up to this point he had kept secreted on his person. He offered it to John Beck, who gratefully accepted.

'Tell me, Father,' said Salty, as he watched him take a swig. 'John Wesley – was he not the founder of Methodism?'

'Yes,' said John Beck. 'That's correct.'

The rum felt good and warming. He passed the bottle back to Salty, who himself took a fulsome draught.

'Unfamiliar as I am with his teachings,' said Salty, 'I believe that Wesley held some pretty strong opinions regarding – well, how can I put it – *licentious behaviour.*'

'That's correct,' John Beck acknowledged.

'By which I mean, gambling, fornicating, turf plunging; the drinking of hard liquor and so forth.'

'Yes, yes, I am clear on the definitions of licentious behaviour,' said John Beck.

'And this is part of what's puzzling me,' said Salty. 'I note that you yourself imbibe liquor with some evident enjoyment.'

'In moderation.'

'Yes, and who's to blame you? Who's to blame you, Father, for having a drink? John Wesley himself would agree, whaling is a thirsty business.'

As if to illustrate this, he swigged again from his rum bottle in a vehement fashion. Then he stashed it away in his coat pocket and pulled out his pipe, which he commenced to stoke.

'Also the card games, Father,' he continued, when he had completed the difficult process of lighting his pipe in the wind.

'What's that?' said John Beck.

'I've noticed you partake of the card games. Occasionally for stakes, I might add.'

'Only when the fellows have needed an extra hand,' said John Beck.

'And very expertly, if I may say so,' said Salty.

'Well, that's as may be –'

'No, no, it begs to be remarked upon; you play with a great deal of *proficiency*.'

His eyes twinkled pleasantly at John Beck across the flickering flames.

'Also,' he added, 'and here's the rub, I could not help but ponder the nature of your attentions to Mary this evening.'

'I was a minister once, but not anymore,' said John Beck. 'Have I not made that perfectly clear?'

'Ah, yes, yes. Perfectly clear. But as I say, it's the *proficiency* that puzzles me.'

John Beck slept poorly on the cold damp sand, and awoke at the first glimmering of the grey dawn breaking over the beach. The other whale men were still sleeping. They were a pitiful sight in the contortions of sleep, having each tried to find shelter by nestling tightly against one another, arms flung across faces, legs entangled. Robert, in the grip of a nightmare – possibly a nightmare about a large black whale – was moaning and muttering incoherently. With a sigh, John Beck unfolded his stiff limbs and clambered out of their dismal grotto. He looked out to sea. It was grey and roiling, its whitecaps blowing foam. He strained to see any sign of a floating whale carcass, but could not. He began to search for driftwood with which to build a fire, for he was keen to put the billy on.

Up ahead in the distance, he noticed a dark stooped figure standing on the shore. His heart started, for from this distance in the ghostly dawn light the figure looked almost like a large black crow, or an undertaker, or some other harbinger of ill fortune. As he drew closer, however, he realised it was Shankly. John Beck had not exchanged many words with Shankly up to now, and those words that had been exchanged had tended to leave John Beck feeling somewhat on the back foot.

'Good morning!' John Beck called out cheerfully, determined that Shankly not get the better of him this time. Shankly turned and surveyed him gloomily. He wore a long black coat that was flapping in the wind, and his thin hair was plastered over his scalp.

'No sign of it,' he remarked, with a sweeping gesture out to sea.

'No,' said John Beck. 'It is not risen yet.'

'Or else it has blown away while we lay sleeping,' said Shankly. This appeared to be an attempt at levity, for he bared his long teeth in a kind of smile or grimace.

'Yes,' said John Beck, with a short laugh. Shankly's grimace vanished.

'A curious thing to find humorous, Father. Given that the livelihoods of twelve men depend upon it.'

'Yes indeed,' said John Beck, annoyed that Shankly had once again got the better of him. 'Well, I am just off to gather firewood.'

'Would it be an imposition if I were to trouble you with a theological question, Father?'

John Beck stopped, and turned back to him.

'In the Methodist church, we are customarily addressed as Reverend,' he responded, somewhat testily. 'You may be thinking of the Catholic or the Anglican faiths, where the priest is referred to as Father.'

Shankly stared at him. 'I understood you had left the church.'

'That is so.'

'But you wish to be still known as Reverend?'

'No, I am simply – I am simply mentioning that it is customary for a minister of the Methodist church to be addressed as such.'

'As you wish,' said Shankly. 'I daresay such questions of nomenclature are important to clergymen, even though they seem of trifling concern to the rest of us.'

John Beck sighed inwardly. He was beginning to wish he had never mentioned his clerical background in the first place, for the whalers could not seem to let go of it.

'In your experience then, Reverend,' Shankly continued, 'how does the Lord regard the act of *mudder*?'

His Scottish accent was such that at times John Beck found him difficult to understand.

'Mudder?' he queried.

'You heard me the first time, Reverend. I will not repeat it.'

John Beck stared at him a moment, nonplussed. Then the penny dropped.

'Oh,' said John Beck. 'Well, not very favourably, I'm afraid. In fact, that is one of His Commandments – *Thou shalt not kill* – so it's something that I think He feels rather strongly about.'

Shankly said nothing, but returned his brooding gaze to the horizon.

'Why do you ask?' asked John Beck, after a moment.

'Well, I killed a man, Reverend.'

'What, just now?'

'No. Some time ago.'

'I see.'

'I killed a man and I ate his kidneys, and then I was satisfied.'

'I see,' said John Beck. 'Did you say that you ate his kidneys?'

'Yes, Reverend. I cooked them up in a frying pan.'

'Well, no. The Lord does not view such things favourably.'

'He was a wretch, Reverend, and deserved his fate.'

'Nonetheless.'

A silence fell between them. They both gazed out to sea. After a while, John Beck felt that he must really resume his search for firewood.

'Well, I'd best be off then,' he said.

'As you wish, Father,' said Shankly.

Twenty-four hours had passed since the whale had been killed, and still it had not risen to the surface. The two whaleboats sat tight by the marker buoys. It had been a miserable day; the wind blew, squalls came and went, and throughout it all, the sea had had a nasty lurching jobble which kept them all in a state of digestive discomfort. As day drew into night, the wind began to freshen once more into a gale. Still their prize lurked deep below. The men stared at the marker buoys as if willing the carcass to materialise. Surely it had to be imminent.

Hungry and exhausted, cold and sodden, the men now barely spoke to each other, and did so only to offer a terse rebuke for some perceived misdeed. 'Shallow Brown' had been cycled through many times now, and they were heartily sick of it; yet none had the inclination to sing anything more cheerful. Not long after midnight on the second night a spat broke out. Robert Heffernan had fallen asleep, and in his unconscious state had slumped heavily against Shankly. When shoved off, Robert had briefly regained consciousness only to slump against him again, and again a third time, and this had roused Shankly to anger and he leapt to his feet wielding a boat spade and shouting: 'Violate me, would ye, so brazenly?' John Beck and Harry managed to wrench the boat spade from him, but in the ensuing struggle, the boat had come close to capsizing. Finally, amidst my father's shouts for calm, some semblance of civility was restored to the second whaleboat. John Beck was instructed to sit between the two men to deter any further infractions. This did not stop Shankly from muttering dark threats at Robert Heffernan out of my father's earshot. Further, as his own weariness threatened to overtake him, John Beck became concerned that he might himself inadvertently violate Shankly. He did not fancy having his kidneys cooked up in a frying pan, no matter how satisfying Shankly might find the result.

For some time, Robert Heffernan could be heard crying softly in the darkness. Far from appealing to their compassion, this seemed to work as an irritant upon the men, yet shouting at him to stop blubbering or punching him hard on the shoulder seemed only to induce fresh bouts of weeping. These small sobs the young man attempted to stifle, producing an effect all the more pathetic and exasperating.

'For pity's sake,' cried Salty. 'This is beyond all endurance!'

'All right,' said my father heavily. 'We'll go ashore and light a fire.'

Once again, they rowed to the rocky and inhospitable beach; once again they almost capsized and drowned in the breakers; once again they lit a scrap of a fire and fell into a deep and dreamless sleep atop the cold wet sand.

Dawn broke to find my father standing alone on the beach, peering out to sea. Amongst the sleeping whalers, Arthur Ashby stirred. Seeing my father, he dashed the sleep from his eyes and stumbled over to him.

'What can you see, Arthur?' asked my father, turning to him anxiously. 'I don't know if my eyes are playing tricks upon me.'

Arthur looked out. It was difficult to see with the breakers and the spray and the size of the swell. His eyes narrowed, and he studied intently for several moments the vicinity where they had left the carcass only a few hours before. Seeing nothing, his eyes shifted out to sea. There he caught a flash of something. It was a marker buoy bouncing jauntily over a wave top.

'She's adrift,' he said.

The Perils of Whaling

N O SOONER HAD THE BLACK WHALE RISEN TO THE SURFACE than a whole gale rose also from the south-west, sweeping the bloated carcass before it and causing it to break free of its anchors. Now the huge body was bowling out to sea unrestrained, its marker buoys crashing along behind it. The whale men set after it, their thoughts focused solely on their vanishing prize: twelve hundred pounds worth of blubber and whalebone, now apparently en route to New Zealand. Once they had made it out of the bay, however, they were struck by seas so vertiginous that the headsmen began to experience great difficulty in handling their boats.

'Pull, for God's sake, men!' cried my father as he grappled with the steer oar. 'Pull! Pull!'

As they bent to the oars, their weary muscles burning, one or other of the men would throw a look over his shoulder and snatch a glimpse of the marker buoys, then turn back to my father in disbelief. Not only were the buoys a great distance away, but the two small boats were pursuing them further and further out to sea. Even if they managed to catch the breakaway whale, they still had to face the prospect of the long and perilous journey back, towing a mountain of blubber. As this new horror dawned upon them, the precarious morale of the new chums began to waver, and the second boat staggered fitfully up each new precipice of water. Even the hardened men of the first boat found their resolve flagging when they realised they had now lost sight of land.

'Keep going!' cried my father. 'Why do you slow down?'

I imagine it can only have been out of loyalty to my father that the men continued to pull at all, for the chase must have surely seemed hopeless.

'I can't see her,' cried Salty from the other boat. 'Where's she gone?'

My father gripped the steer oar for support and squinted against the spray. It was true: the marker buoys and carcass seemed to have vanished.

'Darcy!' he cried. 'Stop rowing and look. Can you see anything?'

Darcy had the best eyes of all the whale men; it was extraordinary what he could see. Where we could see a tree on a distant hill, he could identify the birds that sat in it. He rose to his feet now and stood looking for several minutes. Then he turned and faced my father.

'I see her, boss,' he said. 'She's too far.'

My father stared at him. Darcy was Percy Madigan's boy, cheeky and good-humoured and well-liked by all. But to tell my father that he deemed the whale too far was an act of unheard-of defiance. The other men kept their heads down, even Bastable. In their hearts, they agreed with Darcy; the whale was too far away to catch, and had been from the beginning.

'How far?' said my father, eyeing Darcy steadily.

'Miles.'

'How many miles? Two? Three?'

'Four maybe.'

'But the marker buoys –'

'Those marker buoys have come loose, boss.'

My father reeled. Albert Thomas Senior leapt up to support him, but he regained his equilibrium and motioned him aside, instead leaning heavily upon his steer oar. (We wanted that the steer oar be buried with my father. It was of course twenty-two feet long and would not fit in the grave; but the fact that it seemed appropriate will give an indication of how much a part of him it was.) The men stared up at him. They had been chasing after marker buoys that were no longer even attached to the whale? Then where in God's name was the whale?

'Home,' said my father hoarsely. 'Turn your boat, Salty. We're going home.'

Turning the boats around, the long journey back now confronted them. At best reckoning, they were seven miles out. The wind was against them and every wave that rose up threatened to engulf their frail crafts. There was no choice except to tackle it; their only other option was to sink and drown. It was all too terrible to contemplate. And yet, as they rowed, calling upon every last ounce of energy from their exhausted reserves, the boats seemed to barely progress. Instead, they slid sickeningly up each new wall of water, only to be dashed into the trough below. Then the next wave presented itself.

It seemed impossible that both whaleboats and men could continue to withstand such a battering.

'This isn't funny anymore,' said Robert Heffernan, not that at any point he had shown signs of amusement.

Salty looked at his exhausted men, rowing as if already dead, their faces haggard with disbelief.

'A prayer! That's what we need!' cried Salty. 'Give us a prayer, Father, now as we row! Is there not a special prayer for whale men in distress?'

John Beck looked up at him in dismay. A prayer? When it was all he could do to keep his hands on the oars, he must suddenly come up with a prayer – and not just any prayer, but one appropriate to the dire circumstances in which they found themselves? The fact that the hardened whale man and self-proclaimed Professor of Whales felt it necessary to appeal to the Almighty surely meant that things were worse than he could imagine. The other oarsmen turned to him now, feebly hopeful. They needed something perhaps he alone could give them, some small words of encouragement, some promise of salvation.

'O God,' John Beck began tentatively. 'Give to the wind our fears –'

'Speak up, Father!'

'O God,' he repeated, raising his voice. 'Give to the wind our fears. Hear our sighs –'

'We can't hear you back here in the cheap seats!'

'Hear our sighs and count our tears!' He had to shout to be heard above the elements. 'Lift up our heads and carry us through waves and clouds and storms!'

'Yea, O Lord,' cried Salty.

'Yea, O Lord!' agreed the whale men.

'Dispose our hearts that death may not be dreadful to us –'

'Not that prayer, Father!' cried Salty abruptly.

'No. No, of course,' said John Beck. They were riding up an especially vertiginous wave. The boat hovered horribly at its crest, causing their bellies to lurch with fear, then smashed down bow first into its trough.

'Oh Jesus,' whimpered Robert Heffernan, and nobody blamed him.

'Yes, Jesus, hear us now!' cried John Beck. All this shouting against the elements and rowing at the same time was making him short of breath, and the words came out in staccato bursts. 'You have – taken from us – the great Leviathan – whose empty carcass must now rot – uselessly – upon the ocean floor –'

In fact, he was quite pleased with this style of delivery. It seemed to suggest a passion and urgency that had perhaps been lacking in his sermons, and his straining voice was acquiring a commanding timbre.

'Where once – its precious bounty – might have lubricated – cogs – of great machinery,' he continued. 'Or served perhaps – in the construction of umbrellas – or indeed corsets – to enhance the silhouettes of our womenfolk –'

'Not a sermon, Father, just a prayer if you would!'

'Right, yes,' said John Beck. 'O God,' he commenced afresh, 'who hath embarked our souls in these frail boats – preserve us from the dangers that on all sides assault us – give Your oarsmen the strength to pull against this tempest – that we might arrive at last in the haven of eternal salvation –'

'Haven of eternal salvation, Lord,' cried Salty.

'Yea, O Lord,' cried the whalers, who would welcome a haven of any description.

'Hear the cry of our hearts, and have mercy upon us, Lord. Have mercy upon whale men who have lost their cargo –'

'Yes, Lord!'

'– and seek only to return home.'

And just as these last words blew away on the wind, by all accounts of those who were present, the dark clouds above broke apart just enough to permit a shaft of pale crepuscular sunlight to shine down upon the two small boats. The men gazed up to the heavens in amazement, and none more so than John Beck.

'Amen,' he said.

'Amen, Father,' said Salty.

'Amen,' said the whalers.

Importance of Preserving Memories

I REALISE, ON LOOKING BACK AT THESE PAGES, THAT IN MY anxiety to hurry along to the exciting part of the story, I have moved on from the moment where John Beck kissed me without perhaps acknowledging that this was, and remains, a moment of great significance to me. Our lips met again on other occasions (and I will get to them in due course), but this was the first kiss, and here I will state that it is not for nothing that these first tender caresses between lovers are so treasured. Unlike the time when Burrows had kissed me roughly and conjured up the unpleasant image of the live sea slug or bivalve flailing about inside my mouth, John Beck's kisses on this occasion were more tentative, indeed almost chaste. And yet even to attempt to describe this moment between us seems to diminish it somehow, so I shall desist from going any further. I have only these memories to hold on to, and am anxious lest I wear them out.

Several years ago, in my anxiety over this possibility, I introduced a ration plan whereby I permitted myself to summon these
most precious memories only once a day (usually at bedtime, after
extinguishing the lamp). It was difficult, but I felt I had to do this,
so concerned was I that the *tangibility* of the memory (where I could
bring it to mind so vividly I could smell and taste, and feel the
roughness of his cheek and so forth) was fading, or at least somehow
becoming *less*. Not long after the introduction of this plan, I noticed
that I was beginning to compensate for the deprivation by allowing
myself, once a memory was summoned, to dwell in that pleasant state
for longer and longer periods of time, as if reluctant to relinquish
it for another whole day. Again I had to be firm with myself and
impose a greater self-discipline. That is, I permit myself to linger
in the memory state for a period of no more than two minutes. And
yet, even in spite of these efforts, I find the memories are continuing
to recede. Thus I have put in place a new regime of allowing myself to
indulge in these memories only once every few days, trying
to stretch the period between them for as long as possible each
time. If I catch myself wanting to summon the memory more
frequently, I pinch myself as hard as I can on the underside of my
forearm.

The Whale Men Return

I DID NOT HEAR ABOUT THE SHAFT OF MIRACULOUS SUNLIGHT THAT had answered John Beck's prayer until some time later, and it did much to explain the puzzling behaviour he manifested from the moment of his return.

But I am getting a little ahead of myself. For although the crepuscular beam pierced the clouds so marvellously that bleak morning, inspiring in the men a sense of hope and salvation, the effect lasted barely a minute and did nothing to assuage the wild seas or ameliorate their ordeal. Their journey continued in the same arduous and terrifying manner until finally they reached the shelter of Leonards Island, and then of Twofold Bay itself. Sometime in the afternoon, they made it back to the whaling station at Kiah. We watched much of this last stage of their journey from the headland (where we had been taking it in turns to keep lookout); it was pitiful indeed to see the laborious progress they made in these conditions, the smaller second boat huddling in the wake of the first.

I was unable to linger, though, for it was necessary that I turn my attention promptly to the problem of how to feed them. They would of course be extremely hungry; I had packed only small quantities of salted beef and damper in their tuckerbags, little expecting that they would be gone for two whole nights. In their absence, the family had subsisted on porridge and griddle scones; our stores were getting worrisomely low. Now, as I untied the last of the salted beef, hanging in muslin from the roof of the cellar, I leapt back in fright. The muslin was alive; that is, the salted beef had become completely infested with larder beetles.

'We can't feed them that,' said Louisa, as we stared in horror at the seething hunk of meat, now lying on the floor where I had dropped it.

'Of course we can't feed them that. I had no intention of feeding them that,' I snapped. Leaning in to examine it more closely, we could see that the industrious beetles were busily laying their eggs in it.

'Dan!' I bellowed. '*Dan!*'

'What?' said Dan, from the top of the cellar stairs.

'Run at once and check the bandicoot traps.'

The reader may not be familiar with the long-nosed bandicoot; it is a slight creature, about the size of a small rabbit, with bright eyes, pointy ears and a nervous, querulous disposition. It sleeps by day, and spends its evenings scurrying around in the undergrowth, grunting and squeaking and fighting with other bandicoots. If you come across one unexpectedly, it will jump straight up in the air out of fright; 'Startle the Bandicoot' had long been a popular game amongst the children. I bear no ill-will to the bandicoot, nor is its meat particularly flavoursome; however, 'needs must' and, thankfully for us, Dan returned with one such creature found in the trap. We then sent him off with the rifle to try to pot a rabbit. Not that we held out much hope of this; Dan was somewhat near-sighted, like myself.

Louisa and I stared at the bandicoot in dismay; they do not have a lot of meat at the best of times, and this one appeared to be a juvenile.

'Well, you had best hurry up and skin it,' I told her.

'We can't feed all twelve of them on this!' she cried in a high-pitched tone that was bordering on hysterical. She was right, of course. I turned my attention back to the lump of salted beef, still lying on the floor, swarming with beetles. It looked for all the world like they might at any moment lift it up and carry it out the door.

'Perhaps if we were to wash it free of beetles?' I suggested.

'Have you taken leave of your senses?' cried Louisa. 'Have you gone completely insane?'

'Well, what else are we going to do?' I was beginning to acquire the same hysterical tone that I had observed in Louisa. There was nothing for it; the men approached in their whale boats even as we stood there. Promptly we filled a large bucket with water and a dash of vinegar, and then I scrubbed away at it furiously while Louisa cowered in the corner, covering her eyes and making sounds as if she were to be violently sick.

'Do not tell a living soul about this,' I warned her. I must have made a pretty sight, standing there with my lump of disintegrating beef, surrounded by a colony of drowned and sodden beetles.

We made a kind of hash of boiled bandicoot combined with those portions of salted beef which were not infested with larvae, onions, potatoes, milk, flour and a liberal amount of Worcestershire sauce to improve the flavour.

'It's a pity we can't feed them the larder beetles,' observed Louisa ruefully, as we slid down the rocks towards the sleeping hut. Suddenly we came to a halt. Over in the try-works, the whale men could be seen taking their baths, no doubt in a bid to thaw themselves out. They had filled the try pots with water and lit fires beneath then, and now they were wallowing contentedly.

'*Quelle horreur,*' hissed Louisa. 'Naked whalers.'

We stood there for a moment and watched them. It was not a sight we had ever seen before. There amongst them, I glimpsed John Beck, ladling hot water over his shoulders with a skimming spoon. I will not go into further detail on this; suffice to say, it is one of the memories I am trying hardest to preserve. Rousing myself from my reverie, I nudged Louisa and we continued our journey to the sleeping huts.

'What's this then?' asked Robert Heffernan, as we doled out the hash. He was staring at his plate and, to my horror, I saw what appeared to be a larder beetle lying legs up in a murky pool of Worcestershire. Deftly, I flicked it from his plate.

'Never you mind,' I replied. 'Just eat heartily. We need to fatten you up, young man.'

'Why do we need to fatten him up?' asked Louisa. 'Are we going to cook Robert next?'

I was distracted then by the sound of tapping on a tin cup, and turning, I saw John Beck standing amongst the whale men. There was something oddly cherubic about their appearance freshly bathed, reminding one of large ruddy-faced bad-tempered babies. Except for John Beck, of course. He had a blanket wrapped around him, and a light beard growth, and looked for all the world like Jesus of Nazareth amongst his Apostles.

'Men,' John Beck was saying. 'Perhaps after our experience out at sea this morning, you will permit me to offer a small prayer of thanksgiving.'

There was grumbling at this, but most of the men put down their forks and some even lowered their heads solemnly.

'How typical of the clergy,' muttered Salty to Bastable. 'Give him a little encouragement, now we can't shut him up.'

'Oh, most great and glorious God,' intoned John Beck, closing his eyes and holding up his right hand. 'Who art mighty in thy power and wonderful in thy doings; accept, I beseech thee, our unfeigned thanks and praise for our creation, preservation and all the other blessings which in the riches of thy mercy thou hast from time to time poured down upon us. Amen.'

A mumble of 'Amen's issued forth from the whalers but I found, in my astonishment, that my lips could not form the word. A feeling of bewilderment overwhelmed me. What had become of the John Beck of two nights ago, stealing kisses and forcing me to admire his muscles? Here he stood, avoiding my gaze and offering grace in the most doleful and pious tones. Behind me, I heard a mutter of disgruntlement.

'I'll not be thanking the Lord for a piece of boiled bandicoot,' said Bastable.

Some Words About My Father

I AM AGHAST, LOOKING BACK AT THESE LAST CHAPTERS, AT HOW selfish I appear. Here I am relating the story of the devastating loss of the black whale through the prism of my feelings for John Beck, when in fact my thoughts should have been only of my father. Certainly now, looking back at it from a perspective of thirty years, I wonder that my memories of him at this time are so hazy; the vigilance I have demonstrated in collating and preserving any memory of John Beck has not been exercised to the same degree in the case of my father. The one memory I do have of Father upon their return that afternoon is something of a distressing one. So exhausted was he by the ordeal, both mentally and physically, that he had had to be helped, almost carried, down the jetty. Seeing his bandy legs buckle as the men supported him, I turned and took hold of the little girls and hurried back up to the house so that he would not suffer the embarrassment of knowing we had witnessed him in this condition.

I remember also that Louisa picked the very best portions of bandicoot for his plate, and made sure that he did not partake of any of the beetle-infested beef (she could be a loving daughter in her own way). But these are my only memories of him on that occasion, for I was obviously too preoccupied with my own feelings to think about how he must have been suffering.

The black whale we lost that season was not the only whale that had ever been lost in such circumstances. Allowing the Killers to take possession of the carcass always carried with it the risk that the weather might turn before the men were able to recover it. Perhaps the profits incurred by whaling would have been more consistent if the whalers had been able to tow the carcass back to the try-works immediately after the kill; however, the Killers would never have permitted such a thing and I daresay would have torn the whale to pieces had my father attempted it. Not that he would have dared, of course; he had too much respect for their longstanding 'gentlemen's agreement'. Besides which, as he readily conceded, without the assistance of the Killer whales, they would likely not have captured the whale in the first place.

The point I was getting to, however, is that although we had lost whales before in similar circumstances, I feel I can trace the beginning of the despondency that characterised his later years to the loss of this black whale in 1908, coming as it did in such a poor season, and after the dreadful season of the year before. And although we went on to have some few reasonably successful seasons after this, there was never a return to the great numbers of whales that were sighted and captured in Twofold Bay in previous generations.

On top of this, whale oil no longer commanded the prices it had in former times; for this, my father would always blame the Great War, although in truth the decline had commenced much earlier, with the ready availability of kerosene. Similarly, as the fashion for corsetry diminished, the demand for whalebone also began to decline. (My father strongly disapproved of these advances in ladies' fashions, and would cast a baleful eye indeed over Violet and Annie's short skirts and drop-waists when they were old enough to attend the Kiah dances. Indeed, it was a full year or two after he died before I felt that I could dispense with my own whalebone corset.) Yet although these larger forces of wars and fashion and kerosene were outside my father's control, I think he felt badly that he was the last of three generations of Davidsons to whale in Twofold Bay. By 1929, he had put the whaling station up for sale, although it took some years to sell.

> '*There's many a time I've quivered with fear*
> *As I've passed by Twofold Bay*
> *And many a time I've shivered to hear*
> *"Fearless Davidson's on his way!"*
> *"Look smart, boys!" cries Fearless George*
> *"She's a humpback fifty feet!"*
> *And he holds aloft the piercing steel*
> *His mission to complete.*'

This poem, written from the whale's point of view and published in the *Eden Observer*, continued for some ten to twelve verses, and yet I find I can only remember portions of it. (As a child I knew the entire poem by heart and would stand on the back step and declaim it to the chickens, although I was always too shy to recite it to anybody else.) It described my father doing battle with a particularly ferocious humpback into whose gizzards he plunges his lance in the last stanza, crying out, '*O dark heart, beat no more!*' This caused my father some embarrassment, for of course he knew the humpback to be a mild-mannered creature, nor would he ever cry out such a thing. The only other part of the poem I can recall is:

> '*I beg of you, (something something)*
> *Please heed my anguished pleas*
> *But now he deals the fatal blow*
> *Which brings me to my knees.*'

Which we found very funny at the time, since obviously whales do not have knees. My point is, however, that while not entirely factually accurate, this poem (and there were others in a similar vein) demonstrates some measure of the esteem in which my father was held by the townsfolk of Eden. I suppose his quiet courage and his cool head when confronted by danger were qualities the civic fathers wished to call their own; certainly they made full use of his reputation to advance the public image of Eden.

Thinking about my father, I feel the urge to recount an event which occurred only a couple of years before he died. By then, it was just him and myself living at Kiah; whaling had been abandoned, much of the equipment already sold, even the Killer whales had stopped returning. I was then employed as a teacher at the Kiah Half-time School; my father spent his days now either sitting on the front verandah or 'tidying up' down at the try-works. On this occasion, he had spotted a whale spout from the headland up behind the house. Living where we did, we frequently saw whale spouts during the season; in fact, they seemed especially plentiful now that our livelihood no longer depended upon them. But for some reason, this particular whale captured my father's attention, and he watched it spout and play for some time from the headland. (It is necessary sometimes to remind oneself that these passing whales are undertaking an epic journey of many thousands of miles, for in fact they seem to dawdle and meander in the manner of recalcitrant schoolboys on their way to school; if there was a bottle, they would kick it. It is truly a wonder that they ever get anywhere.) Returning home from school, I saw my father going down to the jetty and getting into his dinghy; I imagined that he was going to row into town, as he sometimes did on the spur of the moment. But instead, unbeknownst to me, he rowed out some considerable distance to where the whale was still idly cavorting. As he approached, the whale sank below the surface; my father – who clearly still possessed an instinct for such things – then rowed to where he believed it might reappear. Sure enough, some minutes later, the whale rose to the surface directly alongside his boat, whereupon he drove his lance into it.

He lanced it just once; the whale immediately dived, then surfaced again in a distressed state and swam off at great speed. My father attempted to pursue it but, needless to say, an old man in a dinghy was no match for it, so after a while he gave up and returned home.

When he came inside for tea, I noticed what appeared to be blood on his clothing, though it seemed he had attempted to sponge it off. When asked about it, he remarked that he had rowed out and lanced a whale, in as casual a fashion as if he had said that he had walked to the letterbox to pick up the mail. I put down my cup and stared at him. For a moment, I truly believed that he might be in the grip of some kind of senile delusion, but his eyes were clear and lucid and he seemed to be entirely his normal self.

'Why did you do that?' I asked, and I realised that my voice was shrill. I did not like whales to be killed for no reason. Besides, it was not as if we had eleven extra men to tow the carcass back and render it into whale oil. Even if we could render it into whale oil, we almost certainly couldn't sell it.

'Why did you do that?' I repeated, and I realised I was angry. I was so angry I felt I could fling something at him, especially since he sat buttering his bread and not responding to my question. He wore a faint, silly smile upon his face, and I noticed his hands were trembling: I suspect he may also have been privately wondering why he had done it, and was unable to provide a satisfactory answer.

Several days later, the dead whale (a young humpback) washed up on the rocks near Green Cape lighthouse, its lance wound plain to see. The story of my father's deed soon became known, and was widely interpreted as somehow heroic; there was even a small article about in the *Sydney Morning Herald*, under the headline: '*Lone Whaler. Veteran's Feat in Dinghy*'. My father's demeanour was considerably more cheerful for some time after this event; he concocted various excuses to go into Eden that he might sit in the bar at the Great Southern and have drinks bought for him on the strength of it. Looking back on it now, I am still somewhat bewildered as to his motive, yet overall more sympathetic in my attitude. I suppose after a lifetime of chasing whales and 'staring down the gaping maw of destruction', it must be difficult to allow them to swim past unmolested. I do not mean to sound glib in saying that; I simply mean that he probably just wished to have one more shot at it.

The postscript to the story is that various attempts were made by my father and his old mates from the Great Southern to somehow float the carcass off the rocks, with the vague idea, I imagine, of rendering the blubber into whale oil. They never succeeded; thus the whale rotted over several months in situ, much to the annoyance of the lighthouse keepers, especially if the wind blew in towards them.

A Missing Clergyman

I T WAS AROUND THIS PERIOD – THAT IS, AFTER THE LOSS OF THE black whale, the period in which John Beck was apparently overcome by a resurgence in his faith – that we first came across the story of the missing clergyman. An old newspaper article had been discovered pasted over a crack in the wall in one of the sleeping huts; the first I became aware of it was overhearing Salty recounting the contents of the article for the other whalers' enjoyment one evening at mealtime. John Beck was subsequently on the receiving end of a good deal of speculative commentary on the subject, and I noted at the time that he became quite 'hot under the collar'.

The next morning, after the whale men had left for the lookout, I entered the sleeping hut, found the article in question (with some difficulty, as there were a great many newspapers plastered over a great many cracks) and copied it out in its entirety.

To summarise the contents of the article: in April of 1906, a Reverend T.A. James, a Methodist minister from Albany, Western Australia, had travelled to Sydney on a visit. Sometime later in the same month, his wife, Mrs James, received a telegram stating that her husband had unfortunately drowned in Sydney and his body had not been recovered. Even amidst her grief, Mrs James considered it odd that the telegram which bore these sad tidings had been posted from Suva, the capital of Fiji, and she at once asked the police if they would commence inquiries. They soon discovered that there had been no drowning accident to speak of in Sydney Harbour at that time. Further, they learned that the Reverend James had last been seen on 15 April, Easter Sunday, at a boarding house in Wynyard Square; he was clean-shaven (up to this point, he had always worn a beard) and, notably, was not dressed in clerical attire. The very next day, a mail steamer, the *Maheno*, had left Sydney for Vancouver. It stopped at Suva on 23 April, the very day the telegram had been posted.

The article concluded with the following postscript:

'Important developments have occurred in connection with the missing clergyman. A photograph of the Rev. T.A. James has been identified as Mr Lee, who, with Mrs Lee, stopped at a Sydney boarding house at Easter week. Inquiries show that Mr and Mrs Lee were amongst the passengers by the mail steamer "Maheno", which left Sydney for 'Frisco on 16 April. There is now not the slightest doubt but that Lee and James are one and the same person.'

The whalers derived a good bit of sport from teasing John Beck on the subject, asking him how he liked 'Frisco and what had become of Mrs Lee and whether he shouldn't let poor Mrs James know his present whereabouts. He had borne all this with good humour initially, but after a while seemed to become irritated by their incessant jibes, and requested somewhat tersely that they desist. (This was not in itself surprising; the whalers would often carry a joke too far, and not infrequently something that had begun as a little light jesting would culminate in fisticuffs.) After a while, the whalers lost interest in the story, and it soon faded from general conversation. As for me, I do not recall thinking there was any great cause for concern; rather, the article simply piqued my curiosity. Yet even as I write these words, it seems to be dawning on me for the first time that given the voyage to 'Frisco occurred fully two years before John Beck came ambling up our front path, then there *was* a possibility, albeit a slight one, that John Beck and Reverend James were indeed 'one and the same person'.

I raise the following points for consideration.

On more than one occasion, John Beck had mentioned Western Australian place names in passing, indicating that he had almost certainly been there. For example, I remember overhearing him mention to my father that Busselton, a town in Western Australia, had a jetty that was a mile long. Another time, he said something about there being a large gaol in Fremantle.

Albany (the town in which Reverend James had originally resided) was a whaling port. So it is interesting that there is a whaling connection.

Also, John Beck was clean-shaven (at least he was when we knew him).

Even so, and all things considered, I find I cannot really believe it. It would mean that he had travelled to 'Frisco only to return to

Australia again within two years. You would think that he would be reluctant to return to Australia, given the dubious circumstances of his departure, but then again, when I think on it, the police were presumably looking for Rev. James (or, rather, Mr Lee) in 'Frisco, and I imagine that could have made things uncomfortable. (Indeed, the West Australian Methodist Conference recommended his expulsion from the ministry, and sent a statement of his offences to be posted in every Methodist church in the United States.) Then there is the whole question of Mrs Lee. What became of her? I can only assume that the pressure of being 'wanted', combined with guilt and shame at his conduct towards his wife – and perhaps even a spiritual turmoil, given that he was a man of the cloth – led to the breakdown of their perhaps somewhat rash and ill-considered liaison.

In truth, it distresses me to think of John Beck as Reverend James in fresh incarnation, with a Mrs James left behind in Albany, and a Mrs Lee lingering in 'Frisco. It conveys the impression that he was some kind of Lothario, yet I cannot believe that of him. It is simply a striking coincidence that both men were formerly ministers of the Methodist church.

The Ungraspable Phantom of Life

I T WAS NOT UNUSUAL FOR THE RIGOURS OF WHALING TO INSPIRE IN new chums a sudden and fervent interest in the hereafter, and for a time I hoped that John Beck's newfound absorption in the Bible, and his readiness with only the slightest provocation to vouchsafe a psalm or lead the whale men in prayer, might simply be another manifestation of this condition. However, it seems that the meteorological coincidence of the crepuscular beam breaking through the clouds in apparent heavenly response to his prayer that grim morning had had the effect of inducing in John Beck a violent reawakening of his faith. This, in turn, induced in me a sense of creeping disappointment. I found I much preferred the old John Beck; the John Beck with the interest in my black silk stockings, the John Beck of the flexing arm muscles; the John Beck with the twinkling eyes and the pleasingly lascivious grin. Most of all, I missed the John Beck who wanted to kiss me, even if it meant risking my father's ire.

I had the distinct sense now that this new John Beck was uncomfortable in my presence. At mealtimes, I gazed at him imploringly as I doled his portion onto his plate, but he kept his eyes firmly downcast, murmured his thanks and moved on. Offering an extended prayer before each meal had become his regular custom now, often taking the opportunity to expound upon theological themes and draw analogies with some small event that had happened during the course of the day. One day, he pontificated for twenty minutes on the fact that just as there were twelve disciples, there were indeed twelve whale men. Needless to say, this sort of talk made the whalers uneasy. Nor did they ever wait for John Beck to finish saying grace before they commenced eating, but I suppose they could scarcely be blamed for that. Thus his invocations were offered to the noisy accompaniment of derisory comments and spoons scraping upon tin plates.

All this was most distressing for me. Was this a repeat of the Burrows episode? I wondered. An ardent pursuit followed by a period of distinct coolness? If so, it seemed very unfair. After all, it was John Beck who had insisted he kiss me; yet now it seemed that I was an unpleasant reminder of a side of his nature that he wished to suppress. At least I was able to examine my own behaviour and truthfully state that, in this instance, I had not thrown myself at him. Certainly, I had acquiesced willingly, but was that the same thing? Did my compliance in allowing myself to be kissed amount to 'throwing myself at him'? If so, I was beginning to grow very tired of the whole thing.

One day some repair work had to be done on the second whaleboat, and the crew of that boat stayed behind whilst repairs were effected. As it happened, that very morning I had come across my mother's flute and decided I would make a renewed attempt to teach myself to play it. I had attempted several times over the years, and had got to the stage of mastering the 'embouchure' and extracting some not unpleasant sounds. Now, with aid of my mother's music book, I intended to work on my fingering. Encouraged by Louisa to move as far away from the house as possible, I took my flute down to the beach below, and there I espied John Beck, sitting alone on a rock some distance away. At first, my impulse was to veer away without him seeing me, but then some contrary spirit within urged me to proceed as I had originally intended. Bonnie, who had elected to accompany me, led the way.

'Oh. Hello there,' I said as we approached.

'Hello, Mary,' he said.

'What are you doing?'

'Well, I am studying my Bible.'

I nodded bitterly. Of course he was. Uncertain as to what to do next but anxious not to end the exchange immediately, I picked up a pebble and skimmed it across the surface of the water. Then I picked up a much larger rock and, with some effort, hurled it into the water. It created a great splash – some droplets even landed on the open pages of his Bible. He glanced up at me briefly, but made no comment.

'Would it be all right if I practised my flute over there?' I asked, pointing to a cluster of rocks a small distance away.

'Yes, that would be all right,' he said.

'I won't disturb your study?'

'No, I don't think so.'

'Will you let me know if it does disturb you? Because of course I would stop right away.'

'Thank you. I think it should be all right.'

I gazed at him unhappily. How handsome he was. I had never noticed it before, but his neck was particularly appealing; strong and well formed, masculine without being bullish. A clerical collar would have set it off to perfection. However, there was little to be achieved by standing there and staring at his neck, so, with heavy heart, I moved off to the rocks with my flute.

I soon discovered that, in the months since I had last practised, my mastery of the embouchure had lapsed, and my attempts at producing any decent sound from the wretched thing were thwarted. I pursed my lips and blew in a variety of different ways through and at and over the mouthpiece, but only the most dismal squeaks emerged. What an infernal instrument this was. How did anyone ever learn to play it? Why must my attempts at self-improvement be continually frustrated?

'May I join you?'

I looked up in surprise. John Beck was standing beside me on the rocks.

'If you wish,' I replied.

He sat down beside me on the rock, his Bible on his knee. I glanced at it resentfully.

'I do hope you have not come to recite psalms at me,' I said curtly.

'No,' he said. 'Not if you do not wish me to.'

I said nothing, but instead pulled my flute apart and proceeded to shake it angrily. I was hoping to convey the impression that there was something the matter with it which prevented me from producing the lilting airs that one normally associates with the instrument.

'Mary,' said John Beck, 'I think you might be annoyed with me. Perhaps if you would allow me to explain myself.'

'I assure you, I am not annoyed with you,' I responded crisply. 'I just find you extremely changeable, much like the weather we have been having lately.'

'Yes. I realise I must seem that way. But you see, something happened out at sea the other day, and I suppose I am trying to make sense of it.'

I said nothing, but put my flute back together. Then I rested it on my knee. I had no wish to embark upon more blowing and squeaking in front of him.

'Up until now, you see, Mary,' he continued, 'I have not always been ... entirely straightforward in the way I have represented myself.'

'Oh yes?'

'Sometimes I find in life we are all too ready to judge a person's worth on what we perceive of their demeanour or appearance or indeed their past history –'

'I'm sorry, you have lost me altogether.'

'I beg your pardon.'

'I hope this is not an indication of what your sermons were like.'

'Not at all,' said John Beck, somewhat tetchily. 'In fact, my sermons were on the whole well regarded. It's just that I am trying to express something rather difficult –'

'Oh, then do forgive my interrupting, simply because I have no clue what you are talking about.'

'Well, to speak more plainly, perhaps you have formed an idea about me –'

'I assure you, I have formed no ideas whatsoever.'

'I mean, based on the fact that I was once a Methodist minister.'

'You are very pleased with the fact that you were once a Methodist minister.'

'But that's my point, you see. Perhaps I have no right to be pleased about it.'

'Then why do you go on about it so?'

The word 'harpy' suddenly leapt into my mind. I sounded like a harpy, sitting there on my mossy rock berating him. Ashamed of myself, I fell into silence. We both stared at Bonnie, who was rolling happily in the remains of a dead mutton-bird she had found on the beach. Every now and then she gave a joyful bark. How nice it must be to be a dog, I thought wildly. Simple pleasures. A nice dead mutton-bird to roll in.

'You wonder why I seem changeable,' said John Beck after a moment. 'It's because I have always been troubled by a kind of restlessness. I have always been in search of something.'

'Goodness,' I said. 'What have you been in search of?'

'I don't know, you see. That's the problem.' He gazed down at his Bible for a moment. 'Perhaps I am searching for "the ungraspable phantom of life".'

He turned to me then, and when I look back at this moment, it seems to me that his face wore a hopeful expression, as if anticipating from me a sympathetic response. A wise nod, perhaps; a gentle smile; a thoughtful word or two murmured in a low voice.

'The ungraspable phantom of life?' I repeated. My voice had now assumed an unpleasantly sardonic tone. 'Do you expect you will find it whaling, amidst the blubber?'

He said nothing. Reaching down into a small rock pool near his feet, he prodded a lowly sea cucumber that resided there. It hunkered down and spat out a murky substance in protest. Then he rose to his feet and walked away (by which I mean John Beck walked away, not the sea cucumber).

I sat on my rock meanwhile, stewing in my own juices. '*Restlessness,*' I muttered to myself scornfully. Was the humble sea cucumber troubled by thoughts of its restlessness? I very much doubted it. More likely, it found contentment within the confines of its rock pool. Had that mutton-bird Bonnie just rolled in been tormented by restlessness also? Actually – I hesitated here – perhaps it had. Perhaps it was restlessness that compelled the bird to fly many hundreds of miles on its annual migration, only to drop dead out of the sky from sheer exhaustion. These hapless whales, driven by an unknown force to travel up the coast each year – perhaps they, too, were plagued by this cursed restlessness, and much good it did them, with the Killer whales waiting to pounce. Such was the confusion of thoughts that darted about in my mind like sheep taking fright in a paddock.

I had failed to recognise, you see, the phrase that John Beck had held out to me. Certainly, I had made several attempts with *Moby Dick*, and in fact I had read that first chapter through on several occasions. But it was only years later, in another of my efforts at improving myself, that I decided once again to make a renewed attempt. And there, in the first few pages, I stumbled across it:

'Why did the old Persians hold the sea holy? Why did the Greeks give it a separate deity, and own brother of Jove? Surely all this is not without meaning. And still deeper the meaning of that story of Narcissus, who because he could not grasp the tormenting, mild image he saw in the fountain, plunged into it and was drowned. But that

same image, we ourselves see in all rivers and oceans. It is the image of the ungraspable phantom of life; and this is the key to it all.'

That night, in the darkness of our bedroom, I confided in Louisa that I had feelings for one of our whale men.

'Which one?' She propped herself up on an elbow to look at me, her interest roused. 'Which one do you fancy?'

Immediately I wished that I had not said anything, for she began poking at me with her bony forefinger.

'Well, John Beck, if you must know,' I finally admitted. It felt thrilling, somehow, to give voice to my feelings, as if in doing so, they might actually amount to something.

'Oh, him.' Louisa flopped down against her pillow. 'But yes, I suppose I can see how he would appeal to you.'

'What do you mean?' I asked.

'Well, he's such an old nanny goat,' she said.

'Hardly!' I cried hotly. 'He is by far the handsomest of all of them.'

'Even if that were true, Mary, it would not be saying much.'

I deeply regretted telling her now, and was thankful that I had not gone into more detail. Although of course now, with the benefit of hindsight, I have come to realise which one of the whalers she personally considered more worthy of admiration.

A Visit From Mr Crowther

I T WAS AROUND ABOUT THIS TIME THAT WE RECEIVED AN unwelcome visit from Mr Crowther. On top of his responsibilities as local agent for Singer sewing machines, Alfa Laval cream separators and Griffiths Brothers tea, he had lately taken on the Wunderlich ceiling account, and 'wundered' whether we did not feel our small homestead could benefit from such an improvement. His habit was to sing out 'Hell-o-o thar!' long in advance of his arrival, in the hopeful expectation that it would allow the lady of the house sufficient time to rustle up a cake, or at the very least a batch of scones. Mr Crowther was a hearty eater, and expected a decent spread; if he did not get one, he was inclined to let the neighbours know that a travelling man could go hungry at the Davidsons', at least since Mrs Davidson had died. He was well known for timing his arrival around three in the afternoon, and then stringing out his stories to such an extent that evening would fall and he would consider it too late to depart. That is, he would gladly depart if it were not for his fear of bushrangers, who would view Mr Crowther's sulky – loaded as it was with tea samples and miscellaneous sewing-machine parts – a welcome booty. Thus his hosts were obliged to offer him a bed for the night and full breakfast.

Upon hearing the first distant 'Hello-o thar!', Louisa and I looked at each other in fright. The men were all at Boyd Tower, and we wondered if we could not perhaps gather the children and try hiding in the store shed. He would sniff us out, though, we conceded, or the dogs would give us away (we had once tried hiding before, and the dogs, thinking it a game, had commenced barking shrilly in their excitement). Besides, if the house was left unattended, he was just as likely to help himself to whatever victuals he might find. He was known to be especially partial to apples; one family had arrived home unexpectedly to find him perched amidst the branches in the process of stripping their small orchard. Thus we found ourselves with little choice but to open the gate for him and greet him in as cheery a manner as we could muster. Our difficulty was this: not only did we not wish to share our dwindling rations, but also our repayments for the Singer were well overdue.

We fashioned an attempt at rock cakes using dripping instead of butter and the last of our currants; they turned out edible enough if partaken immediately and washed down with plenty of hot sweet tea. Indeed, Mr Crowther made no complaints but demolished half a dozen of them whilst allowing us to pore over the catalogue for his Wunderlich ceilings. Louisa expressed her admiration of a frieze representing the four seasons, to which Mr Crowther nodded his approval. 'There is no doubt the Wunderlich ceiling would form the crowning feature of any decorative scheme,' he said, casting a doubtful eye over our kitchen. The whitewash on the walls was in need of fresh application, and there were greasy marks where the menfolk leaned back in their chairs of an evening and rested their heads. 'Further, you will find them durable and fire-resistant; nor will they crack, warp or fall on top of you.'

'I am glad to hear it,' I said. Surely 'not falling on top of you' was the least one could hope for from a ceiling, and not a bonus feature deemed worthy of advertisement? 'Unfortunately, it has not been a good season for whales, so we find ourselves unable to contemplate such improvements just at the moment.'

'But it is only the first week of October,' said Mr Crowther. 'I am surprised at you for taking such a pessimistic view. Is this not the month when the whales become more plentiful?'

'Ordinarily, yes,' I said. 'However, we suspect the Norwegians may have greatly depleted their numbers. They have factory steamers, you know, with explosive harpoons. They capture five whales a day without difficulty, but it is not fair on the rest of us.'

'No,' said Mr Crowther. 'Nor very fair on the whales either. Tell me, how is the Singer running?'

'It is running satisfactorily at present,' said Louisa.

He nodded, eyeing her coolly. Then, briskly wiping the crumbs from his shirtfront, he stooped to pull from his bag his receipt book. Our hearts sank at the sight of it: clearly, all pleasantries were over. He had decided it was a waste of time to tempt us with ornamental ceilings and now, given the low standard of our comestibles, he thought he might just as well get down to the unpleasant business.

'Treadle belt still holding firm?' he enquired, frowning down at his book. He had had occasion to replace the belt once, and had never forgotten it: we had learned from our nearest neighbour that he considered Louisa to be 'very rough on belts'.

'Yes, I have had no trouble,' said Louisa. I could see her cheeks beginning to flush, which was usually an ominous sign.

'Purchased November 1899 at a sum of seven pounds, sixteen shillings and sixpence,' he read from his receipt book. 'To be repaid in quarterly instalments of fourteen shillings threepence. The last payment I have received was . . .' Here he paused, and flicked through the pages of his receipt book. 'Can this be correct? A part-payment of six shillings only, March 1907?'

'No, that's not correct,' said Louisa. 'We gave you three shillings in July.'

'July of this year?'

'No, last year.'

'Ah yes, here it is. Three shillings, 21 July 1907.' He sighed and looked up at us. 'You have defaulted on the last four instalments. Do you have the outstanding amount for me today?'

'What is the outstanding amount?' I asked.

'Four payments of fourteen shillings threepence, plus this quarter's due.'

'And how much is that altogether?'

'Do you wish me to work it out?'

'Please.'

'It may be quicker for you to simply tell me how much you are able to pay.'

'Oh. Well, none of it just now. We have no money at all, unfortunately.'

Mr Crowther sighed heavily and closed his receipt book. 'Then I am very sorry to say I have no choice but to reclaim the Singer.

I have strung you out for as long as is possible. Mr Singer will not tolerate it any longer.'

Here it was: the death knell we had feared. Louisa rose up out of her seat at once and fled the room, which I took to be a sign of her emotion.

'There, you have upset my sister!' I cried. 'I hope you are satisfied.'

And certainly, Mr Crowther seemed concerned, for he broke into a light sweat. I suppose he understood how important the Singer was as a memento of our mother, let alone as the only thing that kept us looking faintly presentable.

'Miss Davidson, I am very sorry about this,' he said. 'But you must realise I am answerable to Mr Singer himself, and he is expecting his money. I have put him off and put him off, but he will have no more of it. You understand, he must pay the wages of his employees.'

It was an odd conceit of Mr Crowther's that he professed to be in direct personal contact with the founding fathers of the firms in which he dealt. He had even gone to the trouble of devising particular character traits for each of them: the brothers Griffiths were prone to spells of nervous disquietude if they learned you had lately been enjoying a rival's tea, and Mr Singer was always fretting about his employees.

Just at this moment, Louisa returned.

'Here,' she said. 'Take this. It might count towards some of it.' And she handed him the gold sovereign awarded her by Mr Caleb Cook for being the best-dressed and most prepossessing young lady at the Eden Show.

Mr Crowther's mood immediately lifted; he thanked her profusely and said that Mr Singer would be delighted; that of course Mr Singer understood about the whales and the Norwegians and whatnot, and that the last thing Mr Singer wanted was for us to lose our machine. Hastily he wrote out a receipt, and then took it upon himself to give the Singer a look-over and apply a bit of oil to its moving parts, and while he was at it he had a look at our cream separator also. By which time, of course, evening had fallen, the men had returned home from another fruitless day on lookout, and Mr Crowther thought he may just as well stay for tea.

We had stewed several rabbits (augmented with giblets and potatoes) for the evening meal, and now Mr Crowther helped us carry the pots down to the sleeping hut. There his interest seemed excited by the spectacle of John Beck saying grace, and in a low voice he questioned me as to the identity of our new whale man.

'That is the Reverend John Beck,' I responded. 'He is an oarsman in the Number Two boat.'

'Reverend?' queried Mr Crowther.

'Yes,' I responded unhappily, for once again I noted that John Beck was avoiding my gaze. 'He was formerly a Methodist minister.'

'How interesting,' said Mr Crowther, stroking his beard thoughtfully. 'Would you be so kind as to introduce me?'

Happy to have a reason to approach John Beck, I led him over. John Beck was now hunched over his plate: he seemed startled by our looming out of the shadows, for he at once jumped to his feet, as if he might run.

'Excuse me for startling you,' I said. 'I would like you to meet Mr Crowther. He is the agent for Singer sewing machines. Mr Crowther, this is Reverend Beck.'

They each said, 'How do you do?', and Mr Crowther shook John Beck's hand in a bracing fashion.

'May I join you?' he asked. John Beck nodded his consent, and Mr Crowther at once sat down beside him in a manner which struck me as oddly familiar. He patted John Beck on the knee, and urged him to eat up and not to mind him.

'I hear from young Mary that you were formerly a Methodist minister,' he remarked, by way of conversation.

'That is correct,' responded John Beck. He seemed reluctant to elaborate more on the theme, although Mr Crowther smiled at him encouragingly. In truth, he was having difficulty with his portion of meat – I noted with dismay that it appeared to be the shoulder girdle of one of the more senior rabbits.

'Tell me, are you aware of the recent scandal involving one of your kind in Milton?' enquired Mr Crowther.

'I have never been to Milton,' said John Beck. 'So I would not know anything about it.'

'Never been to Milton?'

'No.'

'Did you hail from Sydney originally?'

'Yes.'

'Then you must pass through Milton to travel down to Eden! It is a pretty little town – you would not easily forget it.'

John Beck said nothing but instead concentrated on eating his rabbit. The very act of pulling the meat from the bone appeared to be hurting his teeth.

'Are you able to furnish us with some detail as to the nature of the scandal?' asked Uncle Aleck. He was seated nearby and sucking on a thigh bone. 'Did you say it concerned the Methodist minister?'

'It did,' replied Mr Crowther, settling into the story with an air of enjoyment. 'Very popular was he, and well-liked by all. It is a small parish, but the congregation had been steadily growing in numbers since he took it over a year or so prior. This minister, by all accounts a fine-looking man – I have forgotten his name – took it upon himself to start a fund, the purpose being to raise money for a church organ. He worked assiduously at this task, enlisting the support of many of his churchwomen. Letters were written petitioning some of the more prosperous townsfolk. In short order, the fund had reached a little over forty pounds, whereupon the minister absconded –'

'Absconded?' cried Uncle Aleck.

'Taking the organ fund with him –'

But just at this point the story was interrupted, for my father approached Mr Crowther, looking very upset. He had just learned that Louisa had given over her gold sovereign in payment for the Singer, and he demanded that Mr Crowther return it to her at once.

'It is my responsibility to pay for that machine, and pay for it I will. But you will not take money from my children, especially in my absence.'

And opening his leather purse, which he normally kept secured in a safe place, my father emptied its entire contents into his hand and thrust it at Mr Crowther. It was the sum of about twelve shillings and a few odd pence – all he had to see us through till they captured a whale.

'Now give that sovereign back to the girl, and be on your way,' said my father, and his voice shook discernibly.

The scraping of plates had stopped; everyone had gone quiet. It was very unusual to witness my father so inflamed, and the whale men recognised the significance of the occasion. Without delay, Mr Crowther dug deep into his breast pocket and handed the gold sovereign over to me. Then, counting the scattered coins quietly under his breath, he secreted them into his pocket.

'I have no wish to offend, I'm sure,' he said to my father. 'But this is not a full instalment. You are very much in arrears. You will need to pay more next time.'

'Next time I will pay it off in its entirety,' said my father. 'On that I give you my word.' (Unfortunately, the fortunes of whaling were such that my father was unable to pay the Singer off in its entirety for another four years.)

'Very good,' said Mr Crowther. And tipping his cap, he rose from his seat and headed off into the night. He made no mention of what Mr Singer might say about this.

'Gather the pots and get back up to the house,' said my father, turning to me. He seemed embarrassed and irritated that I had witnessed this exchange.

'And if you must feed us these aged vermin, kindly allow the rigor mortis to subside before you stew them,' added Bastable.

Now here is a very odd thing. It took me some several minutes to gather the pots etc., and as I headed back up to the house, I could hear that Mr Crowther was in the process of harnessing his horse as best as he could manage in the darkness. It seemed by the sound of it that the horse was giving him some trouble, for I could hear scuffling noises and low curses emanating from that area. Taking pity on him, I went over with my lantern, and as I did so, I was suddenly aware of a dark figure moving off abruptly at my approach. Mr Crowther himself seemed somewhat agitated, and I noted his shirt was free of his trousers, as if some kind of struggle had ensued.

'Most kind, most kind,' he murmured, but all the while his eyes darted nervously about.

I stood over him till he had lit his lanterns; in fact, I had to take over at one point for his hands were trembling so much he had difficulty in lighting the matches. Then, in great haste, he climbed up into his sulky and drove off into the pitch-black night. The question of bushrangers seemed suddenly not to bother him.

A Sermon Interrupted

J OHN BECK SUGGESTED TO MY FATHER THAT WE CELEBRATE the Lord's day by conducting a short non-denominational service for the whale men and family early on Sunday morning, before the men rowed to the lookout. Perhaps he had hinted that this might be beneficial in terms of whales, for somewhat unexpectedly my father embraced the idea, and not wanting to displease my father, the whale men felt obliged to attend. Benches were arranged on the sand as if pews, and John Beck stood before us. In lieu of cassock and surplice, he had donned a clean white shirt, and it complemented his suntanned complexion admirably.

'Today I would like to talk on the subject of Temptation,' said John Beck, after we had sung what we remembered of 'All Things Bright and Beautiful'. This was in fact only the chorus, and the verse about the rich man in his castle and the poor man at his gate.

'For who amongst us has not been buffeted by temptations?' John Beck continued. 'I know I most certainly have, and sadly I yielded to them, and that is why I am no longer a minister of the Methodist church.'

I found myself sitting upright now. This had become rather more interesting than I had anticipated.

'If you are no longer a minister of the Methodist church, then why are you imposing upon us this sermon?' demanded Bastable.

'Well, I suppose I am acting today as a kind of lay preacher,' John Beck replied. 'But back to the subject of Temptation. Who amongst us has not been buffeted by temptation?'

'Father, since you ask, I have not been buffeted by temptation in a long time,' said Uncle Aleck.

'Me neither,' admitted Arthur Ashby.

'I would very much like to be buffeted by temptation, but sadly no one is buffeting me,' said Salty.

'I wonder if we could get on to the business of praying for a whale,' said my father.

'Yes, in a moment, but first – I understand that some of you may not have been to church for some time and may have forgotten the procedure, but the idea is I talk on a theme for twenty minutes or so – generally there are no interruptions – then we might have another prayer and a hymn or two. Does that sound all right?'

'Yes, yes, by all means.'

'As I was explaining, whilst I was serving as a minister of the Methodist church, I was greatly buffeted by temptation.'

'Bragging,' muttered Bastable, behind me.

'Would this be some of the ladies in the congregation buffeting you, Father?' asked Uncle Aleck.

'Yes, in fact it was.'

Louisa nudged me sharply in the ribs. A murmur of interest passed through the congregation.

'You see,' John Beck went on, 'I have always been greatly susceptible –'

'They're not shy then, Father, the Methodist lasses?'

'As I say, Uncle Aleck, generally speaking a sermon is not a question-and-answer style of discussion. Rather, I expound at length on a certain –'

'Just get on with it, Father, pay no attention to Uncle,' said my father.

'Yes, yes, proceed; pay no attention to me,' agreed Uncle Aleck.

'Thank you. Now, where was I?'

'You were telling us about your susceptibility,' I said.

'That's right,' said John Beck, and here I seemed to notice a flush of colour rising up from his collar. 'You see, my difficulty was that I have always been burdened with a natural susceptibility to whatever is amiable' – here he glanced at me nervously – 'in a woman.'

'More bragging,' said Bastable.

'Well, not really bragging – you see, it was my undoing, and the reason that I stand before you as an oarsman in the Number Two boat.'

'There's no shame in being oarsman, Father,' cried Bastable. 'I have been an oarsman for nigh on fifteen years and proud of it.'

'What he means is, he is only oarsman in the Number Two boat,' said Darcy, who was of course an oarsman in the Number One boat.

'No, no –' John Beck protested.

'Oh, so the Number Two boat isn't grand enough for you?' declared Salty, ever quick to take umbrage.

'No, you have me all wrong. What I mean is, I am now an oarsman – forget the Number Two boat – where once I was a minister of the Methodist church.'

'And that makes you a better man than us, does it?'

'No, not at all, I am simply saying that temptation has brought me greatly undone.'

'Are you referring to your exploits with Mrs Lee in 'Frisco, Father?'

'I have no knowledge of Mrs Lee.'

'Then is it regarding the organ fund?'

'Once again, I must reiterate that I have never been to Milton –'

'Back to the buffeting, if I may,' said Uncle Aleck. 'What were the ladies doing exactly? Were they pressing up against you in the sacristy?'

'I have no wish to go into details – that is hardly suitable –'

'Could we pray for a whale now?' asked my father.

'If you could just let me finish. You see, I thought that God had abandoned me, given the depths to which I had fallen –'

'Is that Tom?' cried Dan suddenly.

'Yet the other day when we were out at sea –'

'I saw him! I swear!'

'– and we prayed – do you remember?'

'Where?'

'Where's Tom?'

'– well, it seemed to me that Somebody heard us.'

And just at that moment, directly behind John Beck, Tom rose out of the water, revealing the full length of his magnificent black and white body. He curved gracefully – surprisingly lithe for such a corpulent fish – and seemed almost to hover in mid-air a moment before re-entering the water and slapping his tail down hard upon it with a sound like the crack of a whip. *Come now!* was unmistakably his terse instruction.

'*Rush oh!*' cried my father, leaping to his feet.

The whalers clambered over each other in their haste to get to the whaleboats. Tom had sounded his clarion; now they must do his bidding. The children ran off, relieved to be let out of church. Only Louisa and I remained in our seats. John Beck glanced over at us, a little embarrassed.

'Well, it would appear that I have lost my congregation to a Killer whale,' he said.

'What a shame, for it was very interesting,' I said.

'Yes, well – I am a little out of practice.'

'No, not at all.'

'It was all right?'

'It was extremely enlightening.'

'Thank you, Mary,' he said, gazing at me earnestly. 'That's kind of you to say.'

'Perhaps you had better go now and catch the whale,' said Louisa, for the whale men were dragging the boats into the water.

'Yes. Yes, I suppose I had better, especially since I am oarsman in the Number Two boat.' He laughed nervously. 'That bit didn't go over so well, did it?'

'Whalers can be very prickly about such things,' I said.

'Yes, I see that now. Well . . .' Here Salty shouted at him to get into the boat. 'Please excuse me, ladies.'

Throwing off his coat and tossing aside his sermon notes, he ran down to the water and jumped impressively into the whaleboat. How magnificent he looked rowing, and how well that white shirt set off his physique. There was certainly nothing of the nanny goat in his appearance today, as I pointed out to Louisa.

'I admit he looks quite nice in that shirt,' she conceded. 'But don't you find him awfully dull?'

I did not find him dull. I was in love with him. And as I watched him bend to the oars as the whaleboats pulled over the breakers, it became clear to me that I could not remain passive; I must act. I must buffet him with temptation as he had never been buffeted before, not even by the good ladies of the Methodist church.

The Boat-Breaker

AS A RULE, WHALES ARE DISTINCTLY BOVINE IN TEMPERAMENT. If they lived in a paddock, they would stand about chewing their cud and staring into the middle distance. If they saw another whale sitting down under a tree, they would think to themselves, 'Maybe I will sit down under the tree also.' Then, when they got to the tree, they would think, 'Why did I come over to the tree again? I can't remember.' And they would start to wander off again. And then they would think, 'Oh, look at that whale sitting under a tree. Maybe I will sit under a tree also.' (I will desist from this allegory now as I feel it is becoming rather strained.) Suffice to say, whales are placid, dull creatures and mean no harm. But every now and then comes a whale different to other whales, and that whale is known as a boat-breaker.

Such was the whale to whose tail, by means of harpoon, my father's boat had just attached itself. As mentioned previously, the harpooner Arthur Ashby was an excellent aim, but so fast was this whale and so erratic its movements that on this occasion his harpoon fell short and found purchase on that narrowing section between the whale's flukes and body. This is perhaps the least desirable part of a whale's anatomy to which to attach oneself, for it seems to be extremely sensitive, as was demonstrated by such wild thrashings on the part of the whale that my father had no choice but to cut loose for fear of damaging his boat. The second boat, in close attendance, was then ordered to fasten on, and here my brother Harry did himself credit by landing his harpoon just at the back of the whale's blow-holes. So stunned was he at his success that he forgot that it was now necessary to change positions with Salty.

'Change over, boy, change over!' cried Salty. 'Oars up, men! Let's let the old girl run!'

The men lifted their oars up high out of the water, locked their handles into the peak chocks and braced themselves for the wild ride. Doing their utmost not to become entangled in this lethal line, the two men scrambled over the oarsmen to assume their new positions. Reaching the bow now and jamming his thigh in the clumsy cleat, Salty took a good look at their adversary. 'Damn it to hell! White spots! Say your prayers, men!'

For sure enough, the monster had two distinct white spots – old harpoon scars – clearly visible on its back. The Killers were doing their utmost to contain the whale's flight, but the canny whale embarked on a series of sharp zigzags in a bid to throw them off. Finally, in desperation, it dived. The Killers dived as well, and for several frightening moments it appeared that the whale might travel down so deep as to pull the entire whaleboat down with it. But the Killers drove it up again and as it broke the surface of the water, it suddenly came to a complete standstill; the second boat, still attached to it and compelled by forward momentum, headed straight for it.

'Stern all, boys! Hard astern!' cried Salty.

The men scrabbled to get their oars back into the water, but it was too late; they collided, the boat sliding onto the whale's vast back. Infuriated, it reared out of the water, lifting the boat up with it. There the boat floundered sickeningly, oars flailing, before sliding down the ridge of its back and smashing into the water.

At once the great flukes rose up and, with a vicious swipe, knocked Harry clean out of the boat. At this, young Robert panicked, and endeavoured to jump out of the boat to avoid being struck himself, but as he did so, the flukes pinned him down on the gunwale, half in and half out of the boat. As he squealed and squirmed, the flukes rose up again and released him; he at once effected his escape into the boiling seas. Only John Beck, Shankly and Salty remained in the boat now, and they stared transfixed as the giant flukes rose with majestic stateliness to a height of twenty feet above them, harpoon and line still dangling.

'Father,' said Shankly, turning suddenly towards John Beck.

'Yes?' said John Beck, feeling a wave of irritation. What in God's name did Shankly want of him now?

'Is it too late to ask for forgiveness?'

As if by way of answer, and with only the subtlest quiver to warn of its impending action, the tail slammed down upon John Beck and Shankly, pinning them to the bottom of the boat. With great presence of mind, Salty set to beating the weighty tail muscle with an oar in a bid to free the men, and at this the enraged creature tipped the entire boat over into the water.

It seems John Beck may have lost consciousness with the first impact of the flukes, but the sudden immersion in freezing water revived him and he opened his eyes to glimpse a flurry of black and white amidst the blood and foam and bubbles. Propelled towards the surface, he came up beneath the overturned boat, so was at once forced to dive again and this time, with the last bit of oxygen in his lungs, came up beneath the whale itself. But the capsizing of the boat had released the tub containing the whale line, and the whale, sensing its chance, gave a last mighty flick of its tail and headed for the open sea, bearing two harpoons, eighty fathom of line (much of it coiled around its girth), and even the tub itself, tumbling along the wave tops in its wake.

Once the whale escaped for deeper waters, the Killers called a meeting amongst themselves and voted to 'down tools'; whales can dive deeper and stay under longer in the ocean and this puts the Killers at a disadvantage. One or two of their number saw the whale off with a nip or two to remember them by, but most of them elected to stay close by the men in the water, both solicitous and curious about their predicament. My father, of course, was wasting no time in effecting their rescue – most of the men wore heavy coats and sea boots, and were in grave danger of drowning.

John Beck was in particular strife; barely conscious, he clung feebly to the upturned hull. Feeling a powerful nudge to the small of his back, he opened his eyes blearily to see Tom's beknobbed dorsal fin close by. A black snub-nosed snout rose out of the water and the famous orca surveyed my battered paramour in evident amusement, for he seemed to be grinning, and he waved a stumpy side fin at him as if by way of greeting. He then opened his mouth to reveal his sharp teeth and made a strange noise as if clearing his throat in preparation for a speech.

John Beck panicked now, for a glimpse of those pointy white teeth brought back memories of the hapless finback he had witnessed torn apart at Leatherjacket Bay. In desperation, he tried to scramble onto the hull, but in his weakened state only slid back into the water. This prompted Tom to embark upon a series of high-pitched squeals, as if sharing a joke with his friends; they responded in a similar vein, and several swam over as if to observe John Beck for themselves. It was at this point that John Beck began to make preparations to die, for he could not seem to keep his head above water; his last conscious thought was that if the Killer whales were laughing at him, then they would surely soon commence to eat him.

Fortunately, my father and his whale men were at once by his side, and pulled him out of the water. Even in his unconscious state, his limbs were still futilely scrabbling, as if trying to get away from the Killers.

Yet he did not need to fear. On past occasions where boats had overturned and whalers had found themselves in the water, the Killers had been known to act with the greatest concern and solicitude, to the extent of propping one drowning whaler up with a side fin till help arrived. According to our Aboriginal whalers, some of their people, in finding themselves in a similar situation, had been towed ashore by hanging on to the dorsal fins of these good Samaritans of the deep. I have no doubt that in this instance Tom was simply keeping a friendly eye on John Beck, ready to offer his assistance the moment it should be required.

It now became apparent to my father that of the five men in the second whaleboat, only four remained; there was no sign at all of the Scotsman Shankly. It was concluded that he had been knocked unconscious by the impact of the flukes, and then drowned amidst the general turmoil of the boat overturning. The men scoured the sea calling for him till such time as it was decided that the surviving whaleboat was in danger of sinking if they dallied further; also, John Beck was injured and in need of first aid. After much time, with the sun sinking low in the sky, they made the sad journey home – eleven men in one boat, the gunwale almost level with the water; the stove-in hull of the second boat towed behind; an escort of Killer whales swimming alongside.

The Sermon Notes

I N THE MEANTIME, WHILST ALL THIS WAS HAPPENING OUT AT sea, we had changed out of our good Sunday clothes and resumed our chores. I was in the process of turning over an area of soil in preparation for planting a new crop of celery and parsnips, and as I tilled the soil, I mulled over the various interesting insights that had arisen during John Beck's sermon. Suddenly a thought occurred to me. As he dashed for the boat, John Beck had tossed aside his sermon notes along with his coat; perhaps if I was to find these notes, they might prove to be edifying in both the personal and the spiritual sense. Abandoning my shovel, I hastened down to the beach and, after some little difficulty, eventually managed to locate the notes floating face down in a small rock pool some distance from where he had discarded them. With great care, I retrieved the sodden, solitary page and took it back to the house, where I allowed it to dry in the sunlight in a sheltered position on the verandah. In fact, I have this same page beside me now as I write; it is the only example I have of his handwriting, which alone affords it enormous value to me. But more than this, the words that I found there on the page – words that were left unsaid owing to Tom's unexpected appearance, and yet give proof positive of the direction in which John Beck's thoughts veered – these have ensured that this tattered, yellowing scrap remains for me one of my dearest personal possessions. It is a simple piece of lined paper, nothing more, seemingly torn in haste from a notebook, on which his thoughts are marked out in pencil, in a neat, forward-sloping hand:

> *'Dangers of Temptation to God-fearing life.*
> *Talk about own exp. & where it has brought me*
> *Matt 26:14 spirit indeed willing but flesh weak etc.*
> *Benefits of marriage in this regard (1 Corinthians 7) let every man have his wife*
> *In conclusion, poss. humorous remark whaling vs marriage? Both fearsome adversary?*
> *(NB pray for whale.)'*

Once again, it is tempting to lay the blame on Tom, for had he only delayed his call to arms by ten to fifteen minutes, then perhaps John Beck might have finally been permitted to get to his point. For close study of his sermon notes seems to make clear: here was a man who had grown weary of temptation, and saw that his salvation could be found within the blessed confines of matrimony. '*Let every man have his own wife, and every woman her own husband*': these were the words he intended, and perhaps his glance would have fallen upon me just as the words fell from his lips, for I have little reason to doubt that his thoughts were beginning to settle in my direction. However, Tom had his business to attend to, and therein lay my misfortune. That, and the blow to the head that John Beck received in the subsequent whale chase, whereby any further thoughts along these lines seem to have been summarily knocked out of him.

Repercussions

WE MADE UP A BED FOR JOHN BECK IN THE FRONT ROOM, and there I devoted myself to the task of nursing him back to health. He was still in a stupefied state when they brought him up and not conscious of his surroundings; I sent everybody away, drew the curtains and set about bathing his forehead where it had been gashed. My tender ministering did not rouse him; occasionally his eyes stirred behind his lids if a drop of water trickled from his brow, but that was all. At one point, he murmured something I could not make out. I leaned in more closely to hear it and felt his soft breath upon my cheek, but he soon lapsed back into unconsciousness. I gazed down at his fine battered features – his blackened eyes, his bruised cheek – and a rush of intense feeling overwhelmed me. How grateful I was that he had been spared, and not banished to the dismal depths like poor Shankly, but *oh!* how anxious I was that he now pull through.

Louisa entered quietly with some clean rags for the purposes of bandaging his head wound. She placed them on the table, then hesitated a moment to watch me.

'Well, you seem to be enjoying yourself,' she said, with an unpleasant smirk.

'How dare you,' I retorted hotly, though still keeping my voice modulated to a whisper. 'The man is gravely injured, and yet you consider it appropriate to make improper suggestions.'

'All I am saying is I have difficulty imagining you tending to the other whale men in this doting fashion.'

Whereupon I pinched her hard on the fleshy part of her arm, so hard that she squealed. Then I instructed her to prepare the supper for the whalers, and to make it a good one, for they had had a bad day. At this she baulked, but I insisted, for I could not be pulled away from my present duties. Amidst vigorous protests and more pinches, she finally submitted and left the room to attend to the evening meal.

Returning my attention to my patient, I found that his eyes were now open and he was gazing at me in a puzzled way. It seemed that our heated discussion had roused him.

'Rest now,' I said softly. 'Do not worry; I have sent her away.'

Thus reassured, his eyes drifted shut again, and I returned to the task of bathing his forehead.

Of this most difficult season, this day – 18 October 1908 – marked the nadir. The experience had shaken the men badly. Morale was at its lowest ebb. To add to their woes, provisions had almost completely run out and Louisa was in charge of the kitchen.

'What is this? Dishwater?' asked Arthur Ashby, gazing down at his soup. A good-natured chap as a rule, he was not normally one of our complainers.

'No, it is soup,' said Louisa crisply.

'What sort of soup?'

'Larder beetle soup.'

At this, young Robert Heffernan, who had just taken a mouthful, spat it out violently.

'Oh, for goodness' sake!' said Louisa. 'I was only joking.'

Darcy was the only one who chuckled; then again, he always seemed to find Louisa amusing.

'I wish it *was* made of larder beetles,' muttered Bastable. 'If it was made of larder beetles, then it might offer us some nourishment. Expecting us to catch whales on a diet of dishwater.'

'Well, if you would only *catch* a whale instead of letting them get away all the time, we might be able to think of offering you some nourishment,' said Louisa, turning upon him. 'Heavens, we might even be able to think of offering *ourselves* some nourishment!'

'Louisa...' said Dan anxiously. She was known for her hot temper, and once unleashed, it could not easily be reined in.

'I never met such a collection of whining, lily-livered namby-pambies!' she continued. 'We'd do a better job if it was me and Violet and Annie out there! I tell you what, we'd have better sense than to let a piddling thirty-foot humpback get away!'

And with that, she threw down her soup ladle and stormed back up to the house, leaving the whalers to stare after her in dismay. A sense of shame overcame them. The young mistress had described them as namby-pambies.

'It's all very well for her to say,' offered Albert Thomas Senior.

'That humpback was at least thirty-five, maybe forty feet. And it was cranky.'

The others said nothing, however, but meekly supped their soup. It was Darcy who later gathered the pots and plates and carried them up to the house.

The Trees They Do Grow High

THAT EVENING, AFTER THE MEN HAD EATEN, MY FATHER TOOK himself down to talk to them. 'Men, I just wanted to say a few words about Shankly,' he said.

'Aye, poor old Shankly,' murmured the men, and some of them lowered their heads out of respect.

'We none of us knew him very well, I know, but I want to pay him tribute nonetheless,' my father continued. 'He proved himself to be a decent oarsman and pulled hard when it counted.'

'Nonetheless, he was a strange one, if you ask me,' said Uncle Aleck. 'There was something about him that made me uneasy. I cannot put my finger on it.'

'He owed me a shilling,' said Percy Madigan. 'I daresay I have no chance of seeing it now.'

'Anyway, he is gone,' said my father, wishing to discourage the direction in which the conversation was veering. 'And, men,

I wouldn't blame any of you if you decided you'd had enough. We are having a bad season, and no mistake.'

'This was the last straw, boss, what happened to Shankly,' said Bastable, and some of the men muttered in agreement.

'I realise that, Bastable. We haven't lost a man in thirty-five years. It weighs heavily upon me.'

There was an uncomfortable silence. My father was a retiring man, and speaking to the men in this fashion did not come easily to him. He stuck his thumbs behind his braces and stared fixedly at the ground.

'Men, I wanted to say this to you. I reckon we should be able to get the second boat back in the water in a day or so – and if you'd consider seeing the season out with me till the end of November, or at least for as long as the Killers stay, then, well, I'd appreciate it. November is usually a pretty good month for whales –'

'Not last November it wasn't,' said Bastable.

'Well, you're right, Bastable, I can't argue with you there. But if November doesn't bring us a whale, then I'll sell the boats and the harpoons and lances, and we'll divide the proceeds up between us. You're good men, all of you, and I feel you should have something for your efforts.'

'You'll not sell the whaling station!' cried Salty.

'I may have to, Salty, if it comes to it.'

'Then you'll have to sell me with it. For I will not be leaving!'

'Hear, hear!' said Arthur Ashby, and several of the other men concurred.

'I appreciate the sentiment, men. But I want you to consider the matter carefully. As I say, I'll not think the worse of any man for quitting, given the circumstances . . . '

And here his voice trembled, so he turned abruptly and marched back up the hill to the house.

Having bandaged John Beck's forehead as best I could, I settled down to watch over my patient. He seemed to be resting more comfortably now and, in the lamplight, I took the opportunity to gaze at him fully. His chest rose and fell as he dozed; a lock of unruly dark hair fell across his brow. One arm rested on the blanket, his calloused palm lying upwards as if in expectation of something being placed in it. Without thinking, I slipped my own hand into his, and his fingers closed reflexively around mine. I sat there for several moments like this, then I leaned forward and kissed his cheek tenderly. He responded with a sigh. Emboldened, I then kissed him full on the mouth – once, twice, and as I kissed him a third time, his eyes flickered open and he looked at me.

'Oh! I'm sorry!' I said, pulling back.

'That's all right,' said John Beck, somewhat dazedly.

'I hope you don't think I was taking advantage of your – of your susceptibility.'

'Oh. Well, I suppose you were a little.'

'Only in that I thought you were deeply unconscious. I do apologise.'

'Oh, that's all right.'

'Are you feeling better?'

'Yes. Considerably.'

'Does your head hurt?'

'A little.'

'Are you hungry?'

'A little.'

'I will fetch you some supper then.'

Only then did I realise that I was still clutching on to his hand, so I released it and hurried towards the door, astonished at my own actions. Had I been taking advantage of him? Perhaps I had. Certainly, I had resolved to buffet him with temptation, but was it appropriate to buffet a person when he had recently been stupefied by a whale? The truth is, the compulsion to kiss him had simply overwhelmed me; I had not considered it, I had simply done it, as if driven by forces I was powerless to fight.

Reaching the doorway, I stopped and turned to him. 'I hope you do not think I am like those ladies who pressed themselves up against you in the sacristy,' I said.

He stared at me for a moment as if confused, then waved his hand wanly. 'This talk of the ladies in the sacristy, that was Uncle Aleck's invention – I would not put too much store in it,' he replied.

I had no sooner stepped out of the room, closing the door behind me, when my father materialised.

'How is he, Mary?' he enquired.

'He is feeling better and about to take some nourishment,' I responded, thankful that it was dark and my father could not see the colour in my cheeks.

'You go and see to it then, girl,' said my father. 'I am going in to talk to him.' And knocking lightly on the door, he entered.

'Sorry to disturb you,' he said to John Beck. 'Is it all right if I have a quiet word?'

'Yes, of course,' said John Beck.

My father sat and gazed down at his battle-scarred hands. Nervously, he rubbed the stump of his right index finger which Tom had famously crushed between his teeth – a habit of his when worried. (That is to say, it was my father's habit when worried – not Tom's habit. That is, it was not Tom's habit to crush someone's finger when worried. I think he had merely been irritable.)

'You're feeling better, I hope?' he said, after a moment.

'Much better, thank you, sir.'

'Mary has been looking after you?'

'She is a tonic for any invalid, sir.'

(To be honest, I am not entirely sure if these were their exact words – I am reconstructing this conversation from an account given to me later by John Beck, and he supplied only the basic details.)

My father nodded absently. It was clear that he was preoccupied with weightier matters.

'Father, the men have just about had enough, and I don't blame them. I've asked them if they'll at least see the season through to the end of November. I don't know how you feel about this, given you've just copped the flukes in the old noggin.'

'Oh, I'll see the season out, sir. No question at all.'

'Well, Father, I appreciate it. I can't promise anything, of course, but we'll . . . we'll do our best.'

John Beck nodded. A short pause ensued.

'Father, just on another note altogether, some of the men have asked if you would kindly stop with the hymns and the saying of grace and what-have-you. It doesn't sit right with them somehow.'

'I see.'

'As I say, it's the men, Father, not me. If I had my way, you'd be singing hymns till the cows came home.'

'Think no more of it,' said John Beck. 'I understand completely.' A silence. 'Do you mean a suspension to the Sunday services?'

'If you wouldn't mind, Father.'

'Of course not. Whatever you think best.'

My father stared down at his hands again. It seemed he might be working up to ask something else.

'Father,' he said finally, 'I wonder if we might pray for a whale, just the two of us?'

'Why, of course.'

'For a good-sized whale, Father, preferably a southern right. I'm fairly desperate, Father, or I would not be bothering you, on your sickbed and all.'

'It is no trouble,' said John Beck, and my father immediately lowered himself to his knees. Yet for some reason, John Beck seemed to hesitate. 'I am happy to do what I can, of course, but there is something I feel you should know,' he said.

'What's that, Father?'

'Well, I must be honest with you. I was never really a proper Methodist minister.'

'Ah,' said my father, and he was silent for a moment. 'Not ordained as such?'

'Not ordained, that's right,' said John Beck. 'In fact, the truth is that I borrowed the papers of an actual Methodist minister who had the misfortune to expire on the passage over, so you see . . .' Here he trailed off.

'Did you say you borrowed them?'

'Yes. Well . . . I suppose it could be argued that I stole them.'

'The gentleman had expired, you say?'

'Yes. The truth is, he fell overboard in mysterious circumstances.'

'I see,' said my father. 'That does cast a different light on things.'

'Yes, it does, sir. I'm sorry.'

My father said nothing. He simply gave a deep sigh, as if this just about capped things off. He had pinned all his hopes on John Beck's celestial connections, and now he found these hopes extinguished. His shoulders slumped; his whole physical demeanour seemed to speak of unendurable weariness and despondency.

'Nevertheless,' said John Beck, who had been studying my father with some concern, 'it is said that God hears us all in our hour of need. You and I are as much entitled to pray for a whale as the Archbishop of Canterbury himself.'

My father looked up at him hopefully.

'A large southern right, if you would then, Father,' he said. 'And long in the whalebone preferably.'

Later that night, my father, Uncle Aleck and Dan sat outside on the verandah together. Nobody spoke; the men simply sat in sombre reflection, smoking their pipes. Dan briefly wondered if the events of the day were such that he might pull out his own pipe without provoking an incident, but better sense prevailed and his pipe remained concealed in his pocket. After ten minutes or so, however, Dan began to grow fidgety. He started breaking a stick into smaller and smaller pieces; *snap, snap, snap!* This got on my father's nerves, and eventually he asked Dan to desist. That was when Dan finally decided he must speak.

'Dad?'

'Yes, son?'

'Now that you are a man short, can I go out, do you think?'

'Go out?'

'In the whaleboat, I mean.'

My father turned to survey him then, his face set grim as granite.

'How old are you now?' asked my father.

'Thirteen. Or at least, I will be thirteen in December.'

'Can you row hard?'

'Yes, sir, I can,' said young Dan. 'And I was only thinking, since you're a man short...' My father gazed at him a long moment and sucked on his pipe.

'Well, Uncle, what do you think about it?' he said finally, turning to Uncle Aleck.

Uncle Aleck shook his head. 'It's a dangerous business.'

'That it is,' said my father. 'His mother would never forgive me. A boy of twelve in a whaleboat.'

'I was eleven when I started,' said Uncle Aleck. 'And I rowed as hard as three men.'

My father nodded. The age at which Uncle Aleck started whaling was a variable thing, but it was consistent in the fact that it was always younger than anybody else's.

'I will row as hard as six men,' averred Dan.

'D'you know what it is to stare down a whale?' asked Uncle Aleck. 'For you must stare down a whale, or they will try to get the better of you.'

'I'm a good starer,' said Dan. 'I can stare down any whale.'

'And how do you calm a whale when he's angry? D'you know that?'

'Sing to him,' said Dan, for he knew all Uncle Aleck's stories as he'd heard them a thousand times.

'Sing to him? What would you sing to him? Just any old song that comes into your head?'

'I would sing to him, "The Trees They Do Grow High".'

'Yes, and why?'

'It will make the whale cry, and he'll stop his thrashing.'

'He'll do,' said Uncle Aleck, turning to my father.

And the saddest part of this whole story is that Dan himself died young, just like the bonny boy in the song, not in a whaleboat but at Pozières, France, sometime around the 26th August, 1916.

Having Gone to be Wasted in Battle

S UFFICE TO SAY, IN WRITING WHAT WAS SUPPOSED TO BE A straightforward account of the whaling season of 1908, I did not intend to be sidetracked by the vagaries of fortune that affected our family as they affect all families. Thus I had not supposed I would dwell upon what happened to Dan any more than I had dwelled upon the loss of our mother. So I was taken aback at the way in which my recounting of that conversation on the verandah in the previous chapter affected me, for it brought my progress with this memoir to a standstill; I found myself tearful and downhearted and had no inclination to return to these or any memories for a period of some weeks. Only now do I feel myself sufficiently strong enough to sit at the typewriter again.

Of course, there is something deeply poignant in a small boy asking the older men if he can join them in doing battle, particularly as for me it brought to mind so many of Dan's qualities: his pluck, his earnest enthusiasm, his eagerness to grow up. But in fact, more than this, I found I was affected by the reference to the song itself. 'The Trees They Do Grow High' was an old song that Uncle Aleck used to sing to us, always with a show of great reluctance and only after the most prolonged pleadings on our part. 'Don't make me sing it for it will only set you to bawling,' he would say, and we would promise that this time we would somehow manage to retain our composure. But of course the power of the song was such that it would inevitably send us flung across our beds and weeping.

> *'The trees they grow high,*
> *The leaves they do grow green*
> *Many is the time my true love I have seen*
> *Many an hour I have watched him all alone*
> *He's young,*
> *but he's daily growing.'*

Uncle Aleck had a thin reedy voice which warbled in a wayward fashion on the high notes, and yet it was capable of making one's heart lurch with sorrow.

> *'At the age of fifteen, he was a married man*
> *At the age of sixteen, the father of a son*
> *At the age of eighteen, the grass grew over him,*
> *Having gone to be wasted in battle.'*

I suppose it is a song about life's hopes dashed, and perhaps that is why it affected us so; as a whaling family, we were familiar with disappointment. And yet I still cannot fully account for the seemingly prescient grief that afflicted us all upon hearing it. For Dan was amongst us then, and as affected by the song as any of us.

When Sergeant Piesley came to Eden to encourage the local lads to enlist, Dan volunteered immediately along with his best mate, Charlie Oslington, and several other lads from the cricket club. It was hardly surprising. As a very small boy, when the Salvation Army missionaries had visited to minister to our Aboriginal whale crew, Dan had been fiercely attracted to the military appearance of their uniforms and had readily joined up, that he might bang his kettle and pipe in his boyish voice:

> '*Thousands of children Jesus has saved*
> *Making them pure and holy*
> *Teaching them how to fight and be brave*
> *In the Salvation Army!*'

Dan with the whale gun.

I remember Dan came galloping home on Trinket (Two Socks had passed away by then) with the news that he would be embarking within two weeks. This came as a terrible blow for my father. I suppose he had hoped that Dan's poor eyesight would prevent him from being accepted; it was right at the beginning of the whale season of 1915, and our father could not easily spare him from the whaleboats. A farewell social for the boys was hastily organised at the School of Arts, decked out with flags for the occasion, and the fathers of each young man took turns in speaking. Mr Oslington said he knew nothing but good of all the boys, and he felt certain there was not a one that would shirk when hostilities got thick. Mr Walsh said he had played cricket with each of them and found them to be true sports. Mr Strickland drew comparisons between whaling and warfare, both starting with the letter W, and went on to liken the humpback with the Hun, my father to Lord Kitchener and Tom the Killer whale to General Douglas Haig. Then Mr English got up and said he felt like the man sitting down to dinner after the turkey had all been served, for there was very little left for him to say. He then went on to expound at length on the theme that the single man had no more duty to go and fight than the married one, and if this war continued, then he would certainly offer his services if he could only pass the medical test. (This produced laughter, for Mr English had only one leg, the other having been crushed by a tree while timber-felling.) It was my father's turn to speak then and he walked in a determined fashion to the stage, but when he turned to gaze upon the five boys all standing there beneath the Union Jack, his lower jaw began to tremble violently.

'I wish you all a speedy and safe return –' was all he could manage to get out, for helpless tears began to slide down his face.

The gathered families and townsfolk stared in dismay; there stood Fearless Davidson, leviathan-killer, weeping into his handkerchief whilst the other fathers patted his back and nodded grimly. Dan himself simply seemed embarrassed. He shifted on his feet and joked about with the fellows next to him while all this was going on.

Sergeant Piesley leapt up then, obviously anxious that the paternal anguish not spread to the room at large, and told the lads in a loud cheerful voice that there was nothing in the world to worry about if they would just heed this one piece of advice from an old soldier, and that was never to become separated from their greatcoat and rifle. The band launched into 'God Save the King', light refreshments were served and a whip-around conducted, with the proceeds of ten pounds three shillings being divided up between the five boys.

Less than a week later, they embarked from Tathra wharf for Sydney. It was a dismal, drizzling day with a bitter wind; we huddled under those umbrellas that had not yet been ripped inside out. Dan was tense and distracted and did not want to linger much in saying goodbye. Also, he had a sweetheart at the wharf, a freckled lass from Lochiel, of whom we had hitherto known nothing. He took her aside, and there was much fervent whispering between them while the family was left to stand about awkwardly. When the ship moved away from the wharf, the girl cried more than anyone.

'God, she is certainly bunging it on,' said Annie.

And yet if we had realised that the offhand wave he had given us from the gangplank was the last we were ever to see of him, we would have howled like babies.

After we learned that Dan was missing in action, the girl came to visit us. (I realise I have completely forgotten her name, but I think it was something like Maud or Maeve.) She said little and refused any refreshments, implying by her manner that she was surprised we could think of such things given the circumstances. Only after much encouragement did she tell us that she and Dan had met at the Convent School Ball only three weeks before he embarked, at which occasion they had shared a piece of jam sponge 'as light as air'. She asked us if Dan had ever mentioned her in his letters, and we had to answer truthfully that he had not. She blushed angrily then, and told us Dan had always said we would try to keep them apart, for she was a Roman Catholic. We told her this was not the case; we had simply been unaware of her existence until her sudden appearance at Tathra wharf. She became upset and left abruptly. I felt bad about it. I imagine she had been fondly nursing the hope that Dan had spoken of her incessantly, a hope we had casually quashed. Looking back, I wish that we had not been so truthful, and simply invented something. All she had to remember her sweetheart by was a shared piece of jam sponge, 'as light as air'. That was not much to keep you going.

The last missive we had from Dan was this postcard:

'Hello All, well, I hope the whales will soon be visiting, say hello to Tom and all the gang for me. London is a fine city but not a patch on good old Eden. There is nothing of interest to tell you so I will ring off, yr affectionite Dan.'

It is undated, but the very fact that he is even talking about whales makes me think it might have been written in early June. In August we heard that he had been wounded. Then we heard nothing whatsoever till the following January, when Reverend Forbes came to visit us, bearing the following cable:

> 'Officially reported that No. 2460 Pte. D. Davidson, 21st Batt, previously reported wounded and missing, is now reported killed in action between 24 August and 26 August, 1916. Please inform Mr. G. Davidson, Eden, and convey deep regret of their Majesties, the King and Queen, and the Commonwealth Govt., in the loss that he and the army have sustained by the death of this soldier.'

Having gone to be wasted in battle, the grass grew over our brother Dan before he reached his twenty-first birthday. Or at least, we can only assume it did, for there were no remains ever to be found; we had simply to take their word for it.

I find myself once again reluctant to go on, except to comment briefly on the effect Dan's death had on my brother Harry. He was six years older than Dan, but had not enlisted, owing to the fact that he was by then married with a small child and working as assistant light keeper at Green Cape lighthouse. In the recent letters leading up to his death, Dan had taken to insinuating that Harry was a shirker.

> 'A toothless old man can keep a lighthouse lamp burning, yes the job is nesessary but it does not take an ABLE BODIE YOUNG MAN to do so, just so long as he can climb the steps. I think if they had a few showers of shrapnel instead of the rain he is always complaining about

at Green Cape, he might realise what we are all putting up with over here and decide to lend us a bit of a hand insted of living the life of Riley.'

We did our best to keep these letters from Harry, but it was difficult. He and Grace would come to visit with the baby and always ask what news of Dan. Letters were so infrequent that when we had received one he would want to read it himself; this he would do silently, and without making any comment regarding the contents. In the awkwardness and embarrassment of the situation, we did not say anything, and I feel now that this was our mistake, for he must have imagined that our silence indicated our agreement with the sentiments Dan expressed. I know my father wrote back to Dan and tried to convey the responsibilities a married man owed to his family, especially since Grace was expecting again; not to mention the responsibilities of lighthouse work for the safety of navigation, never more so than during wartime. But who knows if Dan ever received the letter.

After Reverend Forbes came with the cable, my father and I travelled over to Green Cape to break the news to Harry. I remember it clearly, for we stood on the verandah of his cottage, and force of habit was such that my father kept turning his head to gaze out to sea on the off-chance he might see a whale spout.

Harry stood there in silence for a long time, and then finally he spoke. 'I suppose you're wishing it was me, not him, if I hadn't been such a shirker.'

Well, my father told him not to talk nonsense, but Harry became belligerent then and said he knew that's what we all thought of him; that he was a coward and that he scarcely deserved to be called a Davidson. He turned on me then and said I was right to depict him wringing his hands like a girl in that painting, and wasn't I happy it had turned out to be true? And then he said to my father, who was looking out to sea again, 'That's right, look for whales, at a time like this. And I'll bet if one swam by, you'd chase it.'

Poor Grace came out then, and seeing at once that we had received the news we had been so dreading, insisted we come inside for some tea. Harry, however, went off somewhere on the pretext of work needing to be done, and we did not see him again before it was time for us to head home.

From that point on, Harry seemed to want nothing more to do with the family. I urged my father to write to him to convince him that we had never thought him a shirker, but for some reason my father seemed disinclined to do so and simply responded, 'He will get over it eventually.' Harry took up a position shortly thereafter at Gabo Island and after that we scarcely heard from him except for a card at Christmas, and even that was written by Grace. So, in truth, my father lost both his sons and we girls lost both our brothers. It was another sad aspect of the whole terrible thing.

It fell upon me, of course, to write to Maeve or Maud in order to convey the dreadful news. I spent a good deal of time in drafting the letter, for I wished it to bring her some small measure of comfort, a comfort we had failed to provide her when she visited. One line in particular stands out in my memory: *'I have no doubt that the memory of your dear freckled face provided Dan tremendous solace, even as he faced his final moments.'* I showed the letter to Annie, who urged me to strike that passage out. 'Do you really think now is the time to start concocting fantasies? Besides, she may not wish to be reminded of her freckles.' To which I responded, 'How do you know it is a fantasy? It may very well be the truth, for all we know. He certainly seemed keen on her at Tathra wharf.' Ignoring Annie's continued protests, I went ahead and posted it. I hope it afforded Maeve or Maud some small consolation; at the very least, I hope she did not take umbrage at the reference to her freckles. Perhaps in retrospect, given her sensitive nature, I would have been wiser to omit that particular adjective, or use another expression, such as 'sun-kissed'. In any case, we never heard back and I cannot say whatever became of her.

The Flukes

IT WAS SUNDAY WHEN THE WHALE UPENDED THE BOAT; BY Tuesday the boat was repaired and the men set off to the lookout. Young Dan took the place of Shankly, and Uncle Aleck stood in for John Beck, until such time as John Beck could return to the oars. This was felt to be within a day or so, as he was considerably improved and keen to return; however, my father deemed it prudent that he rest a little longer. Thus John Beck sat on our front verandah in the morning sunshine reading the *Eden Observer and South Coast Advocate*, while Louisa and I laboured over the week's washing.

My father had erected three solid posts, crossed at the top, from which hung a big cast-iron pot, and under this we lit a fire to boil the water. I did most of the hard scrubbing, as Louisa felt that the steam rising off the tub caused an unattractive ruddiness of the complexion (here indicating my own complexion) and that the Rumford's Blue was too harsh on one's hands. Thus she concentrated most of her efforts on jamming the mangle and hanging out the wet sheets in such a pointedly bad-tempered fashion that inevitably a pole would collapse and the whole lot would end up in the dirt. Rarely did we get through washing day on speaking terms with one another.

Normally, as a matter of strong principle, we did not tend to the whale men's laundry, but as John Beck was still recuperating in the front room, it was a small matter for me to ask if he would like me to launder his white shirt. He gratefully accepted and requested that perhaps I might starch and iron it also, to which I agreed somewhat hesitantly, as our laundering standards were such that we rarely bothered with starch and were somewhat uncertain as to how best to get satisfactory results from the process. However, I found a small amount of cornstarch and boiled it up with water and hoped for the best. Whilst I was plunging the shirt into the starch bowl, I noticed it had been darned very neatly near the cuff; perhaps it had become caught on something and torn. As I studied the tiny stitches, I found myself wondering if this was not the handiwork of whichever lady had caused John Beck such problems with Temptation. Certainly there must have been some attentive gentlewoman offering her services, for the needlework was far too dainty to have been done by any man. It was on this matter that I was thus preoccupied when a series of muttered maledictions caused me to glance in Louisa's direction. She was struggling with our mangle, the cogs of which frequently jammed and could only be released by employing a dangerous and intricate manoeuvre involving great risk to one's fingers. My vantage point was such that I saw at this moment a plume of fine spray apparently emanating from the top of her head; that is to say, the plume emanated from the sea directly behind her, at a point behind the breakers, not far removed from where Tom would often come to marshal troops. Saying nothing for fear of having imagined it and thus invoking my sister's derision, I put down the shirt and fixed my eyes upon the sea, waiting for another such appearance. Surely, if I had seen a spout, then it must have been the spout of a Killer whale, for it struck me as remarkably reckless, even fool-hardy, of a whale to swim up to a whaling station and draw attention to itself in this manner. But no, there it was again! The size of the spout and the glimpse of grey bulk beneath the water confirmed it.

'*Whale*,' I said in a strangulated tone, for excitement had gripped the muscles of my throat.

'Whale?' said Louisa.

'There! See it?' I said, pointing triumphantly. For now the mass of whale had surfaced and was rolling idly with the swell.

'Is it dead?' said Louisa, staring.

'No, I just saw it spout.'

'How have the Killers not seen it?'

'I don't think anyone has seen it.' For there was no sign of whale-boats bearing down upon it, nor indeed the familiar tall black dorsal fins.

'Louisa, saddle up Two Socks at once and ride over to the lookout,' I said.

'Are you mad? I will have to take the cow as well.'

'Then – run over!'

'I can't run all that way!'

'Well, what else do you suggest then? Should we row out and catch it ourselves?' And even as I said it, the idea took form before my eyes. 'Yes. We will row out and catch it ourselves.'

'Are you mad?' she repeated shrilly. 'How can we?'

'We'll take the dinghy.'

'But we don't have any harpoons.'

'We'll use the whale gun.'

At this, Louisa gasped and clapped her hand to her mouth, but without waiting for another query as to my sanity, I took off as fast as I could down to the boatshed. Forced to choose between finishing the washing or chasing down a whale, Louisa opted for the latter, for she at once hitched up her skirts and came tearing down the hill after me. Patch and Bonnie rose up in a startled fashion from their sunbathing and joined in the chase, barking excitedly but with little notion as to what they were actually barking about; all the while the Maudrys shrieked their protests.

The whale gun was kept up on a high shelf in the boatshed, wrapped in a blanket and oilcloth. It was rarely used for, as previously mentioned, the loudness of its report was known to scare the Killers away; however, since the Killers had failed to show up at all in this instance, I was not unduly concerned by this. It was also said to have a fearsome recoil, but that too was something I did not pause to ponder, so consumed was I by the desire to surprise our father with a whale. In truth, I suspect that the main reason my father preferred not to use the whale gun was that he felt it somehow dishonourable to do so. Far better to have the battle play out hand-to-hand, as it were, in close quarters, than to fire a bomb at the whale from a safe distance.

My first shock was how brutally heavy was the whale gun – far heavier than you would reasonably expect by looking at it. It was just over three feet in length, with a wide round muzzle and a curious skeleton stock of cast iron. I passed it down to Louisa, who staggered back a little with its weight, then I seized a rectangular wooden box inscribed in my father's lopsided capitals '*BOMB LANCES*', along with a small bottle of Black Powder.

'Well now! How are you going to load the stupid thing?' cried Louisa.

'Oh, I expect it cannot be too difficult,' I responded, anxious that Louisa not detect any sign of uncertainty in my demeanour. I was no expert at armoury, but I imagined I knew enough to load a bomb lance, having heard my father once describe the action and having frequently loaded our muzzle-loading rifle which we used for potting the occasional rabbit. I say 'occasional' because the aim of the ancient rifle was infamous – if one wanted to hit a rabbit, it was best to aim roughly four feet to the right and slightly upwind of it. It was the same weapon with which my great-grandfather, Alexander Davidson, had infamously shot dead Uncle Aleck's beloved pony Nimblefoot when she made the mistake of bailing him up once too often on his morning walk. It was offered in my great-grandfather's defence that perhaps he had only meant to teach Nimblefoot a lesson, and had been surprised when the weapon had unexpectedly fired straight. I know for certain, however, that Uncle Aleck (who had been a small boy at the time) considered this unlikely, and still thought very bitterly of the old man. 'She was the grandest little pony you ever saw,' he would say, if ever the subject came up in conversation, and it did, remarkably frequently. Louisa averred privately that grand the pony may have been, but none too nimble-footed if she had managed to get herself shot by this most unreliable of weapons.

The whale gun required that the sharply fluted arrowhead of the bomb lance be forced down the muzzle with a ramrod. The bomb lance itself was about thirty inches in length and its latter section was hollow to contain a fuse which was lighted by the flash of the powder; this would cause the weapon to explode once embedded in the whale's flesh. Having jammed it in the muzzle as securely as I could, I set the hammer in the half-cock position in readiness. Now gathering up some rope, a marker buoy, the box of bomb lances and a kellick, we hurried towards the jetty, at which the dinghy was moored. Hearing a cry, we saw John Beck running down towards us.

'God help us, not the nanny goat,' muttered Louisa. 'He will want to say a prayer over us.'

'You're not going after it, surely!' cried John Beck as he caught up with us.

'Well, what else are we going to do?' I responded. 'Let go a perfectly good whale simply because no one has seen it?'

'All right – then I am coming with you,' he said, and we clambered down into the dinghy. Compelled by sense of duty to protect us, the two dogs jumped into the dinghy also, causing us to waste several valuable minutes in hoisting them back upon the jetty and sternly admonishing them with little effect, however, for they jumped directly back into the boat again. Fortunately, at this point Violet and Annie appeared and were instructed, by means of our screaming at them, to hold on to the dogs till we had gained some distance from the jetty. We had only managed to row a short distance when Violet must have relaxed her grip, for Bonnie – always a plucky little dog – leapt heroically into the water and proceeded to paddle after us with an expression of deranged determination on her face, intermittently barking and disappearing underwater. This of course necessitated that we turn about and rescue her. All the while, Patch yelped his outrage from the jetty (he had a horror of water, and did not care to get his paws wet).

Realising we had little choice but to continue our mission with Bonnie on board, we squared up to the breakers now, and it was here I felt the first pang of doubt as to the wisdom of our proposed adventure. With three of us on board and one small wet dog, our aged craft sat worrisomely low in the water. In truth, the dinghy, like the rifle, dated back to Alexander Davidson's time and was now mostly retired from use; I was not entirely confident that it would withstand the rigours of crossing the bar. However, it surprised us by ploughing gamely through, although not sparing us from a terrific drenching.

'Ease up now, there it is!' I cried, once I had dashed the stinging water from my eyes and resumed my position at the steer oar. For there indeed the whale drifted, only fifty feet away. I could tell at once that it was a humpback whale, and a very good-sized one at that.

'Let me see,' said Louisa, pausing in her rowing to swing about and look at it.

'Keep rowing!' I hissed. 'But quietly does it. We must sneak up upon it, as a cat would a mouse.'

We rowed to within twenty feet of the vast creature, at which I signalled to my crew to lie on their oars. The three of us now took the opportunity to gaze at the creature in wonderment; certainly it was the first time in my nineteen years that I had ever seen a living whale at such close quarters. It was dark grey in colour and approximately forty or so feet in length, though this was difficult to determine precisely as most of its bulk was underwater. Its back (which was the only part above water) was rounded, yet surprisingly sleek in appearance, its modest dorsal fin forming part of a ridge or 'hump' from whence I suppose it got its name. It seemed perfectly aware of our presence but not in the slightest concerned; it lifted its knobbly head and spouted, *Bosh!*, as if by way of casual greeting. It conveyed no sense of purpose but seemed content to simply drift about aimlessly, as if enjoying the gentle motion of the swell; if a whale could whistle, I imagined it would be whistling just now, or humming to itself some small snatch of song it vaguely remembered. It was remarkable to me how different it was in its affable demeanour to the determined intent and ruthless purpose of the Killer whale.

Having admired it long enough, I reached down now and picked up the whale gun, and at once an odd feeling of calm descended upon me. Given the remarkable ease with which my plan was unfolding, it felt almost as if this day, this moment, had been laid out for me by Fate. I would capture this creature which floated so obligingly within range of my whale gun and, in doing so, I would turn around my family's fortunes. My father would be surprised and delighted; even proud of me in his own quiet way. 'Good work, lass,' he might say, placing his knotted hand upon my shoulder. Perhaps one of the Eden townsfolk would write a poem about me.

'I really don't think we should be doing this,' said Louisa. 'Dad won't be at all happy when he finds out.'

'He'll be happy if we catch a whale,' I responded, moving the hammer to full-cock.

'He won't be happy that you're using the whale gun.'

'May I ask a question?' said John Beck. 'Is it loaded?'

'Of course it is loaded!' I said, turning to him.

'Don't wave it at us!' cried Louisa, and even John Beck cowered involuntarily as if I was about to shoot him.

'Oh, for goodness' sake,' I said crossly.

Raising the gun to my shoulder, I now took careful aim at the mass of grey that lay before me. There was so much of this whale, it seemed almost impossible that I could miss – if I could only control the muscles of my right arm, which had begun to tremble involuntarily with the great weight of the weapon. I braced myself as best I could till the muzzle steadied, but just as my finger moved to the trigger, Bonnie – who had up till then been gazing off eagerly in the other direction – turned about in her seat, and seeing the whale for the first time, took strong and vocal exception to its presence.

'Grab the dog!' I cried, struggling to retain my balance with the weight of the gun and the dog leaping about. 'Shut the dog up! We will scare away the whale!'

But it was too late. The whale curved its back and tipped up its tail flukes, suspending them in mid-air momentarily as if for our inspection, then disappeared from view.

This was the first time that I had seen a humpback's tail flukes in situ, and I remain convinced, thirty years later, that there is no more wondrous and stirring sight to be seen. Though dark grey on their topside, they are quite white on their underside, which is the side the whale revealed to us now. The flukes were outlined heavily in black as though drawn with a thick nib; several splodges of black were speckled across them, as if the artist had been careless with his pen, and yet the end result was as endearing as freckles on a small child. In the delicacy of their movement, the flukes seemed possessed of a charming insouciance; the overall effect was of a strange flower upon its thick stem, its twin petals opening to the sun. They were beautiful flukes, and we were hushed by them, and remained so for a long moment after they had disappeared. Even Bonnie broke off from her barking and stood with her front paws on the gunwale, staring at the water, now oddly still.

'Don't whales look different up close?' I said, lowering my whale gun. 'Alive, I mean.'

John Beck turned to me and nodded. We looked about us at the empty sea. A strange atmosphere of melancholy stillness came over us as we waited, and it brought to mind the feeling as we had sat in church at my mother's funeral, waiting for the service to commence. The organist had played 'Abide with Me', and I suppose he had been instructed to keep playing till the congregation settled, for I remember feeling that he would never stop, and at one point, when we thought he had finally finished and he started up afresh, Harry had got the giggles and had had to be spoken to. Yet as long as that mournful dirge continued and we sat in the presence of my mother (for she lay in her coffin at the front of the church), it felt to me as if the family were suspended together (for the last time) somewhere between the earthly world and heaven. Why I should suddenly think of it at this moment, I cannot say.

I clutched onto the whale gun, its muzzle pointing to the sky. Bonnie leaned her wet body against me and made small anxious noises. *This isn't right*, she seemed to say. *We shouldn't be here.* My eyes scanned the sea for a disturbance of the water, but the conviction I had felt formerly that I was acting upon my Destiny had begun to evaporate. In truth, some small part of me was beginning to hope that the whale might not reappear at all.

But there it was! It had surfaced on the other side of the boat now, some thirty feet away. *Bosh!* it spouted. *Here I am again! Over here!* I recognised that I must summon my resolve; I could do this, if only I steeled myself. Rising to my feet, and lifting the whale gun to my shoulder, I took aim.

Again, the muscles of my arms commenced shaking violently,

and as my finger closed on the trigger, I was struck by how tremendously heavy was its action, almost as if it might have jammed from years of disuse. As I endeavoured to overcome this resistance, I screwed up my face with the effort, and as I felt the trigger begin to give, I thought, *Oh, I must look where I am firing*, and I opened my eyes and saw – at that exact instant, as the whale rolled with the swell – a small calf nestled beneath its side fin. Louisa screamed, 'Don't shoot! There's a calf!' and I at once pulled my finger away from the trigger.

It seemed to me (in retrospect) that the whale did not recognise as threatening the great weapon I was aiming at her; in fact, she had, at that moment, deemed us sufficiently friendly to reveal to us her cherished baby that she had been hiding beneath her fin. She was proud as any mother of her newborn, and with good reason; it was the dearest little thing (when I say little, it was probably ten feet long) and a perfect miniature of its mother. Even its spout was its mother's spout in miniature; the knobbles upon its small head were tiny version of hers. It tipped up its flukes (the prettiest little flukes you ever saw!) and together, in unison, they dived out of sight.

'Why did you not shoot?' said John Beck, looking up at me.

'Because it had a calf,' I responded. 'My father never kills a whale if it has a calf.'

This is indeed what my father used to tell us as children, knowing how sensitive we were to small creatures being left without their mother. But in truth, although he may have wished otherwise, the Killers did not share his compunctions and would set upon a calf immediately.

'Did you see its flukes?' cried Louisa. 'How sweet they were! Oh, Mary, thank God you didn't shoot!'

Just then, John Beck put his hand upon my arm. Surprised by this action, I looked at him. He said nothing, but pointed towards Honeysuckle Point, from where, unmistakably, slicing through the water in their haste to join us, appeared the tall black dorsal fins of the Killer whales. I have never forgotten it, for there seemed a great many of them and they were travelling at such speed. It was as if the Indians were descending from the hills, for if the Killer whales could have waved their tomahawks and hollered their war cries, so they would have. It was a chilling spectacle, for we knew at once that they would tear the baby apart, even before they began on the mother.

Now the next part is difficult to describe for it happened all very quickly. Without being aware of consciously deciding to do so, I found myself lifting the whale gun once again and this time taking aim at the Killers; that is to say, I aimed in their direction, for I must make it perfectly clear I had no wish to kill one; my intention was simply to frighten them away. Again my arms set to shaking, and again I felt the great resistance of the trigger beneath my finger. I was startled by a loud extended squeaking noise, like a creaky door opening, and I realised that this was the call of a Killer whale, now almost alongside the boat. I had no time to stop and identify its dorsal fin, but I felt instinctively that this was Tom, the leader of the pack. At once I felt a great confusion – should I aim four feet to the right of this creature, as if Tom was a rabbit; or should I aim directly at him, if I did not want to hit him – for what if I were to compound the misadventures of this afternoon by inadvertently blowing up this most beloved of all cetaceans, my father's favourite? All this went through my mind in the instant my finger closed on the trigger, and to my surprise, the resistance suddenly gave way.

There was an almighty report, and as if collected by a steam train, I was hurled backwards into the bottom of the boat, which itself rocked violently almost to the point of capsizing.

There I must have momentarily lost consciousness, for I opened my eyes to find John Beck leaning over me, while some great weight sat upon my chest and prevented me from breathing. This turned out to be Bonnie; John Beck shoved her aside and peered down at me.

'Are you all right?' he enquired.

And there I must have passed out again.

I have only the groggiest memories of what followed, although apparently I rallied and indeed set about attempting to load another bomb lance, before John Beck, with some difficulty, removed the whale gun from my grasp. I was told that the Killers had vanished and I have the briefest memory of Louisa crying, 'There they are!' and pointing to something I could not see, which she seemed to think were the whales' spouts, some distance away. Apparently I insisted that we row after them in a bid to ensure the whales' safety, and when John Beck argued that it was not possible to take our dinghy into the open seas, I became agitated. In the end, he had to pretend they were rowing after them in order to get me to lie down again. I spent the remainder of the trip at the bottom of the dinghy, with my arms wrapped tightly around John Beck's boots, while Bonnie licked my face encouragingly.

My father and the whale men had heard the report from Boyd Tower, and thinking it sounded suspiciously like the whale gun, and thinking that it emanated suspiciously from somewhere near home, my father had ordered the men to the boats to investigate. Fortunately, by the time they intercepted our dinghy, the whale and her baby had long since departed. Nor at any time were the Killers sighted after that initial report of the whale gun.

Sensing from his stern expression that my father required an explanation, John Beck proceeded to recount the whole story from the beginning. He had just outlined in detail the moment in which the whale had revealed her calf, and was about to launch into a description of the dramatic approach of the Killers, when Louisa suddenly interrupted him in the midst of his sentence.

'Mary fired at the whale but she missed – she is as blind as a bat,' said Louisa.

John Beck turned to look at her. Of all the Davidson children, Louisa alone had inherited my father's whale-killing gaze; thus John Beck sensed that she was willing him to keep quiet.

'That's correct,' he agreed, though somewhat confused.

'Why did you not then have a shot?' Bastable demanded to know. 'Are you telling me that when the girl missed, you threw your hands in the air and gave up?'

'Yes, I suppose I did,' said John Beck unhappily, his colour deepening.

'Leave Father alone,' said Salty. 'He has just had the flukes to the head. Is it any wonder he does not wish to be blasted into the hereafter by the bomb lance?'

'Did the *Beowas* come?' asked Percy Madigan.

'Beowa' was the native word for Killer whale. Up until then, the Aboriginal crew members had kept quiet, although John Beck noticed that some of them had been surveying the surrounding waters intently.

'No,' said John Beck, for by now he had begun to suspect why Louisa had cut him off. 'No, they did not come.'

'I thought you said something about them coming?'

'No, no,' said John Beck. 'I may have simply said that we . . . we wished they would come. But they did not come.'

I, of course, was still lying on the bottom of the boat, dimly conscious of what was transpiring, yet still not aware of the potential seriousness of the situation. It was thought that I may have cracked several ribs and suffered a concussion; thus, upon our return, I was put to bed at once.

My father had a stern talk with Louisa, who wavered between brazen defiance and pinning the blame in its entirety on me. However, at no point did she let on about the presence of the Killers. (I know all this because Dan informed me later; he and the little girls were eavesdropping in the next room in the hopes that Louisa would get a thrashing.) 'Very well, Louisa, I can see I am getting nowhere with you,' my father concluded. 'You may leave the table.'

To which she responded, in her typical fashion: 'Well, I can't very well take it with me.'

This set the younger ones to giggling; when they were unable to stop, my father gave up and went out on the verandah to smoke his pipe.

Interesting Beliefs of the Aborigines

VERY EARLY THE NEXT MORNING, AT THE FIRST GREY glimmering of daylight, my father came into our bedroom to talk to me. Bidding Louisa get up out of bed to pack the tuckerbags (to which she acquiesced hastily and without complaining), he sat on a hard-backed chair and surveyed me sombrely. Rarely had I seen his countenance so grim as he outlined to me the foolishness of my actions and the gravity of their possible consequences. He was, of course, rightly concerned that I had endangered our lives in going out to sea in the old dinghy; also in using the whale gun, which was strictly prohibited, not to mention attempting to ensnare a whale by ourselves when we should have more sensibly alerted the whale men.

'I just wanted to capture you a whale!' I cried out, unable to halt the tears that were rolling down my cheeks.

'It is not your responsibility to capture me a whale,' he responded. 'Any capturing of whales to be done around here is up to me and the whale men. Just imagine if you had succeeded in hitting that whale. She would have upended the boat in her death flurry and you would all be drowned.'

I nodded mutely, horrified at this possibility, which I had not till this point ever considered.

'Mary, I must ask you this, and I want you to answer me honestly,' he continued. 'Am I right in believing that the Killers were in attendance?'

I hesitated for a moment and then I nodded, for I could not easily lie to my father.

'And is it that you fired upon them to keep them away from the whale calf?'

How was he able to know such a thing? Were my actions so predictable, my motives so transparent? My tears started up afresh; I dabbed at them futilely with a sodden handkerchief.

He sighed heavily and looked down at the floorboards.

'Mary,' he said finally. 'If it happens that you have slaughtered one of the Killers, then I am afraid we have a very serious situation on our hands.'

I stared at him for a long moment and then, suddenly, I saw for the first time, with terrible clarity, what I had done. For it was the deeply held belief of our Aboriginal whale men that each individual Killer whale represented the reincarnated spirit of a deceased tribe member. If I had taken the life of a *Beowa*, their respect and loyalty towards my father notwithstanding, the Aborigines might well feel compelled to take my own life in order to avenge that of their spirit ancestor.

Many years ago, in my grandfather's time, a headsman named Higginbotham, but known affectionately to all as 'Flukey', was in the process of lancing a whale when a Killer whale reared up before him and was accidentally struck by the lance and killed. The natives were so greatly distressed by this that they armed themselves with spears and, by all accounts, would certainly have killed Flukey had not an elder of the tribe intervened on his behalf. His life was spared, but only on condition that he leave the region at once. This he did, with the utmost haste, and was never heard from again. My father was very mindful of this story in his own actions, as amidst the chaos of trying to lance a whale, with the Killers working closely all around, it could easily happen that a Killer be accidentally struck.

I remember when I was quite small, there was an infant Killer whale of whom the Aboriginal crew members were inordinately fond; his name was Jimmy, and it was believed that he was the reincarnation of a small boy of their tribe who had not so very long ago died of sickness. When Jimmy first made his appearance alongside his seniors, the Aboriginal whale men greeted him with loud cries of excitement and recognition, as if overjoyed to be reunited. Whilst out chasing whales, they would call to the infant orca in their own language, 'Jimmy, do this,' and, 'Jimmy, do that,' and Jimmy would respond to the very best of his abilities. (The Aborigines often called to the Killers in their own language; they seemed to be calling instructions, as you would to a sheepdog.) One day, the infant Killer whale was playing with the anchor rope of a whaleboat (for Killer whales have a fondness for ropes and anchors, as we have seen) when he became entangled within these ropes, and drowned. It was nobody's fault, of course, but even though I was quite small at the time, I well remember the terrible grief displayed by the natives over the loss of this young Killer. The men wept openly and wailed, cut themselves with shells until they bled, so intensely felt was their sorrow.

'I must ask you this,' continued my father. 'Can you be sure that you did not injure any of them?'

I shook my head miserably. I could not be sure, for I had been too busy being 'blasted into the hereafter', or at least into the bottom of the boat, to pay much attention to what became of the Killers. Nor did I dare admit to my father how close to the boat one of them had come: the leader, no doubt it was Tom. Nor could John Beck or Louisa say for certain what had happened; their impression was that the Killers had dived. Had the bomb lance itself exploded? Amidst all the smoke and confusion, no one was able to confidently say, least of all myself.

My father eyed me gravely, then stood up. 'You must say nothing of this to anyone, not even the children.'

He and his men, including John Beck, left for the lookout. Bruised and wretched, I dragged myself out of bed and limped through my chores. I felt sick to my stomach at the thought of what I might have done, not just for the terrible consequences I would undoubtedly and deservedly face, but also for the sheer, ghastly fact that I might have, in the heat of the moment, destroyed so horribly such a noble beast. Surely, pray God, I had missed? But what if the swollen corpse of a Killer whale were to wash up on a beach somewhere, a bomb lance embedded in its flesh? And what if the corpse was that of Tom, most beloved of all orcas, himself a reincarnation of an ancient tribal warrior greatly venerated by the blackfellows? What would happen then?

I climbed up to the headland and gazed out, willing Tom to materialise at the breakers. He was welcome to eat as many whale calves as he liked, I thought to myself bitterly, if only he would kindly leap out of the water this instant. Him and all his cohorts, especially Cooper, who was believed to have been a tribal king, and Charlie Adgery, who was known to have been a distinguished and beloved whale man in his former life. But as far as I could see from the headland, the watery world seemed utterly devoid of life, ancestral or otherwise.

Further, I was plagued by the feeling that the rest of the family was avoiding me. Louisa assisted me in completing what remained of the washing, but was churlish and silent throughout. Uncle Aleck stayed in his shed and did not even come down for his lunch. Even Bonnie seemed anxious to stay clear of me, leaping out of the way in a startled fashion whenever I drew near. (We later discovered she had been rendered completely deaf by the explosion of the whale gun.) Thus I passed a most miserable day, compounded by the fact that the injuries to my ribs meant it hurt to draw breath.

That evening, the whale men returned from the lookout to report that there had been no sign of the Killer whales in their favourite haunt of Leatherjacket Bay. This was not in itself completely unusual, as the Killers often occupied themselves with activities elsewhere of which we knew nothing, and yet for them to be absent that day of all days felt to me like the death knell of all hope. There was a degree of tension evident amongst the whalers that evening as I doled out their stew: Arthur Ashby and Percy Madigan, and Albert Thomas Senior and Darcy and Albert Thomas Junior (that is, our Aboriginal whalers) all seemed deliberately to avoid my gaze, while Bastable and Salty were evidently still brooding over the fact that we had let the whale get away.

'As I said to the Reverend, in no uncertain terms,' muttered Bastable, making sure that I might hear it, 'if you cannot find the gumption to kill a whale, then summon the men that can.'

Not surprisingly, perhaps, given that he had passed much of the day being tormented in this fashion, John Beck seemed somewhat withdrawn; he asked briefly if I was feeling better, then retired a small distance away to eat his meal. It was only later when he saw me struggling with the pots that he jumped up to help me carry them. We walked together in silence up to the house, for I felt somehow mortified by everything that had happened and sure that he must think me worthless.

'Mary,' he said finally, when we had reached the kitchen door, 'I feel as certain as I can be that your shot did not injure the Killers.'

'Really?' I said, turning to him. I felt as if a thin shaft of sunlight was revealing itself from behind a bank of dark clouds.

'Yes,' he said. 'I am fairly confident that you missed them by a wide margin.'

'Oh, I hope so!' I exclaimed, and it hurt my ribs so badly to do so that I cried out in pain. That hurt also, making me gasp, which also hurt.

'Are you all right?' he asked. He had been watching my gasping and wincing with some concern.

'Yes,' I said. 'Although my ribs are quite sore.'

He nodded. And then he hesitated a moment before he next spoke.

'Mary, I just wanted to say this also. I thought what you did tremendously brave.'

'Tremendously brave?'

'Yes.'

'Which bit?'

'I'm sorry?'

'Which bit was tremendously brave? I mean, of what I did?' You see, I had to be sure of his meaning, for I knew his words would stay with me for my lifetime, and I could not afford to suffer any confusion about it.

'Well, all of it, really. But especially the action...' (here he looked around to ensure he would not be overheard) '...regarding the Killers.'

'Thank you,' I said.

Such tender memories as I have! So much more fortunate than poor Maeve or Maud, with only her jam sponge 'as light as air'. For although his eyes were still blackened and his cheek bruised, his face as he gazed at me, so troubled and earnest, had never looked more gravely beautiful. And things no longer seemed so terrible nor did it hurt so much to breathe.

An Unexpected Revelation

I N FACT, THE KILLERS DID NOT REAPPEAR TILL ALMOST A WEEK later, and true to form, they made sure to stage their reappearance in the most spectacular of circumstances.

But I am getting ahead of myself. The most pressing problem for us at that time, apart from the non-appearance of the Killer whales, and the non-appearance of whales in general, was in fact our desperate shortage of provisions. We were now at the stage when my father's terse instructions to 'eke 'em out' were to little avail; our provisions could withstand no further eking. Anxious not to miss a day on lookout (and presumably anxious not to have the difficult conversation with Mr Howard, the storekeeper, that I would inevitably have to endure), my father arranged for Mr Caleb Cook to come over in his sulky and convey Louisa and myself into Eden. It is an indication of how distracted my father must have been at the time that he permitted Mr Cook, of all people, to be our driver and escort:

for as observant readers will be aware, it was Mr Cook who had put up the prize money and then selected Louisa as the Best-dressed and Most Prepossessing Young Lady of the Eden Show. I may not have mentioned previously that Louisa had been rather insufferably pleased with herself when awarded this prize, but significantly less so upon meeting her admirer.

Mr Cook had a sheep farm in Burragate, and was very keen to find a wife; it seems that the prize he offered in the Eden Show may have been an opening gambit towards this end. I should explain that Burragate is tremendously isolated and accessible only by the most arduous journey over many precipitous ridges, and if the axle did not snap or the brake fail or the horses take fright at a snake and bolt down a hill, then you considered yourself to have had a reasonable trip to Burragate. It was funny to imagine Louisa spending her days up there married to a sheep farmer and occasionally we teased her on the subject, but only if we wished to have our heads bitten off, for Louisa did not regard the topic as humorous. While happy to accept the prize money and bask in the glory of being Eden's 'Most Prepossessing', she nipped in the bud any further attentions, and Mr Cook had returned to his sheep farm still a bachelor.

He was an extremely tall man of about twenty-eight years with a ruddy face, prominent ears and a diffident manner; his mother had passed away several years ago, and it seems the loneliness was beginning to affect him. He wanted a companion, and who could blame him, for there is not much companionship to be had from three hundred and twenty-one sheep. That is the exact number; I know, because he mentioned it several times during the long trip into Eden.

'Last year I had twenty-eight cows and fifty-three sheep; this year, I got no cows and three hundred and twenty-one sheep,' he volunteered, apropos of nothing, but just because the numbers seemed to appeal to him.

'What happened to the cows?' asked Louisa. 'Did they run away?'

There was once an article in the newspaper entitled *'Women Who Should Never Marry'*, which seemed to have been written by someone of intimate acquaintance with Louisa, for I felt at the time that it described her to a tee:

> *'Sweeping as the assertion may appear at first sight, there are women who should never marry, and whom young men would do well to avoid. Someone has said that a girl who comes under this category is one:*
>
> *Who is so utterly selfish that she could not consider or love another more than herself.*
>
> *Who prides herself on her domestic incompetence, and boasts of her inability to cook a dinner or scrub a floor.*
>
> *Who displays no love for children, and who would rather fondle a pug dog than a baby.*
>
> *Who is cross and miserable unless she is the centre of attention or is engaged flirting with the best-looking man in the company.*
>
> *Who does not hesitate to pronounce old and ailing people "bores", or to show impatience with the recital of their aches and pains . . .'*

I mention this article, because I was reminded of it whilst sitting in the sulky with Louisa and Mr Cook, and I found myself contemplating copying it out in its entirety and sending it to him anonymously. What on earth he was doing driving all the way from Burragate to pick us up and then convey us all the way into Eden, I do not know. I imagine he had hoped that the long trip would give

Louisa ample time to warm to him, but if her frosty demeanour was an indication, this was not eventuating.

'Who is looking after your sheep?' I asked politely, for I felt a compulsion to make up for Louisa's coolness.

But he looked at me in scornful amazement. 'They're not like cows, you know – you don't have to milk 'em,' he said, and when Louisa gave a snort of laughter, he began to guffaw at his own joke, and from then on kept alluding to the fact that I apparently thought sheep needed milking.

After that, I decided I did not much care for him. Let Louisa do her worst, I thought, and sat in silence. (I suppose I will not spoil the ending if I say that Louisa did not marry him, and as far as I know, he remained a bachelor.)

The trip into Eden was uneventful, except for when we came to a dead echidna on the road. Mr Cook's ponies took great exception to it, and would not go past it for anything. Instead, they decided they might simply back up all the way home again, and this they commenced to do, with the unhappy effect of unscrewing the sulky wheels in the process, causing us to have to hastily dismount before the entire contraption fell apart. Fortunately, Mr Cook seemed to have come prepared for an event of this nature, for he produced a large wrench and screwed the wheels back on again. After removing the offending corpse from within a hundred yards of the vicinity of Mr Cook's ponies, we were eventually able to continue.

'Let us try to not draw attention to ourselves,' Louisa whispered to me as we finally approached the post office. 'I would rather not be noticed with Mr Cook.'

No sooner had the words fallen from her lips when, as if to defy her, Mr Cook's ponies began to buck and plunge, and then at once took off at a terrifying speed across Imlay Street, along Mitchell Street and then down the hill towards Aslings Beach. I remember little of the incident clearly except clinging on for dear life and thinking the sulky would surely break apart as we hurtled down the hill. People in the street were screaming and running in all directions. Mr Cook lost his hold of the reins amidst the initial bucking, but I will say this for him: he managed to clamber forward over the dash board and take hold of them again whilst our sulky was careening down the hill. He had almost succeeded in reining the ponies in just as we reached the cemetery, whereupon the ponies slewed sharply to the right, capsizing the sulky and tipping us into the sand on Aslings Beach, directly in front of the cemetery in which rested the remains of our great-grandfather, Alexander Davidson.

At once, a crowd of people came running down the hill in the hope of our having incurred death or serious injuries; many excitedly declared it the worst runaway they had ever witnessed. But in fact, despite a few bruises from being bounced about in the sulky, we were relatively unscathed; shaken up and covered in sand, certainly, but mostly just very annoyed with Mr Cook. To our mind, he did not seem sufficiently apologetic. In fact, he offered by way of explanation that his ponies were used to the peace and quiet of Burragate, and did not much care for town; they particularly did not care for town horses, and it seems a town horse may have slighted them in some way outside the post office.

'Slighted them in what way?' asked Louisa.

'Well, I daresay he looked at them funny,' said Mr Cook.

Mrs Pike, proprietress of the Great Southern Hotel, insisted we come back to her establishment and lie down in a darkened room for an hour or so to recover from the shock. We accepted her offer gratefully, leaving Mr Cook to tend to the injured feelings of his ponies. We were very glad of one thing, and that is that we now had a perfectly acceptable reason not to travel back with him; Mrs Pike kindly offered to make arrangements for us to travel home later in the day by means of Mr Jessop's motor launch. She brought us up corned beef sandwiches with mustard pickles and a bottle of lemon barley water, and when we thanked her profusely, she said that she'd do anything she could for George Davidson's girls, she thought so well of the man, and so did everyone in the whole of Eden and surrounding areas; in fact, she went on about our father to such an extent, we began to wonder if she harboured feelings for him. When she had left us, with assurances that we must consider the room ours for as long as we needed it, we washed up with a soap that smelled of roses and drank our lemon barley water and ate our sandwiches; then we lay down on the big bed with the pink satin eiderdown and giggled about Mr Cook and his sensitive ponies and his three hundred and twenty-one sheep. And that is when Louisa confided in me that she loved Darcy.

I was surprised of course, stunned even; and yet I also experienced the not disagreeable sensation that pieces of a puzzle that had never made sense to me (the puzzle being Louisa) suddenly fitted into place, and I saw her at once clearly and wholly and compassionately, for possibly the first time in her sixteen years. Of course Louisa loved Darcy! It seemed suddenly obvious – and yet not obvious at all. Certainly, they had been great playmates in childhood, for we had known Darcy since he was very small; his father, Percy, had been a whale man for my father for many years. When whaling season came around, our Aboriginal crew members would materialise (their usual home was Wallaga Lake, some distance north); the men would stay in the sleeping huts, but the women and children would often times in those days camp up the hill behind the house. We would rush up to greet them, so excited were we to have our little friends return. After a period of initial shyness, lasting all of about half a day, we would pick up where we had left off the previous year; fishing with spears we had fashioned ourselves and building humpies and 'startling the bandicoot'; all the normal fun of childhood. Louisa was a contrary sort of child, but Darcy seemed to have a knack with her, and her oft-declared boast as a child was that her bare feet were almost as tough as his. At thirteen, Darcy began whaling, which meant we saw a good bit less of him, and if you asked me to relate any particular sign of their enduring closeness, I would say only that they were inclined to surreptitiously toss small stones and sticks at one another whenever circumstances drew them in near proximity.

But now that I thought of it, quite recently, when she had been charged with the cooking whilst I tended to the injured John Beck, I had entered the kitchen to fetch his meal and there they were, just the two of them, for Darcy had carried up the pots. It was odd to see him standing in the kitchen, for he would never normally venture into our house, and seeing him silhouetted in the doorframe made me realise how tall he had grown. However, I was too preoccupied with John Beck at the time (what a familiar refrain this is becoming) to notice anything between them; besides which, Darcy made his excuses and promptly left.

'Does he love you?' I asked Louisa now, as we lay together on the bed.

'Yes, of course he loves me,' she said, and she suddenly looked very sorrowful. By which I mean that the corners of her mouth pushed downwards and her lower lip convulsed violently for a moment before she regained control of it. As a rule, Louisa did not like to cry, and considered it a sign of weakness.

'Does anyone else know?' I asked.

'I think Harry and Robert may suspect.'

'What makes you think that?'

'I don't know. They seem to watch us all the time.'

'Don't let them find out,' I said urgently, and I found I was enjoying my new role as her heart's advisor. 'No one must ever find out.'

'Oh well, they will find out soon enough,' said Louisa.

'What do you mean?' I asked, and even as I spoke the words, I could feel my physical being stricken with a presentiment as to the answer.

'Well, we are going to run away and get married,' said Louisa.

The very first thought that came to my mind, and I am ashamed to admit it, was of the Breelong murders. These had happened some years earlier, for I remember reading about it in the newspaper, and when my mother saw what I was reading she snatched the newspaper abruptly from me and hid it away. However, I found it again and, when my mother was otherwise occupied, I studied the article at length. A young blackfellow named Jimmy Governor had married a white woman (in fact they had been properly married by a Church of England minister), and he and his wife Ethel (who was by all reports a nice-looking and presentable young lady) were camping on the property of the Mawbey family, for whom Jimmy Governor was working. The Mawbey womenfolk taunted Jimmy and Ethel and called them 'rubbish' and said that Jimmy deserved to be shot for marrying a white woman. Ethel began tearing her hair out, and cried, 'Lord save me from the terrible things these people are saying, I cannot stand it.' So Jimmy went up to the house to ask the women to stop their name-calling. But the women taunted Jimmy further, and he became so enraged that he bludgeoned the women to death, and the children also, with a tomahawk. I remember the article vividly for the description of the brains coming out of one of the victims; also because it was the first time I had ever heard of an Aboriginal man and a white woman being married. (In fact, it was the only time I had ever heard of it.)

The second thought that leapt to mind was that it was a great shame that my mother had died when we were young. It was more than a shame; I felt suddenly furious about it, for I was saddled with more responsibility than I was equipped for. Surely if my mother was still alive then she would have taken Louisa in hand, and she would not be now considering running away and marrying a blackfellow and spending the rest of her days in ignominy and ruin. But even as this thought passed through my mind, I realised with a jolt that Louisa was not 'considering' this; she had already made up her mind.

My third thought was this: I had long sought to be close to my sister, but her haughty demeanour and the various differences of our personalities had always kept us at a distance from one another. Here now, as we lay side by side on the pink eiderdown, she was confiding in me, and this she had never done before. I felt honoured and filled with love for her; I was proud of her pale beauty and her defiant spirit. It was somehow of the greatest importance to me to keep this thin new thread of sisterly feeling between us from breaking. I see clearly now that as her older sister, especially in the absence of wise counsel in the form of our mother, I should have urged her to consider more fully the inevitable and terrible consequences of this action. I should have reminded her that she was only sixteen, and that her feelings for Darcy were most probably a remnant of her childish fancies, distorted by the tempestuous emotions common to youth and the relative isolation in which we lived. At the very least, I accept that I should certainly have said something to our father. However, the unexpectedness of the revelation and the pleasure excited in being her confidante prompted in me a loss of reason, and in this moment, when I had perhaps my greatest opportunity, I chose not to attempt to dissuade her.

We lay on the bed in silence together, me absorbing what she had said and having all these various thoughts and so forth when, perhaps interpreting my silence as disapproval, she suddenly leapt up, quite pink in the face, and cried: 'Don't be foolish! Of course, I am only joking! It is only nonsense! I cannot think why you believed me!'

At once, I felt a mixture of emotions, hurt and confusion foremost amongst them, but also a small measure of relief that I did not after all have to contend with such a complicated scenario. To vent my feelings, I berated her harshly for making up fibs and she berated me in turn for believing them and so I punched her, and once again our sisterly relations resumed their normal course. Some small part of me, however, held on to the truth, and the truth was that I had seen her lower lip tremble violently when I asked if Darcy loved her.

Antecedents

I
T IS AN INTERESTING COINCIDENCE THAT, EARLIER THAT SAME day, we had been capsized out of the sulky, petticoats over our heads, directly in front of our great-grandfather's tombstone.

'Well,' said Louisa, pulling her skirt down and dashing the sand from her eyelashes. 'This will certainly confirm the old man's suspicions about us.'

It seems that several of Alexander Davidson's daughters had been notably flighty of disposition, and thenceforth the old man regarded all his female progeny with some measure of distrust. We had only been small children when he died, and yet he would so frequently mutter the word 'harlots' in our near vicinity that for a long time we believed it was the Gaelic word for 'girls'.

Apparently his daughters had a weakness for sea captains and, happily for them, the feelings were entirely reciprocated. How they ever came to meet these sea captains was a source of some wonder to us, for these Davidson girls were stranded and becalmed in Kiah, just as we were. Yet it seems they were somehow more resourceful in their methods, for certainly they succeeded where we did not (I have never even met a sea captain, and short of loitering hopefully about the wharf, cannot imagine under what circumstances such a meeting might ever have transpired). The eldest daughter Margaret married William Greig, the captain of one of Benjamin Boyd's whaling ships. She bore him a son (our own Uncle Aleck), and shortly thereafter Captain Greig sailed to Queensland, from which ill-fated trip he was never to return. It was presumed that the ship had foundered in bad weather and gone down with all souls.

Yet it seems in truth that Captain Greig had somehow convinced his crew that, instead of returning to Sydney, it would be a fine thing to try their luck on the goldfields of California, as had done Benjamin Boyd before them, and thus in that direction they set sail. A hurricane drove them to seek shelter on Fanning Island, and there they found the amenities so pleasing they decided that perhaps they were not in such a hurry to get to the goldfields after all. Captain Greig succumbed to the charms of a native princess (having apparently forgotten about poor Margaret languishing at home), acquired large tracts of plantation land, sired several more children and appointed himself the King of Fanning Island. This was only discovered many years later, when Uncle Aleck happened upon his obituary in a newspaper. As can be imagined, it came as a tremendous surprise to him, for he had laboured under the misapprehension that his father drowned at sea. He had never imagined for a moment that all this time the captain had been lying about under a coconut tree with a bevy of dusky maidens in attendance. Poor Margaret, meanwhile, had died long ago, bereft, at the age of twenty-two. So it is a very sad story, and goes some way to explaining the fact that Uncle Aleck could at times be a difficult individual.

The story of Alexander's third daughter, Jane, had particularly piqued our interest for she had eloped at the age of eighteen with a gentleman considerably older than herself, the sea captain of the *Fancy*. Her sister Elsy had assisted in this illicit conjugation by rowing her out to his waiting schooner. Alexander got wind of the scheme and gamely pursued them, but the sea captain had no sooner hauled Jane on board than he set sail, and Alexander could not catch them. Whenever I hear this story repeated, I always find myself sympathising with the hapless Elsy, persuaded against her better judgement to row her sister to her waiting paramour and receiving, no doubt, little thanks for her trouble; her sister scooting up the rope ladder swung over the *Fancy*'s sides with nary a backward glance. And then Elsy having to turn the little boat around and row back and face the wrath of Alexander Davidson, all red-faced from the rowing and spitting epithets at her. I would not be in her shoes. And yet it was not difficult to imagine myself in a similar scenario, for if any member of our family was most likely to elope with a sea captain and force me into rowing her out to his schooner, it would be Louisa. Except she didn't.

Unpleasant Encounter with the Price-Cutter

WHEN WE HAD DECIDED THAT WE HAD SUFFICIENTLY recovered from our ordeal with Mr Cook and his ponies, we thanked Mrs Pike profusely and made our way down Imlay Street towards the vast emporium of Mr Howard, the Price-Cutter. A sick, heavy feeling of apprehension began to manifest in my belly, for Mr Howard was a trying man at the best of times, and we were already indebted to him to some considerable extent. I had a long list of requirements and no money to pay for them; I could only prevail upon his kindness, the one provision he kept in short supply.

Out the front of his store, we paused to survey a small poster pasted on the window:

- A GRAND -

PLAIN

—AND—

FANCY DRESS

BALL

will be Held at the

Eden School of Arts

— ON —

Saturday 21 November.

—

Double Tickets 5s, Single 3s.

—

First-Class Music and Refreshments.

Glumly, we gazed upon it.

'I wonder if Eunice Martin will wear her cream lustre or her tinsel-thread organdie,' I said.

'I imagine she will have a new dress altogether,' said Louisa. 'It will be sewn together from the desiccated corpses of seventeen bush rats, left out to dry in the sun.'

I snorted gleefully. How fondly I felt towards Louisa sometimes! In her meanness towards Eunice Martin, I saw that she was demonstrating her loyalty and affection towards me. In her own strange way, she was a loving sister.

'Let us look at the muslins and cretonnes and see if there is something we like,' I said, squeezing her arm. 'There is no harm in pretending. And choose some lace and some ribbon to go with it.'

'All right,' said Louisa, although her heart did not seem to be in it. We stepped inside, adopting a purposeful attitude to indicate that we had a job to do and meant to do it. Mr Howard was engaged in serving somebody, and feeling our resolve diminish at the sight of him, we seized the opportunity to lurk amongst the bolts of chiffons and georgettes, muslins and lace. How pretty they were, and how long it had been since we'd had a new dress! After some consideration, I chose for myself a moss-green georgette with cream chiffon trimmings; it was only then that I realised Louisa had moved over to the bridal section, where I found her thoughtfully contemplating an ivory crepe de Chine. Alarmed, I thrust a bolt of pink crinkle marocain at her in an attempt to distract her from the direction in which her thoughts seemed to be wandering. It was at this point that Mr Howard pounced upon us.

'Well, here we are, the Davidson lasses! I was wondering if you'd pay me a visit, for I heard you were thrown face first into the sand at Aslings Beach! I am glad to see that you have sufficiently revived to feel equal to the task of shopping. Are you looking to buy something pretty for the ball?'

'Actually, it is for provisions we have come,' I responded stiffly. 'I have rather a long list, if I could call upon your kind assistance.'

He took the list I proffered and surveyed it at length, and as his eyes travelled down it, his face assumed an expression of mounting incredulity.

'70 lb sugar
2 cwt flour
10 lb Lipton's tea
Rolled oats, 2 bags

3 dozen eggs
vinegar (1 gallon)
condensed milk, 1 dozen tins
jam (1 doz. assorted)
5 lb tapioca
5 lb pearl barley
5 lb split peas
3 lb currants
2 lb cocoa
1 loaf cheese
2 jars mustard pickles
Lea and Perrins Worcestershire sauce (6)
5 large tins golden syrup
Biscuits (Arnotts), 5 lb
Dripping
5 lb bacon
1 side corned beef
2 flaps mutton or mutton shanks
5 bags potatoes
3 bags carrots
2 bags onions
2 lb salt
Baking powder
Tobacco (6 pkts Yankee Doodle dark)
Sunlight soap (4)
Candles (3 boxes)
4 cases Snowflake kerosene
1 bottle raspberry cordial
1 small bag aniseed balls'

'Is there anything you've left off, do you think?' he asked finally.

'I don't believe so,' I responded untruthfully. In fact, we required a great deal more than this, but given we did not have any money, I did not wish to appear too fanciful.

'I note that you request aniseed balls – would you not prefer humbugs instead?'

'No, thank you,' I replied firmly, for I sensed where this was heading.

'Yes, I daresay there is enough humbuggery already in this list,' said Mr Howard. 'Kindly tell me how you imagined you were going to pay for all this?'

'Oh! Well, of course I was hoping that you would extend our credit for just one more month, Mr Howard,' I began, and as he was already starting to shake his head, I continued on quickly: 'As you know, November is traditionally a very strong month for whales –'

'Not last November, it wasn't.'

'Last November was certainly the exception to the rule, I grant you. But all the signs are there for us this year. The Killers are in remarkably fine trim –'

'I heard the Killers have already departed for the season.'

'I refute that utterly!' Just at that moment the bell tinkled above the door and a customer entered the shop.

'Misses Davidson, I have the greatest respect for your father –' said Mr Howard, adopting a more obsequious tone for the benefit of the other customer.

'I am *Miss* Davidson,' I interrupted.

'I meant "Misses" as in the plural, for there are two of you.'

'Mrs Davidson is my departed mother, who had the misfortune to expire far too early,' I continued, ignoring him, for a wave of fury had overtaken me, 'before she could raise her children to adulthood and before she could see the statue in honour of our father that I have no doubt will be erected in the middle of Imlay Street, cast in bronze and standing thirty feet high, with a fountain spouting from it which will represent the spout of the whale, and which people will travel from far and wide to throw coins into, for it will bring tremendous fortune to all who do so.' I remember Louisa staring at me, but the release of all the accumulated tension – of the day, if not of the entire whaling season – was so tremendous I did not seem able to staunch the torrent. I went on to state that while it seemed to me the townsfolk were very happy to bask in the reflected glory of my father's bravery, and write poems about him that were factually inaccurate and did not even rhyme very well, and use his reputation for fearlessness to advance their own ill-fated efforts to have Eden become the nation's capital, no one would offer a hand in assistance if he suffered two bad years in a row and was struggling to feed his family.

And just at this point, the customer, who had been standing about impatiently and shifting his weight from foot to foot, suddenly interrupted me, and said: 'Excuse me, Miss Davidson, your father has a whale in the bay right this moment and it is as big as the S.S. *Merimbula*!'

'*Rush oh!*'

That during last Thursday's whale chase, intense excitement prevailed in Eden.

That, while the chase lasted, business was suspended and homes deserted.

That many families left the dinner table before the meal was completed; and

That as a consequence, before they returned home, the cats of the neighbourhood had 'sat down to all good things provided'.

That two lady visitors had some trying experiences while negotiating the barbed wire and other fences on whale day.

That when the whale was in the vicinity of the wharf, many feared it would be knocked down, and reached the other end, hat in hand, in even time, and

That one was the 'belle' of the Eden Show.

EDEN OBSERVER AND SOUTH COAST ADVOCATE

An Intensely Exciting Chase

I AM NOW GOING TO ATTEMPT AS BEST I CAN TO DESCRIBE THE chase and capture of the whale, and I ask the reader's forgiveness in advance if my abilities are found to be somewhat less than equal to the task. I admit it is a daunting challenge, for I fear it will only invite comparisons with Mr Melville that will not be flattering. (I mean, they will not be flattering to me; they will be perfectly flattering to Mr Melville.) Nonetheless, it is important that I attempt it, as this particular chase was considered by old-timers to be unparalleled as regards its unpredictability and sheer excitement, not least for the fact that the Killers staged their triumphant 'deus ex machina' in the third act. So I shall endeavour to do it justice in my depiction, and if the reader finds it wanting, then they must simply put up with it, as I will have certainly tried my best.

Upon hearing the news of the whale, we took leave of Mr Howard and hastened out of the store, finding ourselves at once amidst a throng of people hurrying in the direction of the wharf and surrounding headlands. Some were running, some rode bicycles or went on horseback; older matrons half ran, half walked in a bid to keep an air of respectability about them. Shopkeepers hastily shut up shop; others climbed onto balconies and rooftops, peering through telescopes and binoculars. Drinkers spilled out of the Great Southern Hotel; children poured out of the school gates in haphazard lines of two by two, herded in as best they could by their teachers. 'Excuse me, excuse me, we are Davidsons, our father is after a whale,' we cried, as we elbowed our way through, and on the whole, the townsfolk were most obliging and made way for us: 'Let them through, it's the Davidson lasses!' Suddenly, there beside us materialised Mr Caleb Cook in his sulky, offering us a ride. I was about to demur, but Louisa, who was slightly ahead of me, at once hitched her skirt up and, taking his proffered hand, clambered on. I followed suit (without any proffered hand, I might add), feeling it arguably safer to be pulled by the sensitive ponies than trampled to death by them. With Mr Cook's encouragement, the easily offended ponies made it down the hill in a matter of moments, whereupon we jumped off and ran full tilt along the wharf, for judging by the screams and shouts that emanated from there, it seemed to be the best vantage point. Some locals were even jumping into their dinghies and pleasure craft, eager for a more immediate experience.

We were about midway down the wharf when we heard the cry, 'Look out!' and, looking out, I saw my father's boat hurtling towards us at such speed that for a moment I genuinely believed it had become airborne. The oarsmen, their oars peaked, clung on to the gunwales with looks of grim desperation on their faces;

my father stood at the bow, lance in hand, and he seemed to be shouting something, for certainly his face was contorting in a way I had never seen before. At once I realised that the whale (to which the boat was attached) was travelling in a direct path towards the wharf, and even if it managed to pass under the structure, the boat would surely collide with the piles. *Cut loose!* I thought to myself. *Cut loose!* It was then I realised that my father was shouting, 'Get off! Get off!' and seeing suddenly that the wharf might well collapse with the impending impact, the crowd turned as one and bolted to safety, clearing the distance, as the newspaper said, 'in even time'. Upon reaching the end of the wharf, we turned around in time to see the whaleboat careening under the wharf. The oarsmen ducked, Arthur and my father threw themselves down to avoid being knocked out; Louisa and I screamed in horror, expecting the very worst. But there, in a second, the boat emerged on the other side, still fast to the whale and the wharf intact. Arthur and my father sprang back up to their standing positions, and the crowd roared its approval.

The whale now headed out to the middle of the bay, causing those eager onlookers in their pleasure crafts to scatter in all directions, rowing wildly as the whale bore down upon them. One hapless man in a dinghy even dived into the water and attempted to swim before remembering that he could not, and was thence plucked out of the water by the nearest boat. The whale cleared all of them with my father's boat hurtling along in its wake, the Number Two boat rowing desperately to keep up with them.

What happened immediately afterwards we did not witness, for at that moment we were running as hard as we could up to Lookout Point, which afforded the best view of the bay. It was en route that we became entangled in a barbed-wire fence, as reported in *'Voices Whisper'* (for it seems the editor of the *Eden Observer and South Coast Advocate* had his opera glasses trained upon us, in preference to the action at sea). Caring not, we ripped our skirts loose and raced onwards, leaving snatches of worn fabric to blow in the breeze like bunting. There was already a crowd up there, waving their hats and shouting and gesticulating. We pushed to the front of them and found ourselves at the very outermost edge of the cliffs, where various men obligingly wrapped their arms around our waists to ensure we did not plunge over. The whale passed close by the rocks down below, and from this perspective we could see the length and breadth of it.

'Oh, Louisa!' I cried. 'It's a black whale!'

'Fifty feet if it's an inch,' offered the stout, moustachioed man who had his arms about me. (Incidentally, I recognised him to be one of the judges at the Eden Show who had deemed *'Stern All, Boys!'* to be worthy only of a Highly Commended.)

'Fifty feet!' Louisa and I exclaimed, looking at each other incredulously. The whale now veered off wildly for the northern side of the bay, before sweeping back to the cliffs again, keeping so close to the rocks that the whaleboat seemed in imminent danger of being smashed upon them.

'Where are the Killers?' cried someone. 'If only the Killers would come!'

Yes, yes, where were they? At once I was stricken with a sharp stab of guilt. For at this time, I was still uncertain as to whether I had scared them off or even inadvertently slaughtered one.

As long as the whale was travelling at this speed, there was little chance of my father gaining proximity enough to lance it. From the shouts of the men below, we gathered that my father was urging the second boat to fasten on as well, in a bid to slow the great beast down. Harry stood up at the bow, harpoon in hand, and seemed about to launch it when a small bent figure rose up behind him and began waving his arms and gesticulating.

'It is Uncle Aleck!' cried Louisa, clutching her face in horror. 'What is he doing?'

Who indeed knew what he was doing? Certainly no one on the Number Two boat seemed to know, for an argument ensued. There was more shouting and waving about of arms, until Dan and John Beck pulled him back into a seated position. (John Beck later informed me that Uncle Aleck had been called in to assist young Dan at the oars. Amidst the excitement, he had risen to his feet to shout advice at Harry, thereby startling him and causing him to miss his chance.) Frantic rowing now ensued in order to catch the whale again. Even from the cliff tops, we could see the spray of Salty's spittle as he urged his oarsmen on.

The next sequence of events happened very quickly. Harry landed his harpoon well, and he and Salty immediately did the changeover, a manoeuvre made even more perilous by Uncle Aleck choosing this moment to take his coat off. ('The old goat! I will kill him!' cried Louisa.) The sting of this second harpoon seemed only to exacerbate the whale's desperation, for it set off on a series of precipitous zigzags in a bid to shake loose its extra burden. The final zag of the series was so sharp and so abrupt that it caused the second boat to swing directly across the first boat's path, its line passing over the men's heads. They had just time enough to duck and thus avoid being decapitated – my father, however, was knocked clean into the water. Immediately the men cut loose in order to rescue him, leaving only the second boat now attached. Of course, our attention was on our poor father; even from this distance, we could see him urging them to row on as he bobbed in the water. His men pulled him back into the boat, and they at once set to rowing to recapture their fearsome quarry.

The whale had meanwhile headed directly for the nearest cliffs, for its intention seemed to be to drive its tormentors onto the rocks. The speed and wildness of the boat's ride as it was towed along behind reminded me of our own experience with the runaway carriage, even to the last-minute swerve executed by the whale. This manoeuvre propelled the hapless second boat headlong onto a rocky outcrop, from which a group of dozing terns rose up in a startled fashion – the boat then slid wildly across the rocks before becoming wedged in a crevice. A strange sight indeed: a landlocked whaleboat with its full crew aboard, its headsman standing at the bow, all looking about in a bewildered fashion. Freed of its burden, the whale headed directly for the open sea, two harpoons rising out of its flesh, fifty fathoms of rope trailing after it. And here at last, just as it all seemed utterly hopeless, the Killers finally made their appearance.

Where had they been? Why had they not participated in any of the preceding chase, which had been underway for over an hour, and crisscrossed much of the bay? Why had they waited till this last desperate moment, when both boats had been forced to cut loose? It was as if they were a troupe of vainglorious actors, waiting for the moment of greatest dramatic effect in order to make their grand entrance. All along the headlands, cheers rose up as those beloved of all dorsal fins revealed themselves, to which the Killers responded by throwing their bodies jubilantly out of the water like tumblers in a Royal Court. Here was Hooky, with Cooper leering cheerfully alongside; there was Humpy breaching and Charlie Adgery and Jackson and so on. Best of all, though, was to see the determined and portly form of Tom, up to his usual antics, with no sign of any ill-effects from the firing of the bomb lance. Perhaps he had simply been nursing a dull headache, and laid low for a while.

After announcing their arrival in this fashion and receiving the ovation they considered their due, the Killers immediately set to work. From here on, amidst the flurry of black fins and white water, it became a great deal more difficult to determine exactly what was happening. Clearly their modus operandi was to contain the whale's progress in order that my father and his men gain sufficient proximity that he might employ the lance, and the gleeful enthusiasm with which they set about the task reminded me of nothing so much as the time that the Bega football team had annihilated Eden in the semi-finals. Bega were the longstanding champions with a reputation for thuggishness; for some reason, possibly owing to being dairy farmers, they were twice the size of our lads and much faster on the field. (Also, their home ground was situated on a hillside, causing visiting teams immense difficulties in having to kick uphill towards the goalposts.) The ease with which they outclassed their opponents was such that they played with a kind of ruthless gaiety, shouting out jokes and pet names for one another, jumping up in the air and spontaneously embracing whenever another goal went through the posts. The delight they took in their play and in one another was not appealing; it was sickening, for it was at the expense of our own boys. The game ended 47–1, with the Eden lads incurring some serious injuries (Harry was amongst them; he had several toes broken when one of his boots came off in the mud and a Bega boy stomped on his foot).

I felt the same sick feeling now as we watched the Killers at work. Their amiable snub-nosed appearance seemed at stark odds with their viciousness; the poor dumb whale was no match for these warriors. Briefly, the embattled leviathan rose up out of the water, rolling its great girth in a bid to shake them free, only to be pulled back down again by the Killers hanging on to its side fins. If it tried to dive, the Killers would dive beneath it and push it back up; if it tried to surface for air, a Killer would leap atop its blowholes and push it down again. Curlicues of crimson appeared amidst the foam. Worst of all, rising up from the water came the most terrible sound – at first we did not understand what we were hearing: the piteous bellowing of the hounded whale.

The men of the first boat rowed gamely (the second boat still wedged upon its rocks) and Arthur Ashby wasted no time in fastening on to the whale again. So sustained was the Killers' attack that the whale had now practically come to a standstill, allowing my father the opportunity to apply his lance. Drawing the weapon up high, he plunged the lance deep into the poor creature; oh, a hideous sight to see. If only once had done it, but again and again he plunged his lance, and each time the heartless crowd cheered as if watching a prize-fighter pummelling his opponent in a boxing tent. The dreadful bellows grew more anguished, its last feeble spouts turned red. 'Stop it!' I heard someone cry, and turning around, I realised it was Louisa, tears streaming down her face. 'Stop it! Make him stop!' (I will say in my father's defence that I believe his frenzy of lancing was born of an urge to expedite the whale's demise and minimise its suffering.)

Mercifully, the poor creature's ordeal ended shortly thereafter and the great body lay lifeless on the surface of the bloodstained sea. Mr Winston, the customs officer, offered me his telescope, and somewhat gingerly I peered through it. There I saw the whale men, bloody and triumphant, slapping each other on the back and shaking hands. The crowds on the headlands offered up a rousing three cheers, and the men turned and waved their caps in response; all except my father. He was leaning over the gunwale, and as I watched, he reached out to touch the fin of a Killer whale swimming close by. It was Tom's fin, I feel sure of that, for I saw that knob on its trailing edge. It was a brief gesture, like a handshake or a pat on the back, a simple moment of acknowledgement between two generals, but done with quiet affection, for my father esteemed Tom above all Killer whales and it would not surprise me if Tom held my father in similar regard. After this brief exchange, my father turned to the men; I could see from his gestures that he was urging them to waste no time in securing the carcass with anchors and marker buoys. They could ill-afford to delay, for the Killers were impatient; it was a matter of barely three minutes before they had pulled the carcass down below.

A Lonely Killer, He

T HINKING ABOUT MY FATHER'S DEEP AFFECTION FOR THE Killer whale Tom, I include in this memoir the following obituary which appeared in the *Eden Magnet*, 20 September 1930, on the sad occasion of Tom's passing.

'*Old Tom: The Last of the Killer Whales is Dead*

For a century or more, there's been whaling – now there's wailing – at Twofold Bay. "Old Tom", the last of the famous pack of Twofold Bay Killer whales, is dead. On Wednesday morning, under the influence of favouring breeze and tide, his body, unheralded, came floating gently in to rest in the bay which had been the killer's battlefield and the scene of many memorable exploits during the last hundred years or more of Eden's history. Old Tom had died at sea a day or two previously, and kind Nature had sent his body drifting in to be disposed of as might seem fit to his allies of old.

It was only last week that Old Tom was disporting off Leonards Island, in the vicinity of which he had caught a grampus, and he was commemorating the event with a display of unusual vivacity. What happened to bring about his demise is a matter of mere conjecture. Master whaler George Davidson does not know and, although he made a post-mortem superficial examination of the body, could form no opinion satisfactory to himself as to the cause of the centenarian's untimely death.

Of Old Tom's sagacity and many deeds of daring there are many yarns extant, but if anyone wants the true version there are few persons to whom one can with confidence apply, and one is master whaler George Davidson, otherwise known as "Fearless George".

Of the old "Orca Gladiator", last of the Twofold Bay killer whales – Old Tom – renowned in war – it may be said that his end was peace, and that he dies regretted by all who knew him.'

There also appeared – on the front page the following week – this poem entitled '*Old Tom*', by Eden's poet laureate, Tom Browne:

'For eighty years or more, Old Tom has whaled off Twofold Bay,
And many a humpback met its fate when passing down this way.
There's "Fearless George" and Aleck Greig who live to tell the tale
Of how the veteran helped them well with many a vicious whale.
And now his carcass lies afloat on peaceful Twofold Bay
Whose waters he so oft has roamed in conflict and in play.
His mates have long since passed away; a lonely Killer, he
Has gone at last to well-earned rest – the whaler's home from sea.'

I don't suppose that there are many fish who could reasonably expect an obituary of several hundred words and a poem dedicated to their memory featuring prominently in the local newspaper. But as I think I have already established, Tom was not like any other fish (or cetacean, to be more accurate); for one thing, he was braver and smarter than most men and, for another, he was more loyal than any dog. I know we are all inclined to eulogise the Dead, but looking back at earlier chapters, I see that I have made much of Tom's undoubtedly more annoying qualities; his impatience at what I suppose he perceived to be petty bureaucracy (the attaching of marker buoys to the whale carcass and so forth), his hooligan antics with the towing of fishing boats and his high jinks with the whale line. But since I am taking this opportunity to mark his passing – and it hit us very heavily at the time, more heavily than even the disbanding of the whaling station and the forced sale of equipment several years earlier – I would prefer to concentrate on his more noble qualities, for there were many of them. He served faithfully as my father's lieutenant year after year as our fortunes waxed and waned; he respected their unspoken agreement, and could always be relied upon to uphold his end of the bargain. Every winter to the end, even when my father had given up whaling, Tom kept returning to Twofold Bay – such was his sense of duty, perhaps unusual amongst his kin, for certainly the rest of the Killers had long stopped coming. Occasionally, as of old times, he would flop-tail at the bar, in an attempt to entice my father out. My father, of course, would drop everything, scrounge together a crew of whoever happened to be about, and off they would go joyously on a whale chase.

Searching for a fitting way of commemorating this friendship, my father settled on the idea of preserving Tom's skeleton, and he towed his body back to the try-works in order to carry out the necessary work himself. How tenderly did he flense Tom of his blubber, and how carefully did he boil his bones. One morning, as I tended to the washing, I heard him calling me down to the try-works; there was something he wished to show me. He had Tom's skull before him on the workbench, and was engaged in the task of polishing his teeth with a rag and some bicarbonate of soda. The skull was long in snout and startlingly prehistoric in appearance; it looked as if it might have been better suited to a crocodile or a dinosaur. The front teeth on both the upper and lower jaws were worn to stumps or broken off; they spoke of a hard life and a great deal of adventure. Only the teeth on the sides of his jaws were of normal length, and here my father pointed to a particular tooth towards the back on the lower left-hand side. There could be seen distinctly a pronounced groove, as if worn down by the repeated friction of a rope; clearly the legacy of his exploits hanging off the whale line. It was a remarkable sight, for the groove was so deep it had practically worn through the tooth; such was the force with which he had been towed through the water in those whaling days of yore. How his antics had annoyed the whalers; such briny epithets as were hurled at his gleaming head! I reached out to feel the smoothness of the hollow, and looked up at my father; he was smiling at me, his eyes shining. We had only Tom's skeleton to remember him by, and yet this rope-furrowed tooth spoke of his very essence, of the foolhardy, reckless and mischievous fish he had been.

Uncle Aleck Takes the Cure

EXTRAORDINARY AS IT MAY SEEM, GIVEN THAT WE WERE the daughters of George Davidson, master whaler, the capture of this southern right was the first whale capture we had ever witnessed, and it is fair to say that we were greatly shaken by the ghastly brutality of it all. The heart-rending bellows of the poor tormented beast seemed to echo around the cliffs and reverberate in our very rib cages. To see this noble creature slaughtered by our own kith and kin was very difficult for us, and we found ourselves unable to respond with any civility to the hearty congratulations that were heaped upon us in the aftermath. Louisa wept openly on the cliff top and would not be consoled by anybody, though many tried, nor even by the thought that we would now be able to pay for the provisions Mr Howard had just refused us; perhaps even, I suggested (feeling it advisable not to mention the ivory crepe de Chine), the pink crinkle marocain that had looked so becoming against her fair complexion.

Upon our return home, she would have nothing to do with any of the whalers – even, I noted, Darcy – but most of her fury she reserved for my father.

For myself, I was not so much angry with my father as stunned that I had formerly been so naive and unquestioning. What had I imagined happened out there? How had I imagined these whales met their deaths? Had I imagined that they passed away delicately of shock like the diamond dove fledgling I had once rescued from the cat? For although I understood in principle the technicalities of whaling – the harpooning, the chase to exhaustion, the necessity of a swift and vigorous lancing – I had never conceived, never understood, never imagined for one moment the horror of it all. Only now did I understand why John Beck had returned from his first whale capture straining to recall that passage from the Bible. I imagine he was trying to find some way to live with what he had just witnessed.

Of course, my father was much too busy to notice – let alone tend to – the more fragile sensibilities of his daughters. The whale proved to be one of the largest black whales ever captured in Twofold Bay. Fortunately the weather remained mild, and when it gassed up a day or so later, it was towed home without incident. It measured fifty-seven feet to the tail tips; its whalebone eight feet in length, and the blubber at its thickest almost sixteen inches deep. It was so large that a channel three feet deep had to be dug at low tide to stop it running aground on the sandy bottom. When finally it was dragged close enough to the try-works, the flensing of blubber commenced, a process that required almost two full days of the most backbreaking labour. Once the flensing was complete, a deep hole was cut into the remaining pile of putrefying flesh and Uncle Aleck duly inserted up to his head, so that the lower part of his body sank down into the whale's intestines.

'How are you feeling, Uncle?' asked Dan, whose job it was to watch him and ensure he did not pass out from the tremendous heat of the fermenting whale.

'I feel like I am roasting in the furnace of eternal damnation, lad, so shut your smart mouth. How long have I been in?'

'Forty minutes,' said Dan, checking Uncle Aleck's pocket watch.

'Is that all? Christ! I will surely die in here and then you will all be happy!'

I noticed that John Beck had emerged from the try-works and was observing this spectacle with some bewilderment. After a while, unable to contain his curiosity, he wandered over to where I sat peeling potatoes for the evening meal.

'Would you mind telling me what your uncle is doing buried up to his head in a dead whale?' he enquired.

'Well, he is what they call "taking the cure".'

'I see,' said John Beck. 'Cure for what, in particular?'

'Cure for rheumatism. You will find him remarkably sprightly when he emerges.'

John Beck stood there a moment, absorbing this information, while I cast furtive glances at him. He had his shirt unbuttoned and his sleeves rolled up, and his forearms were glistening with whale oil.

'How is it supposed to work exactly, this cure?' he asked eventually.

'Oh, well, I think it is something to do with the fermenting gases. Or maybe the heat and the oil. Anyway, it is very beneficial, if you have the lumbago. Although sometimes it can require several immersions.'

'I see.'

'Unfortunately, it can be rather difficult to remove the smell of putrefying whale meat afterwards.'

'From his clothes, do you mean?'

'Oh no, he is not wearing any clothes. If he was, he would have to burn them, for the smell can never be removed.'

'Yet I note he is still wearing his hat?'

We both turned now to gaze at Uncle Aleck. It did seem an odd choice, superfluous somehow, to wear a hat while immersed bodily in a dead whale, but there you have it, that was Uncle Aleck, standing on his dignity at all times. It seemed he may now have had enough, for he was bellowing to be pulled out. Several of the men hoisted him out (not easily, for the whale's grisly innards seemed to have a suction-like grip on him) and mercifully covered his scrawny nakedness with a blanket. He waded limply through the shallows, dripping bodily fluids and entrails, with Dan hovering close by lest he collapse. Various whale men stood about at a distance, offering derisive comments and laughing uproariously. Even the normally amiable Bonnie skulked away as he approached, her tail between her legs.

'Would you give me a dance at the ball, Mary?' asked John Beck, all of a sudden.

'Are you going to the ball?' I asked.

'Yes. Aren't you?'

'Yes, of course.' The capture of the black whale had meant that this was now possible; however, our father had not been persuaded to relent on the subject of new dresses. Our fortunes had improved, but not to the extent of moss-green georgette and pink crinkle marocain.

'It's only that I thought Methodists didn't approve of dancing,' I said.

'Ah well,' he said, making a kind of grimace. 'Maybe I'm not really a Methodist.'

I stared at him. What an odd and surprising man he was proving to be. What had been the excuse that he had once proffered for his changeability? That's right: he was troubled by a kind of restlessness. He was in search of the 'ungraspable phantom of life'.

'In fact, I can't be a Methodist,' he continued. 'I dance too well to be a Methodist.'

'Are you a Presbyterian or something?' I asked.

'I don't think so. Do they dance?'

'No. At least, not terribly well.'

'I see. Well. Perhaps I'm just an oarsman in the Number Two boat.' He looked at me now with a smile. 'Does that sound all right to you?'

I nodded, for my mouth had become suddenly tremendously dry so that I was forced to swallow.

'I will be having a bath, so I don't smell of whale oil,' he added.

Again, I nodded, having apparently lost all ability to form words.

'And Mary,' he said, earnestly, 'if I was to pretend I'm unconscious, do you think you might feel inclined to kiss me again?'

To which I responded readily: 'You will not need to pretend you are unconscious.'

'There, you bantered!' he said. 'You see, you are very good at it.'

He smiled at me then, and a strange, miraculous feeling seemed to overcome me. I watched him ambling back towards the try-works; along the way, he passed Uncle Aleck, who was staggering up towards the house, muttering to himself and clutching his blanket around him. There was a brief exchange between the pair of them, and I remember John Beck threw back his head and laughed, even slapping Uncle Aleck on the back in a good-natured fashion. And remembering how I sat there, potatoes on my lap, my heart bursting with happiness and hope, I realise that all I have achieved in writing this memoir is to reopen a great wound that has taken a very long time to heal over.

Louisa

AS MENTIONED IN THE PREVIOUS CHAPTER, LOUISA HAD BEEN greatly distressed by the killing of the whale, and vowed to have nothing further to do with any of the whalers, whom she referred to as 'a pack of murderers'. By all indications, this included Darcy. Certainly they appeared to have no contact with each other – I know, for I made it my business to keep a close eye upon the pair. Louisa kept herself up in the house and only grudgingly assisted in the preparation of the whalers' meals (which in itself was not unusual), insisting that Dan help me carry down the pots lest one of the 'murderers' should affront her by wandering into her field of sight.

Robert Heffernan came knocking at the back door to ask Louisa if she might give him a dance at the ball, to which she responded bluntly that she would never dance with a whale slaughterer, now or ever. At this, Robert remonstrated that he had only rowed the boat, and not very well at that; she had only to ask Salty, who had called him a 'bl---y incompetent'. Louisa, however, could not be cajoled. She kept to herself, and spoke little to anyone. Our father she referred to as 'George Davidson, master murderer'. When he entered a room, she got up and walked out of it.

For his part, Darcy, normally so full of quips and merriment, now seemed subdued and withdrawn. After several days of having had no sighting of Louisa, he finally asked me if she was sick. 'No, just bad-tempered,' I replied, for her mood was becoming tiresome. Also, I thought it unfair that she was so hard on my father, who after all was only trying to provide for his family. I explained to Darcy that she was upset about the whale, and if she kept to her usual form, would likely get over it in a week or so. He seemed to accept this response but, as I say, he seemed subdued. Like Louisa, he kept to himself.

On about the fifth night after the whale capture, around the same time as John Beck had asked me if I would dance with him, I awoke and realised that the bed beside me was empty. At once, I felt a sickening lurch of my belly; *She has done it*, I thought, *she has run off with Darcy.* And as I lay there imagining various awful scenarios, yet too paralysed with dread to get up and go and look for her, I suddenly heard from the front garden the shrill, infuriated cries of Mr Maudry. Only a few short moments later, the door of our room opened softly and Louisa slipped back into bed alongside me. Feigning sleep, I affected to fling an arm out; sure enough, her skin was cool to the touch, which indicated that she had been outside for possibly some time. I realise now, of course, that she was undoubtedly returning from a clandestine rendezvous with Darcy, in which a great many things had been discussed, arrangements put in place and so forth. But so convinced had I been by her act, by her avowal that she would have nothing to do with any whalers, and so preoccupied was I with my own thoughts of John Beck and the upcoming ball, that I chose not to dwell on the possibilities but simply elected to put the whole business out of my mind. It is highly unlikely, I told myself, if not impossible, that she would ever do such a thing. Had she not told me herself that she had simply been joking?

The next day her mood was greatly improved. She was civil to my father at breakfast; she even braided the younger ones' hair in the popular fishbone style, and willingly helped me with the usual chores. One incident, however, stands out to me now as significant. We had pulled our cretonne dresses out of the trunk to see what we could do by way of enlivening their appearance for the ball. After some experimentation, we decided that my green floral cretonne could be improved if we trimmed the neckline with a small quantity of lace removed from an old blouse of my mother's. I also suggested that Louisa's pink floral cretonne could be brought up to date if we removed the spangled netting from my mother's good hat and arranged it in a fashion at the bodice. At first, Louisa had seemed very tempted by the idea, but as she passed the veil netting between her fingertips, she seemed to change her mind. 'No, it doesn't matter,' she said. 'Let's leave it. I don't mind it as it is.'

This was most unlike my sister, and in itself ought to have been enough to alarm me.

'Well, then,' I suggested, 'you could have the lace trimming, and I could use the spangled netting.'

'No,' said Louisa promptly. 'You use the lace as it suits the green cretonne.'

'It will suit your pink cretonne just as well.'

'No, I have made up my mind. You use the lace, and I will wear my pink cretonne just as it is.'

As I say, this degree of unselfishness was unusual for Louisa. But perhaps, as I reasoned at the time, this was a long-awaited sign of her growing maturity.

The next night, I feigned sleep in the hope that I might catch her sneaking out on another of her midnight assignations. But instead she fell asleep promptly (I could tell by the rhythm of her breathing) and so I fell asleep also, and the pair of us slept through till morning undisturbed. The night after that, however, I awoke from a deep sleep to find her climbing back into bed. When I questioned her, she responded: 'What are you blathering on about? I was just using the potty. Go back to sleep.'

Yet even as I write these words, I am struck by how plainly obvious it all was, and I wonder at myself that I did nothing except vaguely hope that the dark storm clouds that seemed to be gathering might blow away of their own accord. Knowing Louisa as I did, I should have recognised the unlikelihood of this, for she had always been an obstinate, pig-headed girl, determined to have her own way. And perhaps that is the real reason why I did nothing: I knew in my heart that there would be no stopping her.

The Plain and Fancy Dress Ball

I F YOU COULD HAVE SEEN HOW PRETTY OUR SCHOOL OF ARTS
looked, its walls festooned with white clematis blossoms and
gardenias, so different from its usual sombre municipal self!
Immediately I wished that, in matters of costume, Louisa and I
had not settled so readily for 'plain', for certainly the townsfolk of
Eden had embraced the more imaginative option. Everywhere you
looked there seemed to be a picturesque tableau. In one corner,
Pierrot chatted with a bearded Viking; in another, a Japanese Maid
smiled coquettishly behind her fan in the company of a dusky Rajah.
Eunice Martin came garbed as a Christmas Lily, draped head to toe
in Louisa's coveted ivory crepe de chine, for which she won the prize
for 'Best-Sustained Character – Lady'. I realise I may seem churlish
whenever Eunice Martin wins an unwarranted prize, but many of
us considered privately that a more deserving recipient was Elspeth
Gilbert, who put together a very humorous interpretation of 'What

Percy Picked Up in the Park', or indeed Miss Watkins as 'Bermagui Meat Supplies', with a chain of lifelike sausages draped about her neck. (Apparently, she was excluded from consideration because it was decided she was more of an Advertisement than a Character – her father is the actual proprietor of Bermagui Meat Supplies – and this was felt to be spoiling the tone of the evening. The Watkins left the ball shortly after the prize-giving, Miss W. in tears.) Mr Strickland Senior practically brought the house down as the Old Witch, chasing after the children with his broomstick and screaming curses (which was not greatly different from his usual behaviour, admittedly), and for this he won 'Best-Sustained Character – Gentleman', before passing out quietly in the bushes out the back.

Annie

At least the children had entered into the spirit of things – Violet came as a Housemaid in apron and lace cap and carrying a feather duster, and Annie as 'Mary, Mary, Quite Contrary', for which a basket of flowers, a watering can and her customary scowl was all that was required. Harry and Robert Heffernan came as Cricketers, which was not so very clever as they simply wore their cricket whites and leaned about nonchalantly on their bats, as if in the unlikely scenario of waiting for a six to be retrieved from the back of the grandstand. Dan, however, came dressed as the Major of the Artillery, sporting his Salvation Army cap, a painted-on moustache, a riding crop and my father's spyglass; this combined with the authentic manner in which he sucked on his clay pipe ensured that he won 'Best Sustained Character – Boy', much to the Davidson family's delight.

After the Grand March and the prize-giving, the dancing began in earnest. Music for the evening was provided by the Powers family on piano, violin, cornet and tambourine, and with Mr Oslington as MC they galloped through a selection of popular dance numbers. Borax powder had been sprinkled liberally on the dance floor, rendering it dangerously slippery in patches, but this did not deter the scores of dancers, of which none were sprightlier than our own Uncle Aleck. Thanks to the whale cure, he was reeling Louisa about the room with the vigour of a man many years his junior.

'I wonder if I should rescue your sister,' said John Beck, glancing over at them. Louisa certainly looked quite flushed in the face, and had I known what I now know of her condition at the time, perhaps I would have shown a little more sympathy.

'Oh no, she adores it,' I replied. 'The faster the waltz the better. She wouldn't dream of changing partners, not for anything.'

I was fast to John Beck and not going to cut loose if I could help it. It was true, he danced far too well to be a Methodist; certainly he danced far better than the rest of us. Most of us had been forced to acquire what dancing skills we possessed from intensive study of Mrs Chas. Read's *Australian Ballroom Guide*, available for loan from the School of Arts. Louisa and I had struggled at length over the years with her bewildering directions and schematic diagrams, but they simply made no sense no matter which way up you held the book. And yet, in spite of the squabbling she caused at the time, Mrs Chas. Read became one of our greatest sources of family merriment.

If ever we read in the newspaper of some wretched soul's misfortune, we would say, 'I see how Mrs Chas. Read has got drunk again and gone at her landlady with a carving knife,' or, 'I see how Mrs Chas. Read has mixed too much laudanum in her hop beer and been taken to hospital with the nerve trouble'. In our minds, the only possible explanation for her bewildering instructions was that she was either drunk or imbibing opium at the time of writing.

Like most Edenites, we were reasonably competent in the Spot Waltz, the Jolly Miller and the Progressive Barn Dance, but any attempts to conduct an orderly Quadrille descended into confusion and arguments. People were forever adding new parts half remembered from other dances or leaving out entire sections altogether. John Beck was clearly used to higher standards, for he became somewhat terse on several occasions with those other dancers who stood in his path saying, 'What's this bit? Oh! I see! Too late! Should we be –? Oh – sorry! Beg your pardon!' For the most part, I simply clung to him, and when separated in the Quadrille, I made small skipping steps as best I could in time with the music.

The Quadrille having finished, John Beck led me over to the refreshment stalls, past Salty and Bastable, all spruced up with their beards combed and their wisps of hair plastered over their scalps, sitting on the bench eyeing us wistfully. They had placed orange blossoms in their buttonholes in an attempt to mask any remnant of whale smell, but the delicate flowers appeared to have wilted.

Dan had won five shillings as Best-Sustained Character and, filled with largesse, had decided to treat his little sisters to some lollies. Now they held up the queue at the confectionery stall as they contemplated the vast display, seeming to find the choice overwhelming. Violet loved coconut ice, but she equally loved jujubes.

Annie could not choose between Turkish delight and chocolate cara-
mels. Dan was becoming irritated and could be heard threatening
to withdraw his offer if they did not bl---y hurry up about it. How
often one's attempts to behave generously are thwarted, and so often
because of the ungrateful attitude of the intended recipient(s). At the
refreshments stall, I found myself faced with a similar, bewildering
array of choice. The Persian Princess behind the counter eyed John
Beck with interest from behind her spangled veil and why shouldn't
she? John Beck was plainly the handsomest man in the room. Not
wishing to dally longer than was necessary, I selected a blackberry
cordial; a hasty choice and perhaps not the wisest, as it was found to
stain one's lips and not necessarily in a becoming manner. I was not
aware of this until Louisa joined us, having at last broken free from
Uncle Aleck.

'What's the matter with your mouth?' she asked. 'Did somebody
punch you?'

Nonetheless, taking the cordial from my hands, she helped
herself to it freely, for dancing with Uncle Aleck was thirsty work.
Meanwhile, I rubbed at my mouth with a bit of spit on a hankie,
until John Beck assured me that the blackberry stain was 'barely
noticeable'.

'We have to do something about Uncle Aleck,' said Louisa,
having sufficiently quenched her thirst (oddly, the blackberry cordial
left her lips with merely a delicate blush). 'He smells abominable.
Everyone is starting to notice.'

'Surely he's harmless enough,' I said magnanimously. 'Besides,
the whole room smells a little ripe.'

'He smells of *fermenting whale gizzards*,' said Louisa. 'You try it
and see how you like it.'

My time had come, for even as she spoke Uncle Aleck was upon us, tapping at my shoulder. Off I went to face my fate. Robert Heffernan seized the opportunity to approach Louisa once more to ask if she would do him the great honour of accompanying him in the Waltz.

'All right,' she said grimly.

'Gosh, this floor's slippery!' cried Robert as they danced past us. 'It's hard to keep on your feet, isn't it?'

'Oh, I see,' observed Louisa coolly. 'You're deliberately trying to step on my feet, are you? I thought it was merely accidental.'

She made a point of dancing with anyone who asked that night, no doubt in a bid to throw us off the scent. And what else could she do, for she could not dance with Darcy. He sat out the front of the School of Arts with my father and the rest of the whale crew, enjoying the balmy evening and the water views. In fact, a great many of the menfolk of Eden ended up sprawled outside on the grassy slopes. It seems they had secreted their bottles of liquor here and there amongst the bushes.

'Mary,' said Mrs Pike, taking hold of my arm as I lurched dizzily off the dance floor after several rounds with Uncle Aleck, 'where's your father? Won't you encourage him to come inside and have a dance with me?'

'All right,' I said, and I went outside to find him. In truth, I was hoping also to find John Beck, as he seemed to have disappeared for the moment.

My father was in the middle of telling his snake and umbrella story, and so I stood about, shifting my weight from one foot to the other, waiting for him to finish. In essence, it was not a complicated story, but my father paused so often in the telling, remembering small details that he should have mentioned earlier or becoming sidetracked by other unrelated thoughts, that the story went on far longer than it deserved to. It concerned a man who had fallen asleep in the bush, and upon waking up to find it raining, opened his umbrella. It felt rather stiff going up and there was a terrible tearing sound, and suddenly a black snake fell to the ground, split in two from head to tail.

Now while I was waiting for my father to get to the end of his anecdote, I glanced around, wondering where John Beck had got to, when suddenly I espied him, standing in the shadows beneath the mulberry trees. He appeared to be in earnest discussion with someone I could not immediately identify, for this person's back was towards me. I would not have seen them at all, had not a party of ball-goers walked past them, lanterns in hand, and momentarily illuminated them. The other person appeared to be doing most of the talking while John Beck listened intently but with some concern, for his hands were deep in his pockets and he appeared to be slowly shaking his head. The lanterns passed and the two of them plunged into darkness again; in some bewilderment, I turned my attention back to my father.

'You see, it had swallowed the umbrella whole, except for the handle,' my father was saying in triumphant conclusion. And at that moment it struck me with absolute clarity that the person John Beck had been talking to was Darcy, for certainly Darcy was not part of the group of whale men that sat around now, laughing appreciatively at my father's story.

I interrupted the general merriment to tell my father that he had been specifically requested as a dance partner by none other than Mrs Pike, the proprietress of the Great Southern. With a show of bashful reluctance, he rose somewhat unsteadily to his feet and accompanied me back inside.

'Tell us, Mary,' Darcy's father, Percy, called after me, 'how are Salty and Bastable faring in there? Have they had any luck in their wooing?'

'Since you ask, I did notice Salty in the company of a lady,' I said with a smile, to which the whale men responded with ribald glee. In fact, I had seen Salty 'tripping the light fantastic' with the widow Mrs Guthridge; he was surprisingly nimble on his feet for a portly man, and conducted himself very reasonably in the Country Dance. Now it was my father's turn to join them, with Mrs Pike on his arm. He was too stiff-legged to dance well, yet nonetheless he cut a commanding figure. He held himself very upright – 'like dancing with a plank of hardwood,' is how Louisa described it – with a look of fierce concentration on his face, moving his lips as he counted. Regardless, Mrs Pike seemed well-pleased to be in his arms and circling the dance floor.

It was soon midnight, and supper was called; all available hands were summoned to assist. There was tea and coffee to be brewed in four-gallon buckets; cold meat and mustard pickle and fish-paste sandwiches to be served, and sponge cakes (light as air!) to be sliced.

'Where is your sister?' asked Robert Heffernan, who was suddenly standing over me as I attempted to daintily arrange some sandwiches on a serving platter. It seemed he may have had a bit to drink as he was somewhat flushed in the face. 'Have you seen her?'

'No, not recently,' I responded. 'She is here somewhere, I'm sure.'

'Oh, do you mean Louisa?' asked Elspeth Gilbert cheerfully. 'I saw her outside just before with one of the blackfellows.'

'One of the blackfellows?' I cried. 'How peculiar.'

My heart thudded in my chest, for I noted Robert's colour rising.

'I think she may have been taking the poor fellow something to drink, that's all,' continued Elspeth. 'She has always been a thoughtful and considerate lass, taking after your mother in that way,' she added.

Thoughtful and considerate! I thought to myself indignantly. If anything, I was the thoughtful and considerate member of the family, the one that took most after my mother. Why was everyone so inclined to bestow upon Louisa virtues she did not possess? Mind you, it had not occurred to me to take any beverages out to our Aboriginal whale crew, but then that was because our whale men generally looked after themselves in the matter of beverages. It has to be said they would not have greeted my offering them a cordial with much enthusiasm.

'If I were you, I would take your sister in hand,' muttered Robert Heffernan ominously. 'She is in danger of making herself a laughing-stock.' And with that, he moved away before I could think of a worthy retort.

'Well, he is certainly the moody type,' commented Elspeth. 'I imagine he is jealous, over such a petty thing as your sister giving a blackfellow a drink of cordial!'

The conversation changed to the more pressing need of locating more teaspoons so that people might be able to add their own sugar to their tea; Elspeth went off in search of some. I was instructed to take my plate of sandwiches and offer them to anyone who could show their entry ticket, thus easing the crush around the supper table. I set off in hope of coming across John Beck, for I fancied the thought of settling down with him in a darkened corner, perhaps sharing a fish-paste sandwich. However, I had no sooner emerged from the kitchen than I was waylaid by Salty, beckoning me over with some urgency to where he sat with Mrs Guthridge. As I advanced upon them with my plate, I was surprised to hear that Mrs Guthridge appeared to be labouring under the misapprehension that Salty had been, in a former life, a minister of the Methodist church.

'May I ask, what then compelled you to leave?' she enquired, an expression of intense fascination upon her face.

Here Salty passed a hand through his beard and affected a sombre expression, as with his other hand he reached out and grasped several sandwiches from my proffered plate.

'Temptation,' he said finally.

'Temptation?'

'That and a certain ... *susceptibility*.'

Glancing up to find me staring at him in frank astonishment, he broke off and popped a sandwich into his mouth, chewing away vigorously with his few remaining teeth. Just then, an unpleasantness broke out at the supper table; some riffraff had got in without paying and were helping themselves to the cakes and sandwiches. When they were remonstrated with by Mrs Atcherley, one smart alec issued an insolent riposte before flinging a sandwich at Robert Heffernan, who happened to be standing at other end of the supper table, broodingly stuffing his face. Robert howled indignantly and returned fire with a lamington. At once, merry hell broke loose; all available menfolk jumped into the fray to 'sort it out', including my brother Harry. The men who had been drinking outside came hurtling in as reinforcements; punches were thrown indiscriminately, women screamed, china was broken and one hapless Edenite was thrown against the tea urn, thus knocking it over and setting hot tea and tea leaves all over the supper-room floor (miraculously, no one was scalded). The melee seemed to go on for a full five or ten minutes before order was once again restored; however, the supper table was the worse for it, and many tears were shed at the sight of flattened sponge cakes and lovingly prepared sandwiches squashed underfoot. The guilty parties (three young ne'er-do-wells from Pambula) were chased off into the night, whereupon it was later discovered that they must have returned at some point and loosened the wheels of various sulkies, for a number of unfortunate accidents ensued on the journey home. In some ways, however, the supper-room fracas provided a welcome distraction, for in all the excitement, amidst which he incurred a bloody nose, Robert Heffernan seemed to forget about Louisa and Darcy.

Once everything had settled down again and the supper room was put back to rights, some additional entertainment was provided. Mr Oslington attempted a humorous recitation of 'Sandy McGlashan's Courtship', but forgot too many of the words for it to be considered entirely successful. Mr O'Henessey sang 'The Little Irish Girl' to much laughter and applause, and after this our own Eden Christy Minstrel Club proceeded onto the stage. I at once recognised Mr Howard the Price-Cutter leering ominously at the audience, and immediately I resolved not to enjoy them. I did not so much as tap my foot during 'Oh, Dem Golden Slippers', but when they launched into 'My Old Kentucky Home, Good Night', the tears began, inexplicably, to roll down my cheeks.

'They hunt no more for the possum and the 'coon,
On meadow, the hill and the shore,
They sing no more by the glimmer of the moon,
On the bench by that old cabin door.
The day goes by like a shadow o'er the heart,
With sorrow where all was delight.
The time has come when the darkies have to part,
Then my old Kentucky home, good night.'

Perhaps I am more susceptible than others to the effects of a sentimental song, but for me at that moment, it was the humpback and the southern right that they hunted no more, and instead of the Kentucky home it was our little house at Kiah Inlet, and instead of just the darkies having to part, it was the whale men, it was all of us. For it was as if some small part of me sensed all the sadness and loss and disappointment and separation that awaited me. Dabbing futilely at my streaming eyes, I turned to Louisa (for she had suddenly reappeared by this time), expecting to see her similarly affected. But she just sat there with a scornful expression on her face, and when they left the stage to thunderous applause, she remarked, 'Thank goodness for that. I thought they'd go on all night.'

After the entertainment, there commenced a great washing up of the supper plates. Louisa and I were last on the roster, and so found it our duty to wash and dry every last cup and saucer in the building, a task which took us some time. When we had finally lowered our tea towels and removed our aprons, I suddenly discovered, nestling in the corner, a small blue and white teacup that we had somehow overlooked.

'Look, Louisa,' I cried, for I was thinking of our kitchen superstitions. 'If when washing dishes, you forget an item, it is a sign you will hear of a wedding! I haven't heard of any weddings tonight. Have you?'

'No,' said Louisa wearily, and mostly she just seemed annoyed about having to wash another cup. 'Here, I'll do it then,' I said, for a feeling of elation had overtaken me; I proceeded to wash and dry this little teacup with infinite care. You see, I was nurturing high hopes about this wedding I might hear of and, in particular, whose wedding it might be.

When I had finished, I stepped outside. The fat full moon hung suspended over Twofold Bay. The younger lads were out on the street playing cricket; Dan, still dressed as the Major of the Artillery, was arguing the point over a fallen wicket. Bodies lay about, snoring richly. I suppose somewhere in the darkness the ne'er-do-wells from Pambula were loosening the wheels of the sulkies. The whale men sat on the grass, exchanging fond reminiscences from the whaling season just past; someone offered up a toast to whaling season, 1909.

'And may it bring with it a great profusion of humpers!' cried Uncle Aleck.

'Hear, hear!' was the rallying response. But I could not see John Beck amongst their number, so I turned and headed back inside.

The Powers family had retired for the evening, and the last remaining dancers were left to rely upon the vagaries of Mr Aikenhead's drunken piano-playing. Having eaten a great many jujubes and run around madly all night, Violet and Annie slumped, sleepy and out of sorts, on the benches. I went over to join them; no sooner had I sat down than Violet rested her head on my lap and fell soundly asleep. It was then that I saw John Beck come in. He stood in the doorway, casting his gaze about the room, and as his eyes lit upon me, his features softened to a smile to which my heart thumped a joyful response.

'There you are,' he said as he sat down beside me. 'I've been looking for you.'

'I have been doing the washing up,' I said.

'The washing up,' he repeated, gazing at me earnestly. 'Yes. And I'm sure you would have performed the task admirably.'

'Well, I suppose so,' I responded hesitantly. The truth was that Louisa had had to pass back to me several cups from which I had failed to remove residual coffee stains. I had finally had to inform her that some of these marks appeared to be stains of long standing and were simply impossible to remove without resorting to vinegar and bicarbonate of soda, and frankly I had better things to do with my time whilst at the ball. Also, it struck me as something of the 'pot calling the kettle black', since her own washing up left a great deal to be desired and consisted mostly of dipping an item briefly in water and making a slight, half-hearted swirling motion.

'I daresay you have had a bit of practice over the years,' said John Beck, still looking at me intently. 'With the washing up, I mean.'

'Oh yes,' I responded, feeling somewhat bewildered. Why was he so interested in my washing up all of a sudden? Was it possible that men took such matters into consideration when evaluating a future wife? Could this possibly be some kind of preamble in that direction? 'I suppose I am rather good at it,' I added, after a moment's thought.

He nodded, as if satisfied by my response. He looked away briefly, deep in thought, and then he turned back to me.

'Mary –' he began, but suddenly Salty was upon us, all pink and shiny in the face.

'Father,' he hissed excitedly, 'do you have a psalm or a prayer you can lend me quickly? I took your advice, Father, and I think I'm in with a chance!'

Surreptitiously he indicated Mrs Guthridge, who sat on the bench near the door, nodding her head in time with the music.

'Oh. Well. Let me think,' responded John Beck. 'Was there any particular theme you had in mind?'

'No, Father. Just something of a biblical nature.'

'How about this?' John Beck suggested. '*Oh ye Whales and all that move in the water, bless ye the Lord and praise Him forever.*'

'That's perfect, Father!' cried Salty delightedly. 'How does it go again?'

'*Oh ye Whales –*'

'*Oh ye Whales,*' repeated Salty, his face a study of concentration.

'*And all that move in the water –*'

'Would that not be more effective if I was to say "swim" in the water, Father?'

'Well, yes, possibly, if you wish.'

'Not saying I can improve on the Bible, Father. It just rolls off the tongue better, is all. Go on.'

'*Bless ye the Lord and praise Him forever.*'

'That's it?'

'Well, it goes on about Fowls of the Air and the Beasts and the Cattle and so forth.'

'No, no. I can't be bothered with Fowls of the Air, nor the Beasts and the Cattle. Let them look after themselves. It's only the Whales I am interested in.'

'Well, then, there you have it.'

'Thank you, Father,' beamed Salty. 'It will do very nicely.'

'Good luck!'

'Yes, Father. And good luck to you also.' This last delivered with a broad wink, and a nod towards me. And with that, the self-proclaimed Professor of Whales hurried back to Mrs Guthridge.

'Sorry about that,' said John Beck, after a moment, turning back to me.

'That's all right,' I replied. 'But what did Salty mean exactly when he said he had taken your advice?'

'Oh, I don't know,' he responded, somewhat sheepishly. 'But for whatever reason, he appears to be pretending to be a Methodist minister.'

'Good heavens! Him too?' I riposted. 'It is practically an epidemic.'

At which he threw back his head and laughed. And leaning in towards me, he then suggested in a low voice that perhaps it would not be a bad idea to step outside and take some air, to which I agreed that yes, it was really quite stuffy in the hall. Prising Violet off my lap, I followed him out. And there ensued a short stroll in the moonlight, the details of which I shall keep entirely to myself, except to say there was no further talk of washing up; in fact, not much in the way of talking at all.

When To Marry

Marry when the year is new
Always loving, kind and true

When February birds do mate
You may wed, nor dread your fate

If you wed when March winds blow
Joy and sorrow both you'll know

Marry in April when you can
Joy for maiden and for man

Marry in the month of May
You will surely rue the day

Marry when June roses grow
Over land and sea you'll go

Those who in July do wed
Must labour always for their bread

Whoever wed in August be
Many a change are sure to see

Marry in September's shine
Your living will be rich and fine

If in October you do marry
Love will come, but riches tarry

If you are wed in bleak November
Only joy will come, remember

When December's snows fall fast,
Marry and true love will last!

(You will have to reverse the lines to make them appropriate to our
own seasons.)

EDEN OBSERVER AND SOUTH COAST ADVOCATE,
25 AUGUST 1905

If, When Washing Dishes

S OMETIME IN THE SMALL HOURS OF THE NEXT NIGHT – THAT is, the night after the Plain and Fancy Dress Ball – and as foretold somewhat obliquely by the blue and white teacup left unwashed – Darcy and Louisa ran away to be married. I awoke suddenly that morning to find Louisa's side of the bed cold and empty; immediately a sense of unease overtook me. Hastily I dressed, and as I hurried into the kitchen, I saw my father standing there with a note in his hands. His face was drained of all its colour and, without speaking, he thrust the note at me to read.

'*Dear Dad,*

Darcy and I are to be married. We love each other and wish to be together. DO NOT TRY TO FIND US OR KEEP US APART, I MEAN IT. Do not worry as we have some money and will be all right.

Your loving daughter,

Louisa'

'I can scarcely believe it!' I cried, and even as I did so, I was horrified at the falseness ringing out in my voice. My father looked up at me, and for a moment I feared he had detected the falseness also.

'Did you know about this?' he asked. I could barely stand to look at him, for his face was haggard with shock.

'No, I did not,' I responded. My father's grief was bad enough without having to admit to my own foreknowledge.

'Go and wake your brothers,' he said, turning away from me.

When the boys were woken, my father sent Dan to rouse the whalers, for his plan was to immediately send out a search party. But here Harry had a very strange response, for he refused to participate.

'She says in her note not to try to find her,' he said, and he went very red in the face because defiance of this kind did not come easily to him.

'Are you not concerned for her safety and wellbeing?' demanded my father.

'She has Darcy,' said Harry. 'Darcy will look after her.'

'Yes, but who will look after Darcy?' said Annie. (A curious thing happened upon Louisa's departure whereby Annie, just turned eleven years of age, dispensed with all the Whinny and horse-nonsense of her girlhood, and instead assumed Louisa's place as the smart mouth in the family. In some ways, this proved a comfort to my father, although in other ways was an annoyance.)

'Anyway, you are joining the search party, and that is the end of the matter,' said my father.

By this time, the whale men were all getting up, and there was much shouting and commotion and coming and going. My father went outside to speak to Darcy's father, Percy, who seemed very shocked and upset and kept shaking his head and wiping away tears with the back of his hand; others joined them and an earnest discussion ensued about the best way in which to tackle the search. I realised at this point that I could better assist matters by getting the stove lit quick-smart and putting the kettle on, and so I was busying myself with this task when I suddenly turned to see John Beck standing in the doorway of our kitchen. He looked somewhat bleary-eyed, as if he had just woken up, and he was gazing at my father apprehensively.

'You wanted to speak to me?' he asked.

'Yes. What do you know about this business?' said my father.

He passed Louisa's note to John Beck, who read it in silence before passing it back to my father.

'I don't know much,' he said. 'I'm sorry.'

'I saw you talking to Darcy outside at the ball,' said my father. 'That's why I ask.'

My heart started, for of course I realised he must be referring to the exchange in the shadows under the mulberry trees that I had myself witnessed. Perhaps it surprised John Beck too, for it took him a moment to answer.

'Well, it's true, sir. Darcy did tell me he was going to get married,' he said. 'But he did not say who to.'

'He told you he was going to get married?'

'He asked me if I might officiate. But I told him I could not, on account of my not being a proper Methodist minister.'

My father stared at him. 'Did you ask him who he was marrying?'

'No, I didn't. But I never suspected it was your daughter, sir. That's the honest truth. I never suspected for a moment.'

I had my back turned through most of this exchange, for I was now busily occupying myself with the making of damper, so I am not sure exactly what then transpired except it all went very quiet and when I turned around next, I saw that John Beck had in fact left the room. My father stood staring down at Louisa's note, and then a moment later he departed also, without a word, to join the search party.

The runaways had planned their escape with some thoroughness. Darcy had his small portion of the profits of the whaling season (not a very large amount, as can be imagined after such a season), and Louisa had her gold sovereign for winning Best-dressed and Most Prepossessing at the Eden Show. As well – I discovered after taking inventory of our supplies – they had taken half a loaf of bread, a box of matches, a portion of salted beef and some tea. As far as I could judge, however, they had not thought to take any sugar, and this grieved me more than anything, for Louisa had a sweet tooth and needed plenty of sugar in her tea. Dan went so far as to leave a small bowl of sugar on a tree stump at the very top of our property in the hope that they might venture back for it, but of course it just became infested with ants.

In spite of the best efforts of the search parties, it seems probable that the pair of them may have hidden out in the bush for several days before boarding the S.S. *Merimbula* and travelling as far as Sydney. Louisa may have disguised herself by wearing my mother's hat with the veil netting (hence her reluctance to use the veil as a trimming on her dress) and stuffing her other clothes under her coat so as to resemble a stouter person. A 'Miss Nicholson' was recorded in the steamer's log as purchasing a single ticket to Sydney; further, a crew member reports seeing a 'stout lady' in a coat and veiled hat sitting on deck, a sight that struck him as unusual owing to the heat of the day. He also stated that he thought he saw this woman disembark at Tathra, but he could not be sure. He only wished to state that he felt like he might have seen the 'stout lady' walking up towards the township from Tathra wharf in the company of a young Aboriginal boy who he considered to be about fourteen years of age. This was odd, because Darcy did not look like he was fourteen; he was a tall boy who looked his age, which was eighteen. Also, why would 'Miss Nicholson' go to the expense of purchasing a ticket all the way to Sydney only to disembark at Tathra? It made no sense. Years later, when the S.S. *Merimbula* ran aground off Bermagui, this same crew member was found to have been drinking below deck in the company of several women, so it is doubtful whether his story can be entirely relied upon.

Late on the morning of their disappearance, while most of the men were out combing the surrounding bushland in search of them, I stepped outside the kitchen and to my surprise saw John Beck standing there beneath the jacaranda tree. It appeared that he may have been preparing himself in some way, for he seemed startled, as if he was not quite yet ready for our encounter.

'Good morning,' I said, for in truth I was startled also. He stood in exactly the same position as had the old grey kangaroo who had regarded me so contemptuously on the morning of my mother's death. It was odd that I should think of this at that moment, but I did.

'Yes, good morning,' he responded.

'Are you off then with the others to go searching?'

'Yes, I believe we are shortly rowing into Eden.' At this, he turned his head suddenly, and again I was reminded of that old grey kangaroo. But it seemed he was simply checking to see that no one else was in earshot.

'I shouldn't worry,' he said quietly. 'If I were you.'

'Why not?' I responded, for it seemed such an odd thing to say, given the circumstances. As far as I could see, there were a great many things to worry about, whichever way you viewed the situation.

'It will be all right,' he said. 'I feel sure.' And he gave a small nod of his head, as if to reassure us both.

I stared at him. A flower, a small violet trumpet, drifted down between us from the jacaranda tree and, looking down, I saw that fallen flowers surrounded us where we stood. He looked down too. The flower had landed on his boot – he moved his foot impatiently, as if this was the last thing he needed at the present time, a flower on his boot, and then suddenly he spoke.

'Mary, I had been going to ask your father something, but now I find I cannot.'

'Why not?' I asked, for a strange constriction had gripped my heart.

'Circumstances have arisen,' he said. 'And so . . .'

'And so?'

'And so . . .'

We stood there for a moment, the two of us. Then he took my hand and he kissed it, and it seemed for a brief instant that he might be about to say something else. But he must have thought better of the idea, for instead he simply tipped his cap. He turned and headed off down the hill – and that is the last time I ever saw him, with Mr Maudry going after him, wings extended, shrieking shrilly.

A Letter From Louisa

SOME EIGHTEEN MONTHS AFTER SHE'D RUN AWAY WITH DARCY, a letter turned up from Louisa, quite out of the blue, addressed to me:

'*Dear Mary,*

I believe there is a story going about that Darcy and I were never legally married. Will you kindly inform those that seek to spread this muck that we were married by the Reverend John Beck (Methodist), and I have the documents to prove it, which I would be pleased to show anybody upon request. Certain people should spend more time minding their own business and looking after their own affairs than seeking to spread lies about others. I hope this letter finds you all in good health. We are exceedingly well and the parents of a fine fat boy (Albert George) expecting another any day now.

With fondest wishes to all, especially Dad,
Louisa
P.S. We have our own dog now, a cattle dog named Jack he is
100 times smarter than Bonnie or Patch.'

This was the first that we had heard from Louisa since their departure, and it is not untypical of her that she found the space within this brief missive to brag that her new dog was smarter than our own dogs. For some reason, miss her as I did, this boast infuriated me. What did I care about her smart dog? Perhaps Bonnie and Patch were not so very clever, but nor had we ever claimed them to be; still, they were nice enough dogs in their own way, and companionable to a fault. I felt the urge to write back immediately and ask if this Jack could sing along with 'Onward Christian Soldiers', but remembering Darcy's skills on the gum-leaf, the chances were that Jack could sing along, and in harmony. Besides which, Louisa had not thought to supply a return address.

The envelope, however, was postmarked Coonabarabran. It arrived in early July 1910, right at the commencement of what looked to be a promising whaling season; a pair of good-sized humpbacks had been captured right off the bat. While many (myself included) felt that my father should 'drop everything' and travel directly to Coonabarabran to bring her home, he did not. I urged him to at least write to the police sergeant stationed there and beg him to make enquiries as to her whereabouts and wellbeing. Here also my father demurred, and although he said nothing of it to me at the time, I have since come to believe that perhaps he was concerned about the possible ramifications for Darcy if he did so. My father had been fond of Darcy, and although understandably distressed by this liaison, he did not like to hear Darcy referred to disparagingly by others. I remember one visitor, in the weeks following their departure, telling my father he must not blame himself. 'You must remember,' said this visitor, 'that these people are several rungs below Palaeolithic man in the ladder of civilisation. It is a wonder to me that they were able to invent the boomerang.' My father got up at once and left the room, and did not return until this visitor had left.

Instead, my father wrote to a gentleman of Mrs Pike's acquaintance who lived on a property near Coonabarabran and asked that he make enquiries on his behalf. The gentleman responded that he had conducted discreet investigations around the township, but had learned nothing of any white woman living with an Aboriginal man in the area. However, he continued, it was possible that they were living out at the Aboriginal mission at Forky Mountain; he would make enquiries forthwith. A short while later, the gentleman wrote to say that he had visited the mission, and there had been told of a white woman living 'as a lubra' with an Aboriginal man and two half-caste babies; it seems they may have camped there briefly before moving on in search of work. By all accounts, the woman appeared to be in good health, although one of the babies was colicky.

'What will we do?' I asked my father, upon reading this letter.

'Well, there is not much we can do,' he responded. 'She has made her own bed, let her lie in it.'

I cannot adequately describe how dismayed I felt, how sick at heart, to hear this from my father. I wanted more than anything that he go and find her and bring her and her babies home as soon as possible, for I would happily help care for all of them. The thought of Louisa struggling in camp with those two small babies filled me with a gnawing anxiety. How on earth did she manage? My own sister, who would never willingly lift a broom or wipe a dish and had no time whatsoever for small children, how was she surviving out there? Did her love for Darcy make all these hardships endurable? *She has made her own bed, let her lie in it.*

But now I wonder if perhaps my father was right to leave her be, for what point was there in dragging her away from her husband, no matter how reduced their circumstances? This was Louisa, after all, who could never be induced to do anything against her will; she would not come easily, we all knew, and my father had a horror of any kind of shouting or unpleasantness. Looking back, I wonder if my father was not in fact a little scared of Louisa. Well, why not? I suppose we all were. She had a sharp tongue and a very forceful personality.

And certainly, when I went back to reread her letter, she did not sound as if she was struggling, what with her 'fine fat boy' and her smart dog Jack. In fact, the more I thought about it, the more it seemed to me that she was feeling sufficiently like her usual self to stir up some trouble for me. For in stating that John Beck had married them, without parental consent and without the requisite publication of the banns, she was making a very serious allegation; in fact, it was tantamount to accusing him of a criminal offence. And yet for all she knew, given her knowledge of my feelings for him and his attentions towards me at the ball (which did not pass unnoticed by many), I could very well have been married to John Beck by this time. Looking back at our friendship, I do not think I imagined the fact that he had grown fond of me. I may as well admit that since my discovery of his sermon notes, I had begun privately to entertain the possibility that he might ask me to marry him. Furthermore, I know that my father considered it practically a certainty. In fact, he informed me sometime later that, on the occasion of the ball, several of the whalers were wagering even money that John Beck would ask my father for my hand that very evening. Hence, in making these allegations, Louisa must have reasoned that she might be causing a person *who might well be my husband* (but was not) an enormous amount of embarrassment and difficulty. And yet this was so typical of Louisa: although apparently content with her own domestic situation, she wished to set the proverbial cat amongst the pigeons for me.

'Well, at least one thing is clear,' my father said. 'I was a fool to believe a word the Reverend said. That man couldn't lie straight in bed.'

It was distressing to hear my father say this of the man I had nurtured such feelings for, but perhaps it was also understandable. I need to explain, of course, that by the time we received Louisa's letter, John Beck had long since disappeared. Shortly after that last exchange we had shared under the jacaranda tree, he and Harry had rowed over to Eden with instructions to conduct further investigations in town. When John Beck did not return the following day, I learned from my brother that they had met a gentleman in the front bar at the Great Southern Hotel who, upon hearing that they were whale men, had bought them a drink in tribute to their courage. He then offered to give them a ride out to the gold diggings at Yambulla with the idea of pooling their money and trying their luck out there. This gentlemen had made a great impression on Harry, for he wore a snakeskin band upon his hat and his boots were made of iguana, and while Harry had had to decline on account of the fact that they were searching for Darcy and Louisa (although I do not know why they were searching for Darcy and Louisa in the front bar at the Great Southern), John Beck had decided to take the gentleman up on it.

Of course, everyone knew that the goldfields at Yambulla were practically worked out, so although I was surprised and disappointed at his sudden disappearance, I comforted myself with the thought that he would not be gone for long. I even imagined that he might be attempting to 'strike it lucky' in a bid to improve his situation and better provide for me. And although the weeks turned into months, summer turned to spring and spring to autumn, I continued to hope that he would come strolling up the path again, whale bones crunching underfoot, just as soon as the whaling season came around again. But he didn't.

When the whaling season of 1909 passed by and there was still no word of John Beck, my thoughts grew darker. I began to entertain the hope that he may have fallen down a mineshaft and died of his injuries or perhaps inadvertently blown himself up with a stick of dynamite or become entangled in the crushing wheel and pulverised, for such were the only possible explanations I could bear for the fact that he had utterly deserted me. I scoured old newspapers dating back to the time of his departure for reports of calamities. I questioned anybody I met who had been to the area, but no one had ever seen or heard of him. After a while, feeling foolish, I stopped asking.

Did his sudden departure, so soon after that of Darcy and Louisa, add weight to her charge that he had assisted in their elopement? Certainly my father thought so. My own natural inclination was to believe that in denying knowledge of their elopement, John Beck had given a truthful account to my father, and thus I argued in his defence that Louisa had simply invented the story as a way of saving face. (What contact did she have with Edenites, I wonder, to learn of this supposed gossip concerning her marital status? I myself had not been privy to any such talk, but perhaps I was excluded owing to the fact that I was her sister. Certainly I was familiar with the abrupt cessation of conversation whenever I walked into a shop; the glancing over shoulders, the whispering behind hands. Nonetheless, my general impression was that the question of whether or not Darcy and Louisa were legally wed paled into insignificance when compared to the larger scandal of her running away with a blackfellow.)

Besides, I argued to my father, when would this supposed marriage have taken place? Somewhere in the darkness outside the School of Arts on the night of the ball? That seemed preposterous; also, the note that she had left in the kitchen indicated that they were 'to be married', not already married. This leaves us with the unlikely scenario that they had somehow met up in Yambulla, whereupon John Beck had seized the opportunity to preside over their nuptials. It is all simply implausible, or so I argued to my father. But since that time, I have grown gradually less certain. For I began to think about the dates.

Checking the envelope of Louisa's letter from Coonabarabran, I saw that it was postmarked June 1910. She and Darcy absconded sometime on the night of 22 November 1908. In her letter, she writes of having a son, and expecting her second child 'any day now'. It takes only the most rudimentary arithmetic to work out that Louisa was expecting Darcy's child when they absconded; in truth, I imagine the knowledge of her condition is what compelled them to run away in the first place. I can also see how, in desperation, Darcy might have confided in John Beck under the mulberry trees outside the School of Arts, and begged him to marry them so that the child might at least not be born out of wedlock. Clearly plagued with misgivings (for had I not witnessed him shaking his head amidst Darcy's pleadings?), John Beck may nonetheless have seen that he could not well refuse. The horse had already bolted, as it were; confronted with this, he may have felt it his duty, as a decent man and a Christian, if not as an actual Methodist minister, to ensure that at the very least their child was born within the holy ties of matrimony.

As I say, I cannot be certain; I merely see that it is possible now, whereas at the time I could not. In some ways, accepting Louisa's version of events makes his abrupt departure less painful to me, for I can see how he may have feared that his role in events would eventually be revealed, as indeed it was. No doubt the consequences for him – had he stayed to suffer them – would have been calamitous. Thus the unhappy chain of circumstances combined in such a way as to render it impossible for him to stay, even in spite of his evident feelings for me. In seeking happiness with her true love, my sister – who can say? perhaps inadvertently – deprived me of my chance of the same.

Our Aboriginal whale men had a strange story about green frog mussings. I never understood it completely, but they said that if you powdered up a green frog, then put it in a handkerchief and waved the handkerchief around with the 'mussings', people would go all funny. If you liked a woman and you waved the mussings, then she would follow you and never leave you. They said it was possible to get any woman you wanted if you had these mussings. The woman would never even realise she'd been mussinged.

There were murmurings at the time that maybe Darcy had used the green frog mussings on Louisa, but I did not believe this. Those two had liked each other since childhood; it was plain enough to see. But particularly as the years went by, I did sometimes feel as if I had been mussinged by John Beck.

The Silverware in Situ

A FEW WEEKS AFTER THE DEPARTURE OF LOUISA AND DARCY and John Beck, Dan and I were in the kitchen cutting up plums for jam when I heard the first distant 'Hell-o-o thar!' of Mr Crowther's approach. We looked at each other very sadly, for of course this made us think of the handsome Sphinx which sat silently in the front room.

'Perhaps we should hide the plums, or he will eat them all,' said Dan, which we proceeded to do. On this occasion at least, I had no need to rustle up any cakes for Mr Crowther, as Louisa's elopement had brought on a flurry of visitors anxious for more details, each of them bearing fruitcake. I suppose due to its sombre, substantial nature and the fact that it keeps indefinitely, fruitcake was considered the appropriate offering. And yet none of us liked it much. We were much more in need of something really delicious to lift our mood – a good sponge with whipped cream and strawberries, or a chocolate cake. But perhaps that would have seemed too festive, even frivolous, given the circumstances.

My father heard Mr Crowther too, and he came into the kitchen and emptied his money pouch onto the table. He counted out fourteen shillings and threepence, and passed the coins to me.

'Here is our instalment,' he said. 'Tell Mr Crowther that I have gone into Eden. And don't mention the business with Louisa.'

'But maybe we should mention it,' I said. 'After all, he travels all over the district. He might keep a lookout for us. Perhaps he may even have heard something.'

'He is a gossip,' said my father. 'That is why he is coming here in the first place. Normally he would not be expected till the New Year.'

And with that, he headed off to hide out down in the try-works, leaving us to slice the fruitcake and open the gate for Mr Crowther.

It was Mr Crowther himself who brought up the subject of Louisa and Darcy, within minutes of settling himself down to his afternoon tea and asking us once again if we did not consider the Wunderlich ceilings to be at once durable and fire-resistant, and yet stylish and attractive. He accepted the instalment of fourteen shillings threepence with a slight raise of his eyebrows, and as he wrote out the receipt he remarked that he had wondered if we would continue to pay off the Singer's instalments, seeing as how Louisa could have no further use for it.

'No further use for it?' I cried. 'What do you mean?'

'Well, forgive me for mentioning it, but did she not run away with one of the blackfellows?'

I suppose it gives some indication of the efficacy of our self-protective armour that in a bad situation such as this, where something is changed irrevocably, some small part within us keeps desperately hoping that things are not truly as they as seem, and in fact will very soon be restored to order. Although I knew the reality to be otherwise, this small deluded part of me continued to blithely hope, perhaps even *expect*, that Louisa would shortly return and conduct her life exactly as before, scowling and avoiding the dishes and doing battle with the Sphinx in the front room. It was not until Mr Crowther expressed Louisa's departure in terms of 'having no further use for the Singer' that this small hopeful voice within me seemed to finally comprehend the reality of her being gone. It was as if he had slapped me hard across the face. I began to cry and found myself unable to speak for several minutes. Dan stood awkwardly by my side, patting me on the shoulder.

Of course, Mr Crowther was aghast that he had reduced me to tears in this fashion. He leapt up at once and volunteered to give the Singer a look-over and a touch of oil, and then he disappeared into the front room until he considered it would be safe to return. Whereupon he informed us that the Sphinx seemed to be in excellent working order; and that with Christmas upon us, he had much to do and regrettably must be on his way. I was so delighted to hear this that I wrapped up a slab of fruitcake and pressed it upon him, and then I accompanied him to his sulky.

'Mr Crowther,' I said, as he climbed up to the driver's seat, 'if you hear of any news of Louisa in your travels, we would be most grateful if you could let us know.'

'Of course, of course. I will keep my ear to the ground,' said Mr Crowther. 'You may be sure of that.'

'By the way,' he said, as he picked up the reins, 'what became of that Methodist minister fellow you had here?'

'Oh, do you mean John Beck?' I responded, happy to have a reason to say his name aloud. 'I believe he may be currently working a small lease at Yambulla.'

'Yambulla? Is that so?' he said, and a slight smile spread across his face. 'As it happens, I am headed in that direction.'

'Will you please pass on my best to him, if you do see him?' I said.

'Pass on your best? Well, I suppose I could,' he said. 'After I have notified the relevant authorities.'

'What do you mean?'

'I believe him to be an imposter, with a string of prior convictions, including larceny and attempted murder. If he left you with any of your silver, then you can consider yourself very fortunate.'

I stood there and stared at him, my mouth gaping open. He tipped his cap and urged his horse to move; the sulky rattled out the gate. I closed the gate behind him, and stood there waving till the sulky had disappeared around the curve in the road; then I turned and ran full pelt back inside, straight into the front room. The only silver we possessed was a cruet set, some napkin holders and a soup ladle, which were kept in the top drawer of the old bureau. It was a sticky old drawer and required a certain technique to pull it open; nonetheless, using brute force, I managed. There was our silverware, in situ and in need of a polish, just as I knew it would be. Mr Crowther had been wrong about John Beck.

The Rawleigh's Ointment Man

FOR THE PAST FIVE YEARS, SINCE MY FATHER DIED, I HAVE
been living in the suburb of Ryde with my younger sister
Vi (Violet), her husband Jim, and their three children,
Margaret, Lionel and George. It is not an especially large house,
but I have the back room, a covered-in verandah, and I find it quite
suitable for my needs. Certainly it is a thoroughfare, as it leads to
the backyard and the WC; also the laundry. However, I find that by
hanging a thick curtain, which can be drawn or left open, I can retain
a sense of privacy when required.

Further, the house is situated two streets from the Methodist
church, with which I am now quite involved. I am a member of both
the choir and the Ladies' Guild, and for two years now I have served
as secretary of our branch of the Methodist Women's Fellowship,
in which capacity I have taught myself to type. At one point, I was
considering perhaps even becoming involved in missionary work,

inspired by the great work of a visiting missionary, Reverend Loftus, amongst the Aborigines near Alice Springs. (What a great shame there are no whales in Alice Springs, for the Aboriginal people are such excellent whalers.) Ultimately, however, he discouraged me, citing that it was no place really for a woman, and that perhaps I was doing more useful work here with my coconut tartlets (this said with a smile), of which he was a great admirer. A pity, as I should very much like to have seen Ayers Rock. Nonetheless, he was correct in suggesting that we perform our share of good work here on the home front. In fact, I was earlier typing up a list of our activities for our annual meeting (Mrs Lunn, our president, would have me type up the Old Testament if she could, and then roneo a hundred copies – she feels it somehow imperative that I be 'kept busy' with these innumerable petty tasks she dreams up for me). Anyway, I shall copy it out here, for it offers an interesting indication of the breadth of our activities:

'*M.W.F. (Ryde Branch) – Annual Report of Pastoral Activities – 1938*

77 visits to the sick
109 trays of food distributed
26 bouquets
63 visits to shut-ins
48 letters and cards sent
250 garments repaired and sent to Aboriginal Mission (N.T.) and Foreign Mission (East Bengal)
£35 raised for the Church Building Fund through various teas and socials etc., which went a long way towards assisting in the much-needed recent addition of the WC.'

Our minister, the Reverend Davis, is somewhat elderly and his sermons rather dry; however, he is shortly to retire, and we are promised that his replacement is to be a good deal younger and known for his 'great sense of humour'. I confess to looking forward to the change; occasionally Reverend Davis will attempt a humorous quip to enliven proceedings, but mostly he abstains from much in the way of frivolity. He is certainly not the type to roll up his sleeves and show me his arm muscles, nor do I imagine him to be proficient at cards; still, I suppose these are hardly prerequisites for the position.

Vi and Jim run a small printing business which keeps them quite busy, so I have been able to make myself useful by looking after the children whilst they are at work (although admittedly the children are getting older now and don't require much looking after; in fact, Margaret is nineteen and engaged to be married). I would gladly cook for the family except Jim is finicky about food and prefers that Vi do most of the cooking: I sometimes joke with him that he is as bad as the whalers as regards his digestive intolerances. Still, I make a lot of cakes and slices, which keep the boys content, especially after school when they are always ravenous.

I am very fond of all the children, and I like to think they are fond of me; we rub along together reasonably well. The youngest, George, takes a great deal after his late uncle Dan; he is only twelve years old and yet he has taken up smoking! As we are often home alone together after school, it is a secret we keep from his parents: at times, I have even found myself procuring his tobacco. Of all the grandchildren, he is the one most interested in whaling, and I suppose it is particularly for George that I set out to write this memoir. When he was a few years younger, he would insist that I tell him whaling stories at bedtime, particularly those that involved the heroic antics of Tom and his chums. 'What did Tom do then?' he would always ask at the end of the story, with the whale dead and the Killer whales leaping out of the water triumphantly. 'Well, then Tom was feeling very sleepy, and so he took himself off to Blanket Bay,' I would reply. 'Goodnight.'

I often think it a great pity that George cannot bend to the oars and chase down a whale himself, as have the generations of Davidson men before him. I feel similarly about Lionel, who at fifteen is worrying his mother by knocking about with a crowd of local lads who consider themselves hoodlums. There has been some drinking and some broken windows; once a policeman brought him home after he had been caught trying to break into the local bowling club. Vi is very hard on him, understandably, yet I find myself saying to her: 'What do you expect? He is a Davidson! He should be out whaling.' To which she replies, especially if Jim is present: 'He is not a Davidson, he is a McGynty.' Yet I know deep down she agrees with me. There was something about whaling that straightened a boy out.

Telling George these stories and having to go back to the scrapbooks to refresh my memory set me to thinking about writing some of these stories down in more detail, particularly now that I have a typewriter. Jim has even suggested he may print up several copies, so that various members of the family might have one; that is, he always goes on to say with a smile and a roll of his eyes, if I ever finish it. And so almost every morning during the working week, if I have had no other activities involving the church, I have set up my typewriter on the kitchen table, and typed up my recollections to the very best of my ability. Dusty, our house cat, keeps me company, sitting at the back door making small squeaking noises at a pair of mynah birds who visit each day to steal the remains of her cat food. Occasionally she will sit beside me as I type and stare disapprovingly at my work, but as she is not really allowed on the kitchen table, I only tolerate this in small doses. She was sitting here a moment ago, but now she has become bored and jumped down to go and wash herself in the afternoon sunshine spilling through the back door.

The process of writing has brought back a great many memories, and although many of them have been painful, it has nonetheless been a rewarding experience to go back and live for a few hours each day in that particular year of my life. Reading it through, I see that I have gone on about John Beck rather more than I intended, and certainly I will remove those chapters before I allow anyone else to peruse them. After all, it is simply meant to be an account of one particular whaling season, concerning itself mostly with the trials of whaling and the antics of the Killer whales, perhaps lightly touching on some of the characters of the time. I find these days when I tell new acquaintances that my father was a whaler, many of them respond in a horrified fashion, and that is before I even go into the details, and so now I am inclined to keep mum on the subject altogether. I'm sure some members of the congregation would be astounded to learn that Miss Davidson with the grey frizz in the second row of the choir once fired a whale gun at a Killer whale! (And missed, I am relieved to say.)

Quite recently – only a few months ago, in fact – as I sat typing in the kitchen, there came a knock at the front door. I opened the door to find a nice-looking young man in his early thirties, swarthy in complexion. Hung from his neck was an open display case which contained an array of salves and ointments. 'Excuse me for bothering you,' he said, 'but I wonder if I could interest you in some Rawleigh's ointment today. We're also pleased to announce a new product, Rawleigh's Ready Relief, containing eucalyptus oil. You'll find it beneficial for a variety of conditions, suitable for man or beast.'

In fact, we already had an ancient container of Rawleigh's ointment in the bathroom cupboard which Vi used on George's chest whenever he had catarrh; nonetheless, mention of the Ready Relief, suitable for man or beast, piqued my interest. Dusty had at the time a rather large and unsightly abscess on her face from brawling with our neighbour's tabby, and I wondered aloud if this might help her. He listened with interest as I described her condition, and then he enquired if he might have a look at her; 'that is, if she is up to receiving visitors'.

There was something about this young man and his ready smile to which I responded, and so I led him into the kitchen where Dusty lay on the towel I had put down for her in front of the stove, quite wan and miserable and out of sorts. Squatting down, he held out his hand to her. She sniffed it gingerly and then, to my great surprise, stood up, arched her back and commenced to rub against him. Dusty is a stand-offish cat by nature, with little time for anyone except those that feed her, so this display of excessive friendliness was most unusual. She purred and rubbed against his leg and threw herself onto her back and waved her legs in the air; all the while he told her what a fine-looking cat she was and gently admonished her for getting into scrapes. Finally he picked her up and examined her swollen face.

'If you would permit me,' he said to me, 'I'd like to try some Ready Relief on it. I've found it works on Mum's cats, although they don't enjoy it much.'

'All right,' I said.

Removing his jacket and rolling up his shirtsleeves, he asked me for a clean rag soaked in hot water from the kettle, to which he applied a small amount of Ready Relief. With Dusty purring in his arms, he then pressed the rag gently against the swollen area of her face. She stiffened but did not immediately struggle, and after a moment or two, he began gently to massage it.

This caused her some discomfort and so she began to struggle and scratch and loudly protest, but nonetheless he continued to massage, talking to her soothingly all the while. A foul-smelling pus commenced to seep from her face and she began to settle a little, as if sensing he was trying to make her better. He asked me for another rag soaked in hot water to which he applied more Ready Relief, and continued to bathe the area until he had it quite clean. Finally he permitted her to escape, whereupon she shot out the back door like a bat out of the gates of hell. When I looked at him, I saw to my horror that his forearms were covered in scratches and some of the pus had found its way onto his shirt. I directed him to the bathroom so that he might sponge his shirt under the tap, and when he emerged he bathed his scratches with the Ready Relief.

'They will be healed in no time,' he said with a smile.

Seeing as how he had gone to such trouble for Dusty, I felt the least I could do was purchase a bottle of Ready Relief. He accepted my coins, recommending that I use it to bathe Dusty's abscess twice daily for the next day or so, to which I nodded my head in agreement even though I knew privately that Dusty would never permit me to do such a thing, and then he pulled out his receipt book.

'What name should I make it out to?' he enquired.

'Mary Davidson,' I responded.

'Mrs?'

'Miss.'

'Davidson,' he murmured, as he wrote out the receipt. 'Not one of the Davidsons of Eden, by any chance?'

'Yes, as a matter of fact,' I replied.

'Well, that's a coincidence,' he said, looking up at me. And even before he said it, I seemed to know exactly what he was about to say: 'My mother is a Davidson.'

'What's her name?' I asked.

'Louisa.'

And that is the funny story of how Louisa came back into our lives again.

Or, I should say, it is the funny story of how Louisa has *almost* come back into our lives, for she is not quite back yet, although we are working on it. For it seems that her characteristic stubbornness and pride may have only exacerbated over time, and she is proving somewhat resistant to being pulled back into the familial embrace.

In the thirty intervening years, we have had no contact with Louisa, nor had we any idea where she lived; our last communication was the letter from Coonabarabran. When my father died, I had hoped that she might somehow learn of it, for notice of his passing had appeared in many newspapers. As I sat in the front pew, I kept straining around to peer at the front entrance, willing her to materialise. But she did not come. I can only imagine that the thought of being amidst the gossipmongers of Eden, even for my father's funeral, was simply too much for her to bear. And yet now, suddenly and unexpectedly, here was her eldest son, Albert, standing in the kitchen before me.

'She is my sister,' I cried. 'I am your aunty!'

And at once I embraced him. For suddenly I so clearly saw the resemblance that I wondered how I could have not been struck by it the instant I opened the door! He was tall with dark curls like Darcy (although his skin colour was considerably lighter), and yet something about his droll, half-scornful smile as he endured the kisses that I planted on his cheeks was for me the very essence of Louisa.

Of course, immediately I begged him to sit down and stay for lunch, and to fill me in on his mother and father and brothers and sisters, and indeed his own wife and children, should he have any. But the young man – up to that point so friendly and open, and I would say even delighted to have discovered the family connection – grew suddenly wary. He seemed anxious not to stay long, insisting that he had a large area to cover that day and his boss would not be happy if he dallied. However, he stayed for one cup of tea, and in that short space of time, this is the information that I managed to glean from him:

That he has two brothers and two sisters, though not all of them are 'still around'. I do not know what he meant by that; whether he simply meant that they might be living elsewhere, perhaps interstate. His youngest sister Marian (or Maryanne?) is unmarried and lives with Louisa.

That his father Darcy died some years ago. The circumstances of his death Albert did not make clear to me, but I gathered that it might have been from injuries resulting from a fight of some description, for there was an inquest and he mentioned witnesses, or a witness who had failed to show. But he seemed very sad about it all, and I did not like to add to his unhappiness by pressing him for details.

Prior to Darcy's death, the family had been living in Queensland, 'near the border'.

That since Darcy's death, Louisa had moved to Sydney and

was living in Surry Hills. She makes her living as a seamstress in a garment factory, and does some additional piecework on the side, if she can get it. She has been unwell recently with some problem relating to her womb, but seems to be on the mend now. 'She's a tough old lady, that one,' said Albert admiringly.

That Albert himself was married, with four children of his own, the youngest a baby.

At around this point, Albert got up and said that he really needed to get going or he would get a walloping, so I took a piece of paper and hurriedly wrote a note for him to give to his mother. Of course, I had no time to make a copy, but I believe it was something along the lines of the following:

'*Dear Louisa,*

I am so happy to have met your son, Albert, and to hear news of you! I am now living in Ryde, with Violet and family. Anne still lives in Eden, married to a Strickland! We all miss you very much. Please come and visit us soon.

Your loving sister,

Mary'

I pressed the note upon Albert with instructions to pass it on to Louisa. I walked him to the door and made him promise to visit again soon, and next time to bring his mother with him. Just as he was turning to leave, a sudden thought occurred to me.

'Just one more minute,' I implored. 'I need to show you something quickly.'

And taking him by the arm, I ushered him back through the house to my small alcove. And there, removing some small ornaments I had on top of it, I lifted the wooden cover to reveal the Sphinx.

'This belongs to your mother,' I said. 'We have kept it for her. Tell her it is all paid off now. Tell her it is hers whenever she wants it.'

He stared at the Sphinx uncomprehendingly.

'She has a machine,' he said simply.

'Yes,' I cried. 'But this is the Sphinx! Tell her it is the Sphinx. That we still have the Sphinx.'

'All right,' he said, but I don't know if he understood the significance.

When Vi returned home that evening, I rushed to the door and told her the news; we hugged each other in our excitement, and shed tears at the prospect of reuniting with our sister. But as I say, this was some months ago now, and we have heard nothing further of either Albert or Louisa. We have stayed in every weekend, even though we usually like to go to the pictures, for fear of missing her if we should venture out. Every Saturday morning, I bake a cake in expectation, and even as I put it into the oven, I have to caution myself not to allow my hopes to rise along with the mixture. Louisa was very partial to cake – any sort, it didn't matter.

'Perhaps it is difficult for her to get out here,' said Vi one afternoon as we sat in the lounge room, looking hopefully out the front window to the street. It was, after all, a long bus trip from town, possibly even warranting a complicated changeover.

'It is a shame that you didn't think to get her address,' Vi continued, and indeed I regret this bitterly, more bitterly every time she mentions it, which is frequently. It *is* a shame, but was I to be blamed for simply assuming that Louisa would respond as I did – with joy and excitement – at the prospect of a reunion with her kin?

Thinking on it further (although I haven't shared these thoughts with Vi), I wonder if perhaps I have inadvertently offended her with my note. Writing it in haste as I did, with Albert hovering there anxious to go, there were things I omitted to say. I am particularly sorry that I did not pass on my sincere condolences regarding Darcy's passing, or indeed even mention him. Perhaps this seemed callous and hurtful to her. Perhaps Albert did not mention to her the hurried circumstances in which I wrote the note, and so she assumes that the fact that I scrawled it so carelessly is an expression of how little she matters to me. Of course, nothing could be further from the truth.

My other thought is that perhaps Louisa's circumstances are so reduced that she is simply too embarrassed to visit us, for fear we see what has become of her. After all, she was a proud beauty of sixteen when last we saw her; Albert described her now as a 'tough old lady'. Certainly young people are not sensitive to the small but important gradations of age in those older than themselves, but instead regard us all as ancient crones. And yet, at the age of forty-nine, with my hair almost completely grey, I find I hesitate to describe myself as 'old'. I think I would be more aptly described as 'late middle-aged', if there is such a definition. I queried Vi on the subject and she agreed, adding that she herself was in the 'early middle-aged' category, to which Margaret snorted derisively. My purpose here is not to talk admiringly of my own appearance, for I have never been an oil painting, still less so now; I simply wonder if Louisa's difficult life has aged her harshly and whether her knowledge of that is contributing to her apparent reluctance to see us. (She was always very slender, too, and I do wonder sometimes if carrying a few extra pounds isn't kinder on the face in the long run, somewhat softening the effect of wrinkles.)

In any case, I have a plan. I may have mentioned that Margaret is engaged to be married, and Vi and I are planning a kitchen tea in her honour. I had noticed that as well as his ointments, Albert carried an interesting selection of cake flavourings and extracts, along with disinfectants and White Rose perfume. If we don't hear anything within the next month, then I shall call up the Rawleigh's head office and ask that they send their man around again, as I would like to place a sizeable order. I have already looked up the number in the telephone book. And this time I will not let Albert get away without securing Louisa's address.

For I am determined that they be with us this Christmas. I have this picture in my head which only grows more detailed every time I summon it up; it is of the family gathered around the dining-room table for Christmas lunch. It is going to be a challenge to fit everyone, but I have more or less worked out a configuration for the tables. I will put George on the children's table (the card table) with Albert's older three (George enjoys the company of small children and likes to play big brother when he can). The unmarried sister (Marian?) I will seat next to Margaret (in my head, I see them both gossiping about film stars; Margaret is mad on them) with Margaret's fiancé Peter on the other side of her, rolling his eyes in his good-humoured way. On the other side of the table, I plan to place Albert and his wife (whose name I did not catch), with Lionel on the end; he is no great conversationalist, but hopefully Albert will be able to draw him out. We may have to squeeze a highchair in for the baby, in which case I will put Albert's wife on the corner end (I am fairly sure the young family next door may be able to lend us a highchair for the occasion).

At the kitchen end of the table, for convenience's sake, I will place Vi and Jim, for Vi will be up and down and back and forth; and down the opposite end, myself and Louisa. I can almost see her sitting there now. She has a paper hat on her head, and she is leaning her chin in one hand and making her sly jokes the way she used to do; except in my mind's eye, I realise, she still looks sixteen.

In any case, I can't be moping around waiting for her this Saturday. We are having our 'Welcome' afternoon tea in honour of our new minister, the Reverend R.H. Trinder, for which I have been called upon to bring my Chocolate Honey Roll, as well as a plate of cheese and celery sandwiches, the preparation of which will take me a good part of the morning. This will be our first opportunity to meet him, as he does not commence officially until October; however, we have already gleaned some interesting morsels of information. Apparently he has a superb singing voice, and according to Reverend Davis, who has met him, he was very keen to know if any of the congregation possessed a pianola, for he loves a singalong. (Reverend Davis seemed to be offering this up as an indication that Reverend Trinder might be a bit of a Flash Harry, but in fact we could not have been more delighted to hear it. So much so that I found myself suggesting to Vi later that evening that if Louisa does not wish to claim the Sphinx, I might very well sell it and buy ourselves a pianola with the proceeds.)

The other nugget of information came from an acquaintance of our treasurer, Mrs Purcell, whose sister resides in his previous parish of Wangaratta. Apparently, his marriage is not a wholly happy one; Mrs Trinder struggles with various ailments, some of them apparently imagined; in fact, the terms used to describe her by the sister of the acquaintance were 'dreary' and 'a bit of a spoiler'. So that is interesting. Not that I wish them any ill; as I say, I have yet to meet them. Vi likes to tease me on the subject, however, for the other day I happened to comment in passing that after sweeping out the kitchen, I had accidentally left the broom in the corner of the room. I reminded her of our old superstition, to wit: the sweeper would shortly meet her true love. I made no mention of Reverend Trinder, and yet she immediately assumed he was the likely prospect, even in spite of the fact that he is obviously married; all of which is rather tiresome of her. Also, she insists I left the broom in the corner deliberately, but I know for a fact that it was entirely accidental. It has to be accidental, or the effect is otherwise null and void.

The Boat Trip Home

I N FACT, THE MAKING OF THE CHOCOLATE HONEY ROLL DID NOT take as long as I thought it would, and it has turned out very nicely (some slight cracking is inevitable, but I have covered it up pretty well with a mixture of cocoa and sugar). I find I still have two hours before I need to even start assembling the sandwiches, for if I commence them too early, they will simply dry out and wilt or, alternatively, become soggy. I have pressed my brown wool suit and laid it out on the bed, and cleaned my good brown dress pumps. The family is out and about engaged in various errands and activities, and so, finding myself with time on my hands, I have been glancing through some of the previous chapters of this memoir.

I see that in my anxiety to explain the circumstances of Darcy and Louisa's elopement, I had left the chapter concerning the Plain and Fancy Dress Ball unfinished, at the point where John Beck suggested we step outside to 'take some air'. It is tempting to perhaps document in more detail the various small sighs and tender caresses and whispered endearments that followed – yet I must stop myself. After all, there hardly seems much point when I shall simply have to go back and excise these more intimate moments for fear of inadvertently startling my nephews. Nor does it seem entirely appropriate to be lingering amidst such memories when I am shortly to be making the acquaintance of our new minister over cheese and celery sandwiches.

To be honest, I am beginning to feel somewhat impatient with myself about it all. There are moments when I find myself thinking, 'Well, he was simply a cad.' There are even moments when I say to myself, 'He may have been a cad but you, Mary Davidson, were a fool.' Certainly, a wiser, more experienced reader might conclude that John Beck led me up the garden path and back again. I, of course, have drawn my own conclusions and, on most days at least, am inclined to give him the benefit of the doubt. So I will provide this one small detail before moving on with the story: that upon kissing me beneath the mulberry trees that night, he murmured softly that my lips tasted deliciously of blackberry cordial (excise all this later).

The Plain and Fancy Dress Ball drew to a close around three in the morning with 'Auld Lang Syne' and 'God Save the King', and then the Davidson clan and the various whale men who were not immediately departing us made our way down Imlay Street to the wharf, where the *Excelsior* awaited us. It is a funny thing, but whale men were always hard to dislodge at the end of the season (like splinters, is how Louisa referred to them). They had grown used to the food and the lodging, and they had come to rather like it, as much as they complained about it. It suddenly seemed a big effort to have to go and worry about sleeper-cutting or whatever it was that they were going to busy themselves with in the meantime.

My father, ever mindful of the difficulty of procuring whale men next season, was never one to peremptorily boot them out, and often the situation dragged on like this for several weeks. So in fact the only whale man we had succeeded in shaking off that evening was Robert Heffernan, who went home to his mother, but not before accompanying us to the wharf. He had drunk so much liquor that he now felt exceedingly affectionate towards everyone, including Darcy, whom he embraced and called 'brother' and told him he was 'a fine gentleman, I don't care what anyone says'. He then stood on the wharf and waved forlornly as the men tossed off the ropes and the motor launch putt-putted out.

The full moon was high in the sky and the bay unusually illuminated by its eerie silvery light. A great weariness, a kind of happy exhaustion, descended upon us. Dan and Violet and Annie fell asleep almost immediately on the bench seats, covered over by blankets. Harry and Uncle Aleck appeared to have passed out altogether, and lay snoring underfoot; in fact, we left them there, covered in blankets, when we got home. Of the rest of us, no one talked much, but instead just sat staring out to sea, listening to the gentle sputtering of the motor as we crept across the bay.

'Well, Father,' said Salty after a while, slapping John Beck companionably upon the knee, 'how did you enjoy your first season whaling?'

'I've enjoyed it very much,' replied John Beck. 'It has truly been a memorable experience.'

'Indeed,' said Salty, taking out his pipe and proceeding to light it, enveloping himself for a short while amidst a cloud of smoke. 'I daresay you fancy you know a bit about whales now?' he continued, once his pipe was lit.

'Oh well,' said John Beck. 'I suppose I know a little more than I did before.'

'I see.' Another cloud of smoke. 'Then I wonder, Father, can you tell me why it is that whales breach?'

'Breach, did you say?'

'That's right. By which I mean leap out of the water in their entirety.'

'Yes,' said John Beck. 'I am aware of what breaching is.'

'You are aware of what breaching is, but are you aware of what causes it?'

'No, I am not.'

'Hazard a guess, if you will.'

'I'm sure I do not know.'

'I imagine you might think it an expression of high spirits. Glad to be alive, is that it? Possessed of the *joie de vivre?*'

'Perhaps,' said John Beck in a noncommittal tone.

'*Perhaps?* Of course it is obvious! Here is a lovely big humper swimming along with not a care in the world! Why shouldn't he leap up in glee?! He would click his heels, if he had any.'

'I suppose so.'

'Then you suppose incorrectly, for that is not the reason,' said Salty. 'Hazard another guess. For example, perhaps the whale is of a sportive disposition?'

'Why don't you just simply tell me why the whale breaches?' A note of irritation had crept into John Beck's voice. 'It would save a lot of time and effort.'

'Very well then, I will,' said Salty, smiling pleasantly. 'It is because the whale has an earache.'

At which Darcy, who had been following the back and forth

between the two men in some amusement, burst into a peal of laughter. For some reason, the idea of a whale having an earache tickled him enormously.

'An earache?' queried John Beck, and he was smiling a little because Darcy's laughter was rather infectious. Others began chuckling also. In fact, even my father was smiling.

'Yes, that's right, an earache,' said Salty, seeming a little annoyed at all the merriment. 'And I can assure you, young man' – turning to Darcy, and becoming more vehement in his tone – 'that it is no laughing matter for the whale. A minuscule crustacean is pestering the poor beast to the point of endurance, scampering up and down in the ear cavities. The whale is breaching in a desperate bid to rid himself of the pest.'

'I was not aware that whales had ears,' remarked John Beck.

This set Darcy off again.

'Indeed they do,' cried Salty. 'Indeed they do have ears! Granted, they do not have the fleshy appendages of land mammals –'

And just at this moment, as if directly refuting Salty's claim, we heard a mighty and unmistakable *Bosh!* and a plume of fine silvery spray rose within twenty yards of the launch. At once we all cried out, and there we saw in low silhouette against the water the sloping curve of a humpback commencing to dive. Up turned the insouciant flukes, a glimpse of their snowy undersides in the darkness, then down they slid into the water, disappearing from view.

'Well, that is a very late whale,' said Arthur Ashby thoughtfully. 'A straggler of sorts.'

The men turned to my father at the wheel. I suppose they were wondering whether they would now be expected to give chase. My father desisted from the throttle and let the motor idle. The little ones roused blearily from their sleep.

'What's the matter? Why has the boat stopped?'

'Sshhh. We are waiting for a whale to reappear.'

At once the children sat up, wide awake. They were not going to miss seeing a whale close up.

'There she is!' cried Darcy. The whale had reappeared a short distance ahead and lolled about, spouting amiably. The children hastened up to the bow and clustered together there, watching it reverently.

'Gee, I wish I had my whale gun,' said Dan earnestly.

'It's a juvenile,' said my father. 'I suppose that's why it's lagging so far behind the others.'

'It is Robert Heffernan, in whale form,' remarked Bastable.

'What do you think, boss?' asked Arthur Ashby, and all eyes turned to my father in trepidation. I suspect none of them felt very much like having to suddenly do battle with a whale. Really, everyone wanted to just curl up in their beds and sleep for twelve hours. 'We try calling the Killers?'

'Well, we could try, I suppose,' said my father. 'But I doubt they'll come.'

He did not sound very enthusiastic himself. Perhaps he was aware of the stony disapprobation rising up from Louisa, who sat quietly at his side. Or perhaps he also wanted to go to bed. After a good bit of fumbling about in the dark, the men unclipped the *Excelsior*'s oars and slapped them over the side in a haphazard attempt at unison. Then they all stood around and scoured the water, waiting for the happy miracle of those raking dorsal fins. The children and I waited too, wrapped in our blankets.

'Come on, Tom,' urged Annie in a small voice. 'Come on, Hooky. Come on, Humpy.'

'And Kinscher and Cooper,' continued Violet. 'And Jackson and Little Ben and Jimmy and Charlie Adgery and Stranger and Typee...' In fact, she went on to list nearly every Killer whale she could think of, living or deceased, and was admonished for her errors by her brother.

Minutes passed. The men tried slapping the oars a couple more times, increasingly more half-hearted and less in unison at each successive attempt. No Killers came; nor was anyone much surprised, for they hadn't been sighted now in well over a week. They had moved on to colder waters, presumably, to wherever Killer whales liked to go when the whaling season was over. Meanwhile, Robert Heffernan in whale form drifted further away, ambling along in his aimless, distracted fashion, making his journey south.

'We'll let him go,' said my father, opening up the throttle. 'He'll be bigger next year.'

Author's Note

George 'Fearless' Davidson, Master Whaler, was born in 1863, in Eden, New South Wales. He was the grandson of Alexander Davidson, a Scottish immigrant who was the first in the line of Davidsons to take up whaling in Twofold Bay. In 1890, George married Sarah Galli, who bore him eight children. George and Sarah both lived to a ripe old age. In 1936, several years after he had put the whaling station up for sale and by now an old man, George rowed out in a small dinghy and lanced a whale single-handedly. '*Davidson's feat of attacking and killing a whale without assistance is unparalleled in the history of local whaling,*' claimed the *Sydney Morning Herald* (12 November 1936).

In the interests of fiction, and with sincere apologies to the descendants of the Davidsons, I have taken a few liberties with some details of his life, in particular by making him a widower and inventing a whole new set of offspring for him.

Regarding the killer whales, however, I have endeavoured to be as truthful as possible. Much of my research centred on the local Eden newspapers of the time, held in the archives of the State Library of New South Wales. Here I discovered an abundance of extraordinarily vivid and detailed eyewitness accounts of the whale hunts, often referring to specific killer whales by name. These newspapers seem to have followed the ups and downs of the Davidsons' fortunes and the killer whales' activities obsessively, even to the extent – in this instance – of documenting the killers' pursuit of an unfortunate 'grampus' (most likely a minke whale):

> *'After travelling somewhat about a mile he again altered his course for North Head expecting to get away, but his attempt was foiled by the appearance of "Cooper". He then trended his way towards the entrance to Curalo Lake, only to find laying in wait for him on the verge of the breakers, "Typee". By a skilful bit of manoeuvring, the grampus succeeded around the killer "Typee", who, finding himself outclassed, immediately took up a position with his confederates. After travelling slowly along the breast of the sandy beach, "Humpy" thought he (the grampus) was not going fast enough, so he took a hand in the game, and gave the unfortunate grampus a reminder that he was in close attendance ... After floptailing a while, there were to be noticed Hooky, Cooper, Jackson, Typee, Tom, Kinscher and other killers known by their distinctive dorsal fins, ranged in semi-circular form between Lookout Point and North Head ...'*
> *Eden Observer and South Coast Advocate, 3 August 1909.*

The whale chases themselves make tough reading, at once exciting and horrifying:

Author's Note

'...the Killers were attacking them in the most ferocious manner, and the unfortunate creatures seemed lost as to which course was best to get rid of their tormentors. The bellowing the whole time was of the most awful and pitiful nature, and it would be a hard man indeed who could not bestow a little sympathy on the poor harassed creatures. Getting slightly away from the Killers, the whales made for East Boyd Bay. There a number of erratic movements were made, but the whales, getting out of the bay, steered a course for the open sea...instinctively (the Killers) knew that if the whales were once outside the bay in deep water their chances of capture were limited and so, like dogs on a beast, they were at the whales' heads and, after a great effort, turned them around again. During all this time, many efforts were made by George Davidson and his crew to fasten to one of the whales, but in vain. Their constant twistings and turnings rendered it impossible...After a while the whales and Killers took a course direct for Quarantine Bay, the whaling crew following in hot pursuit. Here success crowned the efforts of the crew, and one of the whales had the harpoon driven well home into its body, and the hopes of the crew went high; but only for a few minutes as an event, not uncommon, happened. It is well known that the Killers will often take hold of a piece of line hanging from a boat, or at times a kellick, and run away with it; and this is just what one of them did on Sunday night; and the extraordinary sight of a Killer having the whale line in his mouth and being towed about by a whale was witnessed. The result of the Killer taking the line was that the crew had to take the oars and row hard for about two miles before they managed to again secure the whale line...'

Eden Observer and South Coast Advocate, 1 September 1905.

In fact, I found several examples of frolicsome Killer whales taking the whale line:

> '...*At this stage an incident occurred which fortunately is not frequent although a similar one took place last season. A Killer, known to the whaling crew as Tom, took the whale line in its mouth, dragging it out of the boat, and for a while threatening the loss of the whale. Fortunately Tom held fast to the line, the whale towing him about the bay, and presenting an unusual sight to the few onlookers who were about at that early hour ...*'
>
> *Eden Observer and South Coast Advocate, 3 August 1906.*

Here is the famous Tom making an appearance! On the same page of the very same newspaper, in miniscule print, I found this fascinating tidbit:

> '*A painful, but fortunately not serious accident happened to Mr George Davidson on Friday afternoon last at the site of the dead whale off South Head. While explaining the names of the Killers, one of them rose immediately at the bow of the launch and catching the whale line of which Mr Davidson had hold, in his mouth, crushed his finger in such a severe manner that the top of it burst. For his playful habits, Tom, the name by which this particular Killer is known, received sufficient anathemas to last him till his dying day – and after.*'

Tom died in September 1930, and the obituary and poem included in this book are taken verbatim from the Eden newspapers of that month. His skeleton was preserved by George Davidson, and is on display to this day at the Eden Killer Whale Museum. Although other explanations have been offered for it, there appears to be a conspicuous rope groove on one of his back teeth.

George Davidson's whale crews appear to have consisted of various Davidsons, a few itinerants and, notably, a regularly returning group of Aboriginal whale men: Arthur Ashby, Albert Thomas Senior (Charaga) and Albert Thomas Junior (Boukal) among them. By most accounts (although this is difficult to verify), the Aboriginal whale men received the same pay and conditions as the white whale men. Certainly, they were highly regarded for their superior eyesight and ability, and Arthur Ashby in particular is mentioned in newspaper accounts for his skill as a harpooner (or boat-steerer). Of particular interest is the great significance that the killer whales held for the Aboriginal people:

'The older race of aboriginals around Eden had strange beliefs about the Killers, holding the opinion that when they departed from this sphere of usefulness they at some time later returned as Killers, and the one which bears the name of Cooper was so-called after an old aboriginal who had in the flesh been king of the Kiah River tribe. Just as a small Killer, on being seen for the first time, was said to be the recently deceased child of one of the natives changed into a Killer. There is no doubt that these animals are looked upon as being supernatural, and held consequently in great reverence. Many years ago, an old whaler named Higginbotham (Flukey), in throwing the lance, by accident caused the death of a Killer. The same night, the natives armed themselves with spears, with the intention of taking his life in revenge for what they considered a great crime, and it was only owing to the intervention of some of the more powerful of the tribe that Flukey was allowed to live.'

Eden Observer and South Coast Advocate, 27 November 1903.

It is informative of the times to note that 'Killers' warrants a capital letter, while 'aboriginals' does not.

Further study of these newspapers reveals that whaling in Eden does not appear to have been a hugely profitable enterprise in the early 1900s:

> *'The whaling season at Twofold Bay was practically brought to a close with the ending of last week, when the two crews dispersed to their homes. Mr Davidson will keep a lookout for chance whales a little while longer, but the fact that the Killers have not been seen for some time renders it probable they have taken their departure for other fields and oceans blue, and there is poor chance of obtaining whales without their assistance ... The season opened auspiciously with the capture of ten whales between July 19 and September 5, the last being a black whale ... Since the latter date, however, the long weary watches have been fruitless. During 1903, not a single whale was taken, with the exception of a small finback, which was driven ashore by the Killers at Haslems Beach. After all expenses are paid, there will unfortunately be small profit for the adventurous work of whaling in the last two years in Twofold Bay. The total quantity of oil secured was 25 and a half tons. Had the Killers remained and the last two humpers and right whale been captured, the story would have been slightly different. As it is, we can only hope that captures may yet be made, late as the period is, and that next year's work may recoup plucky George Davidson for past losses.'*
>
> *Eden Observer and South Coast Advocate, 11 November 1904.*

In fact, 1905 proved to be worse than 1904: only five whales were captured, quite late in the season, and two of these were blown away in gales before they could be towed to the try-works. These losses were a bitter blow for the whalers, but perhaps even more disappointing for the gentleman below:

> '*Mr James Hogan, of Moruya, who came to Eden this week to be immersed in one of the whales as a cure for rheumatism from which he is a great sufferer, returned to his home on Monday. Owing to the loss of the whales after they were killed, Mr Hogan could not try the remedy.*'
> *Eden Observer and South Coast Advocate, 15 September 1905.*

For those interested in reading further about the Davidsons and the killer whales of Eden, I recommend the following:

Tom Mead, *Killers of Eden*, Angus & Robinson, 1961; re-published Dolphin Books, 2002

Danielle Clode, *Killers in Eden*, Allen & Unwin, 2002

Rene Davidson, *Whalemen of Twofold Bay*, self-published, 1988

W.J. Dakin, *Whalemen Adventurers*, Angus and Robertson, 1934; re-published Sirius Books, 1963

www.killersofeden.com

It is well worth visiting the area, not only for the Eden Killer Whale Museum, where Tom's skeleton may be admired and much of the Davidson whaling paraphernalia is on display, but also for the charming, rough-hewn Davidson cottage at Kiah, which stands preserved just up the hill from where the try-works used to be. At South Head, it is possible to visit the whaler's lookout post of Boyd Tower, where one can plainly see, carved into the sandstone, an epitaph for the whale man Peter Lia, who died when a whale smashed a whaleboat with its flukes in 1881. There's even the faded remnants of an old draughtsboard, painted on a flat rock – no doubt a means of whiling away the long hours, waiting for a whale.

Happily, these days during whale season there always seem to be plenty of whales passing through Twofold Bay, relatively untormented – even the whale-watching boats must keep a respectful distance. Killer whales, however, are much less frequent visitors. While one would never wish for a return to the brutal days of whaling, it's hard not to be slightly nostalgic for a time when the killer whales' annual arrival in Twofold Bay warranted an excited snippet in the local newspaper, under the headline 'Voices Whisper':

> '*That the "Killers", true to their custom, are about, and whales may be expected soon to show – or cry "hello" and bellow.*'

Shirley Barrett